searching blind

Tonya Burrows

part one
disaster

There's nothing like a jolly good disaster to get people to start doing something.
King Charles

chapter
one

CONSCIOUSNESS CLAWED its way back to Sawyer Murphy as the world shook around him. Dirt and debris rained down on his head, dust filling his lungs as he gasped in a sharp breath.

Earthquake.

The memory came rushing back, intense enough to cut through the fog of confusion. He'd been on the mountain searching for Pierce and had run into Lucy Harper and her hiking group—city folks mostly, out of their depth. And then, a thunderous roar as the mountain shook under their feet like it was trying to buck them off. He remembered the snap of a redwood branch, remembered the startling sharpness of seeing it materialize out of the soup that was usually his vision as it fell toward one of the hikers...

Well, fuck. No wonder his head was pounding like a drumline at a college football game. He'd pushed the guy out of the damn way.

The tremors subsided, leaving an eerie stillness in their wake. Not another full earthquake, then, but just an aftershock.

"Christ," he muttered, the word scraping his throat raw as he tried to sit up. Pain lanced through his head. He stopped moving, waiting for the world to stop its sickening spin, and convinced his stomach he didn't need to revisit his last meal. His body ached all over, and he felt blood seeping from a cut on his forehead. Taking a breath, he reached up and gingerly probed the injury. His fingers came back slick and warm with blood. It wasn't a deep gash, but it had bled plenty and was still trickling.

Zelda.

He reached out, feeling the rough grain of wood beneath his fingertips. Okay, so he wasn't outside anymore. Where was he? His ears registered the soft drip-drip of water from a ceiling crack, the creaks and groans of an old building settling on its haunches after the earthquake. Every sound amplified to painful levels. A metallic tang of blood filled his nostrils; he tasted it too, coppery and bitter.

His dog wasn't at his side.

Where was his girl?

Panic surged through him. Zelda was more than just a pet. She was his partner, his confidante, and his eyes. She had brought him back from the brink of a very dark place. She had given him something to live for and made him realize he was still the same capable man he'd been before he lost his sight. She was his lifeline. His sanity. If he lost her…

Pushing past the throbbing in his skull and the flaring pain in his left side, Sawyer got to his feet. Or at least, he tried to. His legs crumbled beneath him like wet paper, sending him sprawling on the dust-laden floor. He gritted his teeth, white-hot pain radiating from his ribs as he collided with the ground.

A wet nose pressed against his cheek, nuzzling gently. Zelda. He buried his hands in her dirty fur and choked on a sob of relief.

She was okay. She was safe.

She whimpered softly, nuzzling closer, her tail thumping against the floor as if to reassure him.

"Good girl," he whispered. "That's my good girl."

Her body trembled slightly beneath his hands, and he knew she was as scared as he was. But she was here with him, alive and whole, and that was all that mattered at that moment. He ran his hands over her back and down her sides, feeling for the stickiness of blood or the deformity of a broken bone. His heart clenched as his fingers found a small cut on her leg, but it was clean and shallow. The blood had already dried.

"Okay. We're okay. We got this, Zel."

Slowly, gingerly, he pushed himself up again. This time, his legs held, though he swayed unsteadily on his feet. He waited for the world to stop its nauseating tilt-a-whirl routine before he took a step forward, Zelda's familiar bulk pressing reassuringly against his side.

"Where are we, girl?" He tilted his head, tuning into the ambient noise around him. The building—it definitely sounded like they were inside some kind of wooden structure—groaned, its bones creaking as it settled. The faint crackle of debris falling filled the silence. And then, underneath that, he heard the murmur of voices. Human voices.

Lucy.

Jesus, was she okay?

He reached out, blindly groping forward until his hands met the cool, rough surface of a wall. His fingers traced over the splintered wood as he moved along it, using it as a guide. Zelda stayed close, brushing against his side, her presence a comfort and an anchor.

The building creaked and groaned as the aftershocks continued to ripple through the earth. Each tremor sent pulses of pain lancing through his skull, but he kept moving, adrenaline and worry for Lucy propelling him forward.

The murmur of voices grew louder. He heard the faint strains of a woman's voice—was that Lucy? — followed by the lower tones of a man responding. There were other voices, too, muddled and indistinct in the echoing room.

"Sawyer!"

He recognized the voice as Lucy's, full of worry and sharp-edged fear. He turned in her direction and saw her rushing toward him, her long ponytail swinging. But then she stopped moving and vanished into the muddled soup of colors and shadows that made up his vision.

"Hey." He tried for a reassuring smile. "Anyone get the number of that bus?"

She let out a breathy laugh that was more from relief

than humor. "Dammit, Sawyer, what the hell do you think you're doing?"

"Just taking my dog for a walk on this beautiful day." He tried to sound light, tried to reassure her with humor. Things were always easier when he was joking. But another ripple of pain coursed through his body, ruining the delivery with a wince he couldn't hide.

Zelda whined and pressed closer to his leg.

"God. You shouldn't be up," Lucy scolded. He could hear the rustle of fabric as she moved close again. "And this isn't the time for jokes."

"Then you're really not going to like the next one. Did you hear about the earthquake that— "

"Enough, Sawyer," she snapped. Then she inhaled sharply and exhaled long and slow. "Just... enough."

He dropped the forced smile and reached out until his fingers brushed against her hand. "I'm okay."

"No, you're not." She quickly pulled her hand away and pushed the hair from his forehead to examine the wound. She was close enough that he could smell the faint scent of wildflowers on her. He knew it was her soap, something from the artisanal shop in Steam Valley, but it made him think of her as part of the landscape, as though she'd bloomed from the very wilderness that surrounded them.

He swallowed hard, allowing himself to lean into her touch, just for a moment.

"Will be," he murmured. "Just need a minute."

"No, you need medical attention. You've been unconscious for nearly an hour. You have a concussion and need stitches." She pressed a hand to his shoulder. "Sit down."

He allowed her to guide him down to a worn wooden seat, a sigh escaping as he leaned back, the wall cool against his burning skin. He hoped she couldn't hear the small sounds of pain he made as he moved, but he knew she probably could. She was observant like that. It was one of the things that made her an excellent park ranger.

"Is everyone..." he began, trying to push himself upright again.

She pushed him back down gently. "Some bumps and bruises, and Joel broke his ankle, but everyone is alive. Thanks to you. If you hadn't pushed Joel out of the way..."

She didn't finish the thought.

He didn't remember who Joel was. One of her hikers, he assumed. "Just did what anyone would've done."

"No, not anyone."

He could hear Lucy rummaging through a first aid kit—the rustle of bandages, the clink of metal on metal —but it felt like it was happening somewhere far away.

Jesus, maybe she was right, and he wasn't okay.

"Do you make a habit of running toward danger?" Her hands were gentle as she cleaned the cut on his forehead. The antiseptic burned, but he didn't pull away.

"Only when there's a pretty girl to impress," he said, trying for a grin.

She snorted softly, but he felt her hand still on his

forehead just for a moment before she continued tending the wound.

Zelda nudged her head under his hand. His sweet girl, always worrying about him. He gave her a quick scratch behind the ears before letting his hand drop back onto his lap. It was heavy, like it was filled with lead, and his fingers were trembling. Pain radiated from every corner of his body, but it felt distant, almost dream-like, as if he were floating in a foggy sea.

His hand found its way to Zelda's head again, curling into her soft fur. He needed the grounding connection, the constant reminder that she was okay, that they were alive. The tremble in his fingers seemed to ease the more he focused on the steady rhythm of her breathing.

Someone else joined them then, a heavy set of boots stomping across the wooden floor.

"Ranger Harper, how's he doing?" It was a woman's voice, but it was deep and commanding.

"He'll be okay," Lucy replied, her hands never leaving his face. "He's just a little loopy right now."

"I'm right here, you know. And I'm not loopy, just..." He trailed off. Even he wasn't sure what he was. Worn out? Shaken up?

"Concussed, most likely," the woman suggested. "Do you know your name?"

"Sawyer Murphy." It came out sounding more like a question than a statement of fact.

"Uh-huh. And who's the president?"

"Probably some old guy that should've retired twenty years ago."

The woman let out a deep belly laugh that echoed around the room. "Yeah, he'll be okay. No doubt about it, you're one tough son of a bitch."

He looked toward her voice and wished he could put a face to it. He imagined a big, muscular woman who towered over everyone else, with laugh lines etched deep into her face and crow's feet at the corners of her eyes from years of squinting against the harsh sunlight. "And you are?"

"Beatrice Carter. Friends call me Bea," she said and held out a hand he couldn't see.

After an awkward moment, Lucy guided his hand to meet Bea's.

"Oh," Bea said, sounding embarrassed. "Forgot about your blindness. My apologies."

"It's fine." He shrugged, but the movement sent a hot wave of pain searing through his side. He clenched his jaw against it, but he knew they noticed.

Bea's grip tightened on his hand. "You're one hell of a stubborn man, aren't you?"

"Been accused of it a time or two."

"Good. We're gonna need that stubbornness if we're to get everybody safely off this mountain, ain't that right, Ranger Harper?"

Lucy's reply was slow in coming. "Yes, we will. All right," she said like she'd made up her mind about something and drew in a deep breath. "I'm going to stitch you up, Sawyer. It's going to hurt."

"Hell," he said with a lightness he didn't feel. "You think a little needle will scare me?"

"No," she admitted, and there was a softness there that made his heart stutter. "But it scares me."

"Why?"

There was a beat of silence, and he had the feeling Lucy and Bea were exchanging a look.

Then Bea said softly, "I'll go check in with the others," and her heavy footsteps faded away.

"Why?" he repeated when Lucy still didn't respond.

"Because... I owe you my life," she finally confessed in a whisper.

"Luce—"

"No, listen. I do owe you my life, and instead of repaying that debt, it feels like every time we meet, I'm always putting yours in danger."

"What debt?" His laugh was a small, pained sound in the quiet room. "And how are you putting me in danger? Did you force me to come up here looking for Pierce? No," he said before she could respond. "And it's not your fault my dumb ass decided to play hero and jump under a falling branch."

"Still," she protested. "I can't help but feel— "

"What? Responsible? Are you going to blame yourself for the earthquake next?"

"No, of course not."

"Then why are you blaming yourself for the rest of it?"

She growled softly in annoyance. "Why do you make everything sound so simple?"

"It's because things usually are. Now, are you going to stitch me up or let me bleed to death?"

chapter
two

LUCY HUFFED OUT A LAUGH. "You're not bleeding to death."

A smile flitted over his lips. "Good to know. But I'd still prefer not to be bleeding at all."

"Okay." She opened the sterile needle with shaking hands and told herself to breathe. She had seen worse injuries and stitched up nastier wounds. But somehow, this was different. This was Sawyer. He was different. Not just a random hiker in distress, but a friend, a familiar face. A man who had once saved her life, who had been her rock in her darkest hour. And now, as he sat there, smiling despite the pain, it was her turn to be his rock.

"I'll do my best." She poised the needle at the edge of the wound and swallowed hard. It was suddenly difficult to breathe. To think.

"You always do," Sawyer said quietly.

When she didn't move, he reached out and found her

hand again, gripping it like he had when she was trapped in that dark cave, freezing and bleeding out. Like he had in the cold hospital room where she'd spent what felt like an eternity after her rescue.

His touch sent a shiver up her spine despite the summer heat that was beginning to seep through the cracks in the shattered windows of the ranger station. She looked at him, his pale blue eye focused on a point over her shoulder, his face ashen against the grit and grime that smeared his cheeks.

He grinned. "Try not to scar my handsome face. It's all I got going for me."

"Don't be an idiot," she said, though there was no real heat behind it. Her hands were steady now. She took a deep breath, feeling the weight of everyone's gazes on her, then pressed the sharp point to his skin.

The first stitch made him hiss in pain, and Lucy flinched, but she didn't stop. The cut was deep and ragged, and if they didn't close it, infection could set in. She worked fast, making each stitch as small and precise as possible to minimize scarring.

Sawyer remained silent throughout the procedure, his hand gripping Zelda's harness so tightly that his knuckles turned white. The dog whined softly and laid her head on his lap, offering what comfort she could.

By the time Lucy was finished, beads of sweat dotted her forehead, and her shoulders ached from the tension. She cut the thread and removed her gloves, studying her handiwork.

"Okay," she said finally, pulling back. "All done."

Sawyer let out a long breath, his body visibly sagging. "That wasn't so bad."

She rolled her eyes. Men and their bravado. But she knew he was hurting. It was in every line of his face, etched in the tight set of his jaw. Yet he managed a weak smirk, an attempt to keep up the facade. It was so Sawyer of him.

Standing, she moved over to their makeshift first-aid station and grabbed a bottle of water, two painkillers, and a thin blanket. She returned to his side, pushing the pills into his hand. "Take these, and drink plenty of water."

He tried to give them back. "Nah, I'll be fine."

"You're not a superhero, Sawyer. Take the damn pills."

He held up his hands in surrender. "All right, all right. Bossy," he muttered and tossed the pills into his mouth.

Lucy watched as he swallowed them with a grimace, then reached out and gently touched his cheek, turning his face toward her to inspect the stitches one last time. Sawyer didn't shy away from her touch. Instead, he leaned into it, a soft sigh escaping him.

And she felt it. The sparks. The heat that had been simmering beneath the surface since their first meeting. She knew it was why he'd disappeared from her life as soon as she was well enough to leave the hospital. He was afraid of it, this thing between them. Afraid of the vulnerability it demanded. In truth, so was she, which was why she never reached out to him after he left. She'd made some really horrible decisions regarding men in the past, and she had promised herself she wouldn't make the same mistake again.

But Sawyer is different.

She ignored the faint whisper of her heart and withdrew her hand quickly, not trusting herself around him anymore.

"Get some rest." Her voice came out raspy with emotion, and she cleared her throat as she draped the blanket over him. His hands caught hers before she could pull away, a simple gesture that sent another bolt of electricity through her veins.

"Don't go," he said quietly, his thumb brushing against her knuckles in an achingly tender motion.

Lucy hesitated, torn between her need to check on the others and the warmth radiating from Sawyer's touch. She looked at him again, his handsome face pale but calm despite the pain he must be in. His quiet strength was one of the many things she admired about him.

"I won't," she promised softly, pulling a chair closer so she could sit beside him. Her hand stayed locked with his, and she leaned back in the chair, her gaze fixed on his peaceful face. She would remain at his side, just as he had stayed by hers all those nights in the hospital. His throat bobbed slightly as he swallowed, a remnant of pain possibly, and then his grip loosened as sleep took him.

A gust of wind blew in through the broken window, carrying with it the scent of fresh rain and fallen redwood needles— nature going about its usual business as if nothing had happened. Lucy closed her eyes for a moment, taking in the familiar smells of the forest. It was a harsh reminder of how they were, once again, at the mercy of nature, their lives hanging in the balance. But there was also a strange comfort in it, a reassurance that even after disaster, life finds a way to go on.

"Is it raining?" Sawyer asked, startling her. She looked at his face again. He hadn't opened his eyes, but his mouth curved into a small smile, "Smells like rain."

"Yeah, it's working up to it."

His smile dimmed. "The ground's unsteady."

"I know." She was fully aware of how dangerous their situation was. The quake had weakened the terrain, and a heavy downpour could trigger landslides.

"Fuck." Sawyer lay his head back against the wall, a low groan escaping his lips. "Where are we?"

"A decommissioned ranger station. We took shelter here after the first quake. It's not much, but it has a roof and four walls... somewhat."

Sawyer's brow furrowed. "The quake... How bad was it?"

Lucy hesitated. The truth was, she didn't know, couldn't tell from their vantage point. But the station–a sturdy, well-built structure–had taken a brutal beating, and the trail down the mountain had collapsed, so she suspected the valley below hadn't fared well, either.

"Bad," she admitted finally. "The trail is gone, and aftershocks have been happening pretty regularly, causing rockslides. It's dangerous to move, and we can't contact anyone."

"Your radio's dead?"

"No, but it's just static. We... we're trapped here, for now."

A hiss of air slipped past Sawyer's teeth, and for a moment, he looked like he was about to argue. But then he just exhaled a long breath. "What about Pierce and Raszta? Did anyone find them?"

"No. I'm sorry."

"Fuck," Sawyer said again, very softly.

"Maybe they made it off the mountain before the quake. Mr. Grassley said he saw him going down the trail. Maybe they're safely back in town."

"Yeah," Sawyer breathed out, a note of forlorn hope tingeing his words. "Maybe." His hand tightened slightly around hers, a silent plea for reassurance she didn't fully have herself.

"Once the rain stops and things settle down, we'll find them."

His fingers relaxed under hers, and he turned his head in her direction. She knew he couldn't see her, but she met his sightless gaze anyway as if trying to communicate with him through sheer will. After a moment, he gave her a small nod and lay back again.

"Why are you so worried about him?" she asked. "Pierce seems like the kind of guy who can take care of himself." She'd met most of the men and women of Redwood Coast Rescue when they rescued her last summer, and they were all strong, capable people. Most of them were former military and could hold their own under even the toughest circumstances. But Sawyer's concern for Pierce seemed to go beyond that to something more personal.

Sawyer was silent for a long moment. "He's... he's more than just a friend. He's my brother in every sense of the word except blood. He's been there for me ever since I lost my sight. We were both at Landstuhl at the same time, recovering from our injuries. The man had damn near been decapitated by shrapnel and had lost his voice, yet he still helped me adjust to losing my sight and made sure I didn't lose myself in self-pity and bitterness. Without him..." He trailed off, his throat working as he swallowed. "Yeah. I wouldn't be here. But he went through some bad shit recently, and... he hasn't been the same since."

Lucy felt a painful tug in her chest. She could picture it so clearly, the two battered soldiers bonding in a military hospital over their trauma. She squeezed his hand again. "We'll find him. If he's on this mountain, I promise we won't leave him behind."

Sawyer released her hand and scrubbed at his dirty face. "I feel like I let him down. He needed a shoulder to lean on, and I didn't notice until it was too late."

She knew he was wiping away tears but didn't call him out on it. Instead, she glanced away, giving him a moment of privacy.

"What if he couldn't take it anymore and came up here to—" He stopped short, leaving the thought unspoken.

"He didn't." She didn't know Pierce, but he didn't sound like the kind of guy to take the easy way out.

"From what you've told me, he's a fighter. He's survived hell and came out still swinging. I don't believe for one second he'd come up here to end his life. Especially since he had his dog with him when my tour group spotted him."

Sawyer let out a shaky breath. "Yeah. Yeah, you're right. He wouldn't do that. He wouldn't leave Raszta up here alone."

There was a silence, the room filled only by the patter of falling rain and the murmurs of her tour group in the other room. The quiet moments were Lucy's least favorite. It was during those times that she could hear her own thoughts too clearly—the fear, the uncertainty. But for Sawyer, she would endure them. She reached out to touch his hand again.

And then, from beyond the battered walls of the ranger station, came a sound that made her blood run cold. The sound of rocks sliding and earth moving, a low rumble growing into an earsplitting roar.

Sawyer's head snapped up, and he turned towards the noise. "What's that sound?"

Before Lucy could answer, the ground beneath them shifted violently. A wave of icy terror washed over Lucy as the wooden boards beneath them bucked and tilted.

Pain blossomed in her shoulder as she collided with the wall, her breath leaving her lungs in a sharp exhale.

"Landslide," she gasped, scrambling to her feet. Sawyer was struggling upright as well, his face pale and strained.

"Everyone!" she shouted, rushing towards the door

that led to the rest of the shelter where the others were huddled. "We need to move! Now!"

Chaos erupted as they tried to evacuate. Chuck Grassley helped his son to his feet, draping Joel's slender arm over his burly shoulders. Bea rushed over to help, wedging her shoulder under Joel's other arm. Between the two of them, they all but carried the kid out. Bea's husband, Theodore, brought up the rear.

The thunderous noise outside continued, shaking the station and drowning out their panicked shouts. Dust filled the air, making it hard to breathe. The world tilted sickeningly as the ground beneath them gave way.

Lucy gripped a wooden beam for support, nails digging into the splintering wood. "Sawyer! Get to the door!"

He seemed momentarily disoriented, swaying on his feet. Zelda was already by his side, her body tense and alert. With one hand on her harness and another outstretched to find the door, Sawyer slowly navigated through the chaos.

Suddenly, with a horrific groan that resonated deep in its bones, the station tilted dangerously sideways. People screamed as they lost their footing, falling towards the collapsing wall. Zelda whined urgently, leading Sawyer towards the rapidly narrowing exit.

As if in slow motion, Lucy watched as Sawyer stumbled, his hand brushing the door frame. He was so close... yet the world continued to buckle beneath them. Pushing off from her support beam, Lucy launched herself at him. Her body collided with his, and they tumbled out of the station moments before the structure gave a final, anguished groan and collapsed in on itself.

They landed hard on the rain-soaked earth, Lucy still clutching onto Sawyer. Disoriented and gasping for breath, she rolled off him and lay there for a moment, blinking up at the smeared sky as the rain pelted down on them.

"Sawyer? Are you okay?" She turned her head, finding him prone beside her, his face white in the dim light. Zelda whined again, her nose nudging at his cheek. He reached up and gave her a reassuring pat.

"Fuck," he muttered, his voice strained.

Lucy sat up, ignoring the pain radiating from her shoulder as she scrabbled over to him. "Are you hurt?" Her hands ghosted over his body, seeking wounds against the wet fabric of his clothes.

He waved her away and sat up with a wince. "I'm okay. Just winded. Landed hard."

She released a sigh of relief. She looked around, the reality of their situation sinking in. The ranger station was gone, swallowed by the landslide. The mountain had reclaimed its own with a vengeance.

Chuck and Bea settled Joel against the thick trunk of a nearby tree. Theodore stood in the rain, staring at what was left of the ranger station, his eyes wide and horrified behind his crooked glasses.

"How bad is the damage?" Sawyer asked.

"It's gone. We need to find shelter. Can you move?" She noticed he was trying to stand and hurried to his side. He waved her away.

"I'm not helpless," he said through his teeth.

Right. Okay, he had a point. He wasn't helpless. He'd lost his sight, not his ability to function. Still, a part of her wanted to shelter him from this disaster.

She stepped back, her hand retracting from his arm, but her eyes never left him as he pushed himself upright. He winced, leaning heavily on Zelda for a moment before he straightened with a determined look on his face.

"We need to move higher," she called over to the group, raising her voice over the rain and the blood pounding in her ears. She still heard the roar of the landslide in her head, a horrifying reminder that the earth under their feet wasn't as stable as it should be. "We can't risk setting up camp near another landslide. If we go up to that ridge over there..." She pointed to a rocky outcrop. "We should be able to see a fire watch tower."

If it's still standing.

She saw the same doubts on Sawyer's face, but he didn't voice them.

No. She put the doubts out of her mind. It was made of steel, reinforced against earthquakes. It *was* still standing.

She turned back to the group. "We can take shelter there."

"What if there's another one?" Joel asked, his voice shaky. His gaze, though directed at Lucy, kept darting back to the pile of rubble that was the ranger station.

Lucy wasn't sure how to answer that. The truth was, the mountain was unpredictable on a good day.

After the earthquake and onslaught of rain… it was a landslide waiting to happen. The only question was when and where. However, she didn't want to add to the teenager's already palpable fear. She decided on a partial truth.

"I can't predict what the mountain will do next. But moving away from *this* unstable area is the most sensible thing we can do right now."

Joel nodded and swallowed hard.

"Is there a radio at the watch tower?" Theodore asked, taking off his glasses to try and wipe off some of the dirt smudging the lenses.

"There should be. As well as food, medical supplies, and everything else that we'll need to ride this out until rescue arrives."

"All right," Bea said and clapped her hands together. "Let's do this. Which way?"

Lucy looked at Sawyer again. What if this wasn't the right call? Her instincts had been fucked since her encounter with the Shadow Stalker last year. She barely trusted herself to cook dinner, and now all of these people were relying on her to lead them to safety. The weight of it made her stomach churn.

What if her decisions cost them their lives?

What if it cost *Sawyer* his life?

Oh, God.

Sawyer, his pale blue eyes hidden behind the curtain of his wet hair, gave her a nod. "You got this, Luce."

His words sent a warm shiver through her, chasing away her doubts for a moment. She took a deep breath, rolled her shoulders back, and scanned the mountainside, picking out a relatively safe path that they could take.

"We go up there. Over the ridge and through that pass," she said, indicating a narrow gap in the line of trees. "From there, it should be a straight shot to the tower. Stick close together and watch your step. If you see anything unusual, like water flowing over the ground where it shouldn't be or new cracks in the earth, shout out."

The group gathered their meager belongings and set off into the rain, following Lucy's lead. She held her flashlight high, sweeping its beam over the slick, uneven ground. Theodore and Bea supported Joel between them while Chuck hovered close behind, glancing anxiously over his shoulder every few steps. Sawyer gripped Zelda's harness and matched his steps to hers, trusting the dog to guide him safely through the treacherous terrain.

The rain seemed to intensify as they ascended the mountainside. Thunder rumbled menacingly overhead, and lightning split the sky in jagged forks, briefly illuminating the dark, dripping trees that loomed over them.

"How are you holding up back there?" she called over her shoulder to Sawyer.

"We're managing," he replied through gritted teeth.

Lucy could tell he was struggling. She longed to go to him, to offer a steadying hand, but she knew he would refuse it. His pride and fierce independence were part of what she admired in him. Still, she found herself glancing back frequently to check on him, watching as he picked his way up the steep incline with a surprising amount of grace and confidence.

That man was full of surprises. Despite his blindness and his concussion, he navigated the treacherous terrain with more ease than her hikers. He was practically a mountain goat. A very stubborn, very capable mountain goat.

And he'd hate that she just likened him to a goat. She laughed softly to herself at the thought.

"Want to share the joke with the class?" he asked, coming up beside her.

The startle of his voice so close to her ear made Lucy jump. She hadn't heard him approach, the rain hammering on the leaves above drowning out any other sound.

She shook her head, even though she knew he couldn't see it. "Nothing important. Just a thought."

His eyebrow arched in curiosity, the small ghost of a smile playing on his lips. "Were you thinking about me?"

Caught off guard, she fumbled for a response. "What? No!"

Sawyer's grin widened. "The lady doth protest too much."

Lucy felt her cheeks burn but couldn't tell if it was from embarrassment or the cold rain pelting her face. "Oh, shut up."

Sawyer chuckled as he continued onward, his grip shifting on Zelda's harness. His amusement warmed Lucy in a way the rain couldn't wash away.

Dammit, she liked him. Had always liked him from

the moment he squeezed into that cave and promised he wasn't going to leave her until she was safe.

But then he had left her once she was healed. She had to remember that. As far as he was concerned, his job had been done, and he had moved on. She'd been left to figure out the rest on her own.

And fair enough, really. He was a rescuer, not a babysitter. He had lives to save and people to help.

So why was she still bitter about it?

She shook her head. It wasn't the question she needed to focus on right now. She needed to focus on getting the group to safety. She glanced back, watching as the rest of the hikers picked their way up the trail.

The incline grew steeper as they climbed, their progress slowed by the slick footing and by having to help Joel navigate the difficult terrain on a broken leg. More than once, Lucy had to stop and help the others haul the kid up over a boulder or fallen log blocking their path. She tried not to dwell on the nagging thought that this route may prove too difficult for them in their ragged state.

But what choice did they have?

Going back was not an option.

chapter
three

AS THEY REACHED THE RIDGE, Lucy paused, squinting through the rain to try and spot the fire watchtower in the distance. But the stormy gloom obscured their view, and all she could make out was a vague dark smudge rising above the trees that she hoped was their destination.

Beside her, Sawyer stood still, gaze turned towards the heavens, letting the rain kiss his face. His nostrils flared as he inhaled deeply, capturing and cataloging every scent that the rain carried.

How was he so calm?

The air was thick with the storm's wild energy, and yet Sawyer seemed as serene as ever. His presence beside her was grounding, a sturdy pillar in the chaos of the storm. He turned towards her, sensing her gaze on him. A wry smile touched his lips.

"Can't see a damn thing through this rain, can we?" Sawyer's calm voice pulled Lucy from her thoughts. His face still tilted upwards, an almost serene expression across his features.

"No," she admitted. "We can't."

"The storm is lessening. I can feel the shift in the temperature and the wind."

She could barely hear him over the roaring gusts of wind but took some comfort in his certainty. "I hope you're right."

Sawyer gently grazed his fingers over her trembling arm, causing an unexpected spark of warmth to shoot through her body. "Trust me," he said softly. "And trust yourself. You know where we're going. Let's keep moving."

Lucy swallowed hard. Trust wasn't something that came easily for her anymore. But there was something in his unwavering confidence that began to soothe her gnawing doubts. "Okay," she said, nodding more to herself than to him. She turned to the group. "We'll keep heading east."

"Where's the tower?" Chuck Grassley asked.

"It's there. We just can't see it yet." She gestured vaguely in the direction they'd been hiking.

Chuck glowered. He wasn't convinced. But as Lucy looked back toward Sawyer, she was met with a reassuring nod. That was enough.

"We can't just keep dragging my boy all over this mountain with a broken leg."

"I'm okay, Dad," Joel said faintly.

"No, you're not," Chuck said, leaving no room in his tone for argument. He turned back to Lucy, fire blazing in his eyes. He pointed at Joel's leg. It was wrapped up as tight as they could get it with what they had on hand. "You're supposed to be guiding us out of here. You're supposed to know what you're doing. Instead, you're leading us in circles!"

"Easy now," Sawyer said, his voice still calm. "We're all scared and—"

Chuck's face went red, and he took a step toward Sawyer, his chest puffing like a rooster's. "I'm not scared."

Zelda's ears flattened, and a low grumble pumped from her throat. Sawyer set a soothing hand on her head.

"Of course not," he said, still in that steady, placating tone. "We're all relying on each other here. So, let's stay calm and focused. It's the best thing we can do for Joel right now."

Chuck jabbed a finger toward Sawyer. "I don't know why anyone is listening to *him*. He's fucking blind. We should be going down the mountain."

"Dad, stop," Joel said.

"Because he's blind, not stupid," Bea said from the back of the group, her face as hard as granite. She stepped forward, squaring up to Chuck in a show of solidarity with Sawyer. "And I'd follow him and Ranger Harper into hell a million times over before I'd follow you anywhere. They're more capable than you've ever dreamed of being."

Chuck opened his mouth to retort, but nothing came out. He sputtered, face red as a cherry. With an angry huff, he turned to help Joel up. "We'll see who's more capable when the shit hits the fan." Chuck grunted, heaving Joel onto his feet despite the younger man's protests of pain. They trudged ahead, heading east, their forms swallowed by the misty veil of rain.

"It'll be okay when we get to the tower," Theodore said and scurried after them like a frightened rabbit.

Lucy looked at Bea in silent gratitude. Bea nodded before turning to follow her husband. "Hang on, Theo. Let me go first."

Sawyer and Lucy hung back a moment longer. She squinted toward the watch tower again, but still couldn't pick it out of the gloom.

God, she hoped it was still standing.

Zelda sat at their feet, her tail brushing over the wet grass as she watched them with her intelligent eyes.

"It's not going to get any easier," Sawyer finally said, and she turned to look at him. For once, he didn't look calm. He was worried, too. Even without sight, he still seemed to see everything. "The longer this drags out, the more unhinged he'll get. Guys like that don't handle powerlessness well."

Lucy nodded, tugging nervously at the end of her ponytail. She was very aware the situation was a powder keg and Chuck was the lit fuse. One wrong move, one wrong decision on her part and the group would explode into chaos.

"I can handle Chuck," she said, trying to sound more confident than she felt.

"Who's going to handle you?" Sawyer asked gently.

She frowned at him. "What?"

"You're taking too much on your shoulders, Luce. You can't carry the weight of each one of us."

She whirled on him, outrage burning through her. "Are you saying I'm not strong enough?"

"No," he said quickly, reaching out to grasp her arm. Once he found it, his hand slid down to hers, his fingers lacing through hers. "I'm saying you don't have to be. Not all the time. Lean on me. Let me take some of that weight."

She stared at him for a heartbeat then looked down at their clasped hands, her throat suddenly dry. She swallowed hard, the words "I need you" threatening to tumble from her lips. She couldn't say them, though. Wouldn't allow herself that vulnerability.

"We should catch up with the others," she said, her voice surprisingly steady considering she was shaking all over. "If we hurry, we'll reach the tower before nightfall."

He nodded and let her pull her hand from his. His fingers hovered for a moment in the air before he dropped his hand to his side. "You're right. Lead the way."

They found the rest of the group huddled under an overhang of rocks providing some protection from the rain. Chuck was pacing like a caged animal while Bea and Theodore exchanged worried glances. Joel lay propped against a boulder, his face pale and drawn with pain.

"We can't stay here long," Lucy said. "We're too exposed and the terrain is unstable. We're moving to the tower."

"But it's pouring buckets," Chuck protested, his

hands on his hips. "Joel can't walk all that way. We barely made it a hundred yards before he had to stop."

"As much as I hate to agree with him, he's right." Bea swiped the rainwater from her face. "The kid can't make the walk."

"I'm sorry," Joel muttered, his eyes brimming with tears.

"It's okay," Sawyer said easily. "We can make a stretcher. It won't be comfortable, but it will save you from walking and—"

"Easy for you to suggest," Chuck spat. "You won't be carrying it."

"No, not unless you want more broken bones," Sawyer said with a lightness that didn't quite match the hardness in his eyes. "But I can help make it, and I can help guide. I know these mountains."

"He does," Theodore spoke up. "He knows his stuff. He's hiked the entire Pacific Crest Trail and the Colorado Trail through the Rockies."

When everyone looked at Theodore, he flushed.

"I... I've read all the articles about you," he added faintly. "What you do, how you do it, is fascinating."

There was a beat of silence as Chuck stared at them all incredulously. "You're not seriously suggesting we let the blind man lead us."

"*I* will be leading us," Lucy said. "But Sawyer does know these mountains as well as I do. Maybe better. So I'd appreciate it if you kept your disparaging comments about his abilities to yourself from now on, Mr. Grassley."

Chuck sputtered, cheeks puffed up with indignation. But before he could retort, a violent wind whipped through the space, snatching away his breath and words. The hikers instinctively huddled closer together, Lucy and Sawyer on either end of the huddle anchoring it.

As the wind subsided, Lucy let out a shuddering breath. "We can't afford any more delays. We don't want to be out here when the sun sets. Bea, Theodore, find something sturdy to use as poles."

Chuck scoffed loudly from where he was stooping over Joel but didn't bother retorting. Lucy was relieved; risking another argument could cost them precious time - time they didn't have.

Sawyer slid his pack off his back and knelt to open it. Zelda sat by his side, his faithful sentinel, her ears perked up and trained on the storm.

"Help me with this," Sawyer said, drawing a folded tarp from his bag and shaking it out.

Lucy stepped forward and caught the flapping edge of it. Together, they stretched it out and began to fasten it to the thick branches Bea and Theodore had found. With each movement, Lucy was acutely aware of Sawyer's firm, steady presence beside her. His fingers brushed against hers as they worked, the contact fleeting but sizzling.

Finally, the stretcher was ready. It was a crude contraption but sturdy enough to hold Joel's weight.

Joel's face had lost most of its color and he was breathing heavily. Chuck stood watch over him, his usual bluster replaced with a palpable fear. For all of his faults, the man did care about his son.

"All right," Lucy said. "Let's get you on this, Joel. We need to move out."

They moved as gently as they could, but Joel still hissed in pain as they shifted him onto the makeshift stretcher.

Sawyer crouched at the head of it, his hand resting on Joel's trembling shoulder. "Hang in there, buddy. We're going to get you out of here."

Chuck took the back end of the stretcher while Bea stepped up to help guide at the front. Theodore walked alongside them, his eye on their footing as they navigated the rocky terrain.

They descended the ridge, the storm slowly blurring into a fine mist around them. Lucy led the way with Sawyer and Zelda close behind, his hiking stick clicking rhythmically against the rocks.

Suddenly, he stopped and cocked his head, his brow furrowing as something caught his attention. "Do you hear that?"

Lucy strained her ears, the steady patter of rain against the leaves of the towering redwoods all she could detect at first. Then, subtly, it came to her— a voice. Female. Calling for help.

"Stay here," she told the group, and without a second thought, she was off, her worn hiking boots skidding over the wet underbrush. Sawyer was right behind her, his sure-footed stride never faltering. He moved with a fluid grace that never failed to amaze Lucy; she knew he wasn't seeing the world as she did, but he navigated it just as deftly— perhaps even more so.

"I told you to stay behind."

He snorted. "And I didn't listen. Let's move. Someone needs help."

"God, you're stubborn."

They picked their way through the undergrowth, following the fading voice.

A fallen tree blocked their path.

And beneath it, trapped and crying out for help, was a woman clothed in torn hiking gear. Her pale face was dotted with grimy tears, and she gasped for breath, her eyes wide with fear. "Help! Please. Help."

"Fuck," Sawyer murmured. "How bad is she hurt?"

Lucy skidded down a short embankment to the woman. "Hi, my name is Lucy. I'm a park ranger. What's your name?"

"Maya," she gasped. "Maya Thompson. I was... I was here taking pictures. I'm a photographer. And the earthquake hit and—and I can't feel my legs."

"Okay, Maya. Let me see what we're dealing with here." She moved around Maya's head and looked down the length of the tree. It was a massive redwood, its roots uprooted by the earthquake. "It's got you pinned, huh?" She tried to keep her tone as light as possible even as her heart threatened to pound out of her chest.

This was bad.

Maya nodded, her eyes glassy with pain and fear. "It... hurts."

"We need help!" Lucy shouted over her shoulder,

hoping to hail their group up the slope. But before she could make out any response, Sawyer skidded down the embankment and crouched beside her.

"Hey there, Maya," he greeted congenially. "Sawyer Murphy. I can't see you, but my dog Zelda here can give me a good idea." He gestured toward the lab who nuzzled Maya's cheek and made her sob out a short laugh. "Zelda and I are with Redwood Coast Rescue. We're gonna get you free."

Maya exhaled a shaky breath, looking between Lucy and Sawyer with relief in her fear-filled eyes. "Please hurry. I'm scared."

"I know." Sawyer touched his stick to the tree trunk several times as if he were assessing, then he put a hand on Lucy's arm and moved her down the length of the tree toward Maya's feet.

"Where are you going?" Maya cried.

"Just over here," Sawyer said, still in that steady, calming tone. "I promise we won't go far, and we'll be right back to you."

"Fucking hell," Lucy muttered as she joined him, her gaze riveted on the trapped woman. The situation was dire, and they both knew it. The tree was colossal; even with everyone's combined strength, they wouldn't be able to lift it off her.

"What do you think?" she asked Sawyer, keeping her voice low.

His head cocked to the side as he let his hand trail over the bark of the tree. His face was set in a contempla-tive frown, his sky-blue eyes distant and unfocused.

"Zelda," he said suddenly. The labrador perked up at the sound of her name, her tail wagging once before she settled back down, ears pricked attentively. He looked back toward Lucy. "Guess her favorite pastime."

"Sawyer, we don't have time for—"

"Digging."

"Oh." Then his meaning hit her. "*Oh*. We dig Maya out."

He nodded. "The ground is soft enough for it."

"Also soft enough to cause another landslide if we don't do it right. Or the tree could roll onto her and crush her. Or us. There are a million ways this could go wrong."

Sawyer's calm smile didn't falter. It was both reassuring and annoying as hell. "And one way it could go very right," he said. "It's a risk, but leaving her is certain death."

He was right. She knew it, but it didn't ease the knots in her belly. "Stay with her. Talk to her. I'll get the others down here."

SAWYER LISTENED until he could no longer hear Lucy's departing footsteps, then used the tree to find his way back to Maya. He sat down in the dirt beside her. "Okay, we have a plan. We're going to dig you out, but we need to make sure the tree is secure first."

Maya's breath hitched. "I-I don't want to d-die, Sawyer."

He reached out to find her hand. Her fingers were cold, trembling. "Hey, we're not going to let that happen."

Maya's hand tightened around his. "Promise?"

"I promise," he said, giving her a reassuring squeeze. "Just stay awake for me, okay?"

Lucy returned moments later, her breath coming in hard gasps as if she'd run the whole way. "Everyone's coming. They're gathering anything they can use to dig."

"Good," he murmured, rubbing Maya's hand between his, hoping to lend a fraction of the warmth circulating through his own veins. "Tell me about your photography, Maya."

She sniffed. "Wildlife mostly. I... I love capturing them in their natural habitat. Are you..." She sounded bewildered and trailed off.

"It's okay." He knew exactly what she'd been about to say. He got it a lot. "Go ahead and ask."

She exhaled in a rush. "Are you really blind?"

"Yes."

"What are you doing up here?"

"It's a long story, but it boils down to hiking was my favorite thing to do before I lost my sight, so I decided I wasn't going to give it up after."

"But how do you..."

"Navigate? I got real comfortable not knowing where I am." He felt Lucy's stare on him like an electric current down his spine, but kept all of his attention on Maya. He was afraid if she stopped talking, they'd lose her. "And I have Zelda."

At the sound of her name, his dog inched closer, her nose nuzzling under his and Maya's clasped hands. Her tail thunked against the tree.

"She's sweet," Maya said and released his hand to pet the dog.

"Yep, the sweetest. She's my best girl." Again he felt Lucy's eyes on him, that quick sizzle of electricity across the back of his neck, and wondered what she was thinking.

Then movement caught his gaze, rocks coalescing and taking form before his eyes as they rolled by.

Oh, fuck. Another landslide?

But then he heard voices and looked toward the sound. He watched as the hikers moved down the hill one by one, the rocks dislodged by their sloppy footsteps. Bea Carter looked about like he imagined her—big, burly, with tattoos and spiky hair. Theodore Carter was a small, thin man with glasses—a seemingly strange match for Bea, but sometimes love was ever blinder than him. Chuck Grassley also looked exactly like he sounded—balding, beefy, more fat than muscle, a jock aged past his prime. The blue tarp of the makeshift stretcher hung between Bea and Chuck, but Sawyer couldn't see Joel nestled inside.

Then, as each member of the group reached the downed tree and stopped moving, they disappeared from his view again.

Sawyer squeezed his eyes shut and pinched the bridge of his nose. It was always disorientating when he saw so clearly one minute, and the next, everything dissolved back into vague shapes, colors, and shadows.

"You okay?" Lucy asked at his side.

"Yeah. Just... a headache." It was the truth and seemed an easier explanation to give rather than trying to explain the faulty connection between his eyes and his brain.

Lucy's voice softened. "I'll get you some more painkillers..."

"No." He shook his head a little too quickly, which didn't help the throbbing. "I'm fine."

"You're not fine, Sawyer. You have a concussion.

Under normal circumstances, you'd be resting in a hospital."

"These aren't normal circumstances."

"I'm aware. But you won't do anyone any good if you collapse."

"I won't collapse." At least, he was about eighty percent sure he wouldn't. Okay, maybe sixty-five percent. "Let's focus on getting Maya free."

Lucy grumbled something under her breath that sounded like "stubborn ass," then moved past him, her wildflower scent somehow not dimmed by sweat and grime. The scent lingered in his nose, and desire swirled through his stomach, goosebumps prickling his skin.

Dammit. Now was not the time or the place for his body to betray him like this. But his brain seemed unable to override the primal response, however misplaced it was.

"You like her," Maya said, a smile in her weakening voice.

He took a deep breath, reining in his unruly thoughts, and refocused his attention on the injured woman. "That obvious?"

"If I were you, I wouldn't play poker."

He chuckled. "Yeah, well, I've always been more of a chess player."

"Hey! Everybody, listen up!" Lucy's voice rang out, clear and commanding. "If you followed my packing list, you should have all brought a collapsible shovel. We need to brace the tree, then we'll dig under Maya until we can pull her out. Hey, Maya?" she added softly, and knelt next to the trapped woman again. "I'm gonna give you something for pain, okay? It might make you feel a little sleepy, but that's all right."

While Lucy tended to Maya, Sawyer straightened and reached out to his dog. He ran a hand over her soft head, taking comfort from her steady presence. She whined and licked at his fingers before pressing up against his leg. He pulled his own shovel off his backpack.

Lucy was suddenly at his side again, her hand wrapping around his wrist. "What do you think you're doing?"

"Helping." His tone was sharper than he'd intended, his arm muscles tensing under Lucy's grip. He was resourceful, independent—he didn't need anyone to remind him of his limitations. And he especially didn't want to hear it from a woman he was attracted to.

"You're hurt."

"I can still shovel."

"No one's doubting your ability, Sawyer," Lucy said, her voice all patience even as her grip on his wrist tightened. "You were *unconscious* a few hours ago. I'm just trying to keep from adding to our injury list. Joel's not helping either."

"Joel has a bone sticking out of his leg. I'm whole. I have four working limbs. Use me."

Lucy's grip tightened a fraction more. She drew a breath, and Sawyer could practically hear the gears shifting in her mind as she weighed the merits of fighting him on this.

Finally, with a sound that was somewhere between a

sigh and a growl, she released him. "We don't have time to argue. Just... be careful."

He wasn't sure if it was a victory or not, but at least he could do something. He heard the shuffle and scrape of shovels, the occasional grunt or curse as they hit a rock. He joined in with Zelda at his side.

"Dig," he ordered. She didn't have to be told twice. The only thing she loved more than digging was policing the squirrels that always tried to steal the bird seed out of the feeder at Redwood Coast Rescue.

The next few hours were a blur of hard work and quiet determination. Sawyer dug methodically, his hands blistering, his muscles screaming in protest from overuse and fatigue. But he refused to stop, refused to show weakness.

He'd spent too many years after losing his sight thinking he was useless. Too many years of letting his disability define him. That had all changed when he got Zelda. She'd given him his freedom back. Then he'd met Zak and Anna Hendricks and joined the Redwood Coast Rescue, and he'd found purpose again.

Now, here, on this mountain, he had a chance to prove himself again. To save a life. And maybe, just maybe, win Lucy's respect in the process.

Lucy was a constant presence at his side. Their elbows brushed more than once as they dug. He felt her attention on him often—that gaze that prickled his skin and made him aware of her in a way that was becoming harder to ignore.

"Easy, big guy." Lucy's voice was tight, her lips

pressed together as she watched him. "You're about to collapse."

He could feel beads of sweat trickling down his brow and the persistent ache in his head had become a dull roar, but he wasn't about to admit it. Not now.

"I'm good," he replied, grunting with effort as he shoved another heap of dirt away from Maya's trapped legs.

She didn't call him on the lie. Instead, she left his side, presumably to check on Maya. His suspicions were confirmed a moment later when she asked, "How are you doing, Maya?"

Silence.

His heart pounded, every beat echoing inside his skull like a hammer striking an anvil.

Then, finally, he heard a shallow, ragged breath and the quietest whisper of a response. "Okay."

"She doesn't sound good," he murmured when Lucy returned.

She said nothing for a beat, then her shovel dug into the earth with a renewed ferocity that made his heart clench. "She doesn't look good. We have to hurry."

Lucy was tough, tougher than anyone he'd ever known. And she bore the weight of everyone else's problems like they were her own. But now he could hear the strain in her voice, the slight tremor that she couldn't quite hide. He wanted to comfort her, to say something that would ease her fear, but he didn't know what to say. So he used his strength instead, clawing through the dirt and rocks with a relentless determination.

Finally, their efforts paid off. With one last Herculean pull from Bea and Chuck, they hauled Maya out.

The tree groaned ominously.

"Get back!" Lucy shouted as the branches they'd used to prop up the tree snapped, the sound echoing like gunshots.

Sawyer grabbed Zelda and realized he had no idea which way to go.

"Left!" Lucy grabbed his arm and yanked him sideways just as the tree moaned one last time before it rolled downhill with a thunderous crash.

"My God," Theodore breathed.

"Anyone hurt?" Lucy demanded. "Sawyer?"

He checked in with his internal pain meter. Other than the persistent throb in his head and some new nicks and scratches on his face from flying debris, he wasn't much worse off than before. "No, I'm good."

"Zelda?"

He ran his hands over his dog. Her heart was thundering, and she was panting hard from stress, but she wasn't injured. "Zelda's good."

"We're all okay," Bea said.

Rocks tumbled and crashed somewhere close by.

"Without the tree, the ground's too unsteady here," Lucy said. "We need to get to the tower."

"How?" Chuck demanded. "Now we have two people who can't walk."

"We make another stretcher," Sawyer answered.

"Who's gonna carry it? Theodore? He'd snap faster than a twig. You?"

As much as Sawyer loathed to admit it, the man had a point.

"I'll walk," Joel said suddenly.

"The hell you will."

"Dad, look at her. She's really hurt. She needs the stretcher more than I do. I can walk."

"You're sure?" Lucy asked.

"I can walk," he repeated, determination in every syllable.

Strong kid. Stronger than his dad seemed to give him credit for. Braver, too.

Sawyer turned toward Joel's voice and held out his hiking pole. "Use this as a crutch."

Joel hesitated. "Don't you need it?"

"I have Zelda." He patted the dog's side. "She won't let me walk off a cliff."

Lucy exhaled sharply. "You're not funny."

"I'm hilarious. You just don't appreciate my comedic genius."

Lucy didn't respond. Sawyer figured she was probably rolling her eyes. He held the pole out and, after a moment, felt Joel take it from his hand.

He lifted his other hand off Zelda and his fingertips felt wet and sticky. He frowned, bringing his hand closer to his face, sniffing the substance.

Blood.

His heart plummeted. Had he missed something earlier? Was his girl actually injured? But a quick inspection assured him that she was unharmed. This wasn't her blood.

"Lucy?" he called out in a low voice. She was at his side in an instant.

"What's wrong?"

He held out his hand. "Zelda's covered in blood."

Lucy's sharp intake of breath was his only answer. He heard the rustling of fabric as she presumably knelt beside Zelda, her touch gentle yet firm as she examined his dog.

"It's not hers," she said after a tense moment.

"I know."

She straightened. "Whose is it then? Maya's not bleeding that badly—at least not externally."

"Pierce." It was the first thought that popped into his head and no matter how illogical—Pierce was probably safely down the mountain helping RWCR with the rescue efforts—but he couldn't shake the chill of dread it brought.

There was silence except for the distant sound of rocks still tumbling down the unstable mountainside, and then Lucy responded, her voice taut. "We don't know that. It could be from anywhere. It's most likely animal blood. She probably found a dead deer or something while we were distracted with Maya."

But Sawyer knew Zelda, and Zelda didn't roam. She didn't abandon her charge to go sniff out carrion. She didn't leave his side unless commanded... or unless she saw a friend in need of help.

A friend like Pierce.

Sawyer lifted his head and squinted at the blurred shapes around him, trying to force them into focus. If

Pierce was somewhere nearby, he wouldn't be able to call for help. And if they walked away...

He couldn't bear that thought. He'd already buried too many friends. He wouldn't—couldn't—leave Pierce alone and injured.

"WE NEED to search the nearby area," Sawyer said, his voice firm despite the worry gnawing at his insides.

Lucy took a moment before answering, her tone unreadable. "We need to get Maya and Joel to the tower."

His hand tightened around Zelda's harness. "I have to look."

A silence hung between them, heavy as the mountain looming overhead.

Finally, Lucy sighed, her exhaustion evident even in that small sound. "We don't even know Pierce is up here."

"But we don't know for sure he isn't, and he could be injured. He can't speak, so he wouldn't be able to call for help."

Lucy hesitated again before she muttered a low curse under her breath. "All right. Ten minutes. It's all we can risk."

Ten minutes was better than nothing.

Turning to Zelda, he smoothed his hand over her head and whispered commands in her ear. Her tail thumped the ground twice in response before she shot off in the direction from which she'd returned. Sawyer gripped his spare hiking pole tighter and followed her with a determination born of desperation.

"Everyone, wait here," Lucy called to the group. "We'll be back in ten minutes."

They traced their path back to the fallen tree, Zelda leading the way with an uncanny sureness that Sawyer had learned to trust long ago. Every so often, she would stop and sniff at the ground, her body tensing before she picked up the trail again.

The mountain loomed ominously in Sawyer's limited vision, its jagged silhouette like an insurmountable wall.

"Sawyer," Lucy's voice was low, gentle like she didn't want to upset him. "We're running out of time."

"We have a few minutes left," he countered, unwilling to abandon their search just yet. Two minutes were as good as two hours if it meant finding Pierce. His hand grazed the coarse bark of a pine as they moved through the underbrush.

A yelp pierced the stillness around them.

"Zelda!" Sawyer called out, fear creeping into his voice. "Zelda!"

The barks were more urgent now, a frantic symphony that echoed from the dense forest. Without thinking, Sawyer surged forward, putting all his trust in his remaining senses to guide him. He heard Lucy shout after him, but he was already gone, following the single-minded drive to find his dog and possibly his friend.

He stumbled and fell, hands sinking into a bed of damp leaves and slick mud. He wiped it off on his trousers and pushed himself back up, not caring about the grit that lodged itself underneath his nails or the twigs scraping against his already-blistered hands.

"Sawyer! Wait!" Lucy skidded to a halt next to him, gasping for breath. Her hand was warm on his arm, steadying him.

"Where is she?" he asked, his voice tight with worry. "Where's my dog?"

Lucy didn't answer immediately. Instead, he heard the rustle of leaves and the crack of twigs underfoot as she moved ahead. After what felt like an eternity, her voice floated back. "Here."

Sawyer followed her voice until he bumped into her, reaching out tentatively to find Zelda's form on the ground. He ran his hands along her fur, noting the steady rise and fall of her chest. She was fine. Then, his fingers brushed against something wet and warm - more blood, but this time it wasn't just smeared on her coat. His heart clenched in his chest as he traced the source to a shallow cut on Zelda's foreleg.

"She must have run into a sharp branch or something," Lucy said gently, coming up behind him. "It's not deep. She'll be okay."

He nodded, pressing on Zelda's wound gently with his bandana to help stop the bleeding while Lucy fetched her first aid kit. The dog whined, but stayed still under his touch. He could feel her trembling, hear her frantic panting.

"Wait a second," Lucy muttered, her voice tight. "Sawyer, move your hand."

He obeyed, retracting his hand to let Lucy inspect the cut further. She gasped softly and he tensed, fingers curling into Zelda's fur.

"What is it?" he asked, fearing the worst.

She was silent for a moment before answering, her voice heavy with disbelief. "A branch didn't do this. The wound is too clean. Like... she was cut by a knife."

Lucy saw the flash of pain cross Sawyer's face, followed quickly by fury.

"Someone hurt my dog?" His voice was low, a dangerous rumble that sent a chill down Lucy's spine.

This was not the happy, easy-going Sawyer she knew. This Sawyer was the soldier, the warrior. This Sawyer was dangerous.

He surged to his feet, his hands balling into fists at his side. "Who the fuck would do this?"

She drew a steadying breath and focused on bandaging the wound. The first thought to pop into her mind was one he definitely didn't want to hear, but it had to be said. "What if Pierce—"

"No." As expected, he rejected the idea instantly. "He would never hurt an animal."

"I'm not saying he would normally, but you seem to think he's not acting like himself. Maybe, if he is up here, he doesn't want to be found and just meant to scare her away."

"He wouldn't—" He broke off. Hesitated. Shook his head. "No. He wouldn't hurt Zelda. He wouldn't hurt any dog. It's not him."

"Well, then, if it's not him, then there's someone else dangerous up here with us and we need to get back to the group. There's safety in numbers."

Sawyer took a moment, visibly struggling with himself. His hands clenched even tighter, knuckles turning white.

"Fuck," he finally muttered and rolled his shoulders back, shook out his hands.

Lucy's heart went out to him. She could see how much he wanted to argue, how much it meant to him to find his friend, and how much it was killing him not being able to protect those he held dearest.

But she also saw the moment when he accepted that they couldn't stay, not without putting themselves and the rest of their group in danger.

"Fuck," he said again with feeling. "Can Zelda walk?"

"Yes. She'll be all right."

Sawyer gave a small nod, trailing his fingers lightly over the bandage Lucy had secured around Zelda's wound. The dog gave a soft whimper, nuzzling her head into Sawyer's hand.

"My sweet girl," he whispered and pressed his forehead to hers before giving her a kiss between her brown eyes. Then he straightened. "Let's go."

They left the cover of the trees and made their way back toward the group. The rain had slowed, just as Sawyer predicted it would, softening into a misty drizzle that shrouded the dense forest in an eerie veil. Somewhere, a great horned owl hooted, the haunting notes echoing through the damp air.

Sawyer had traded his hiking pole for his white cane, using it to navigate with Zelda limping bravely beside him. Lucy followed behind, her gaze scanning their surroundings for any signs of danger. Every rustle of leaves, every snap of a twig set her nerves on edge.

God, she hated this.

The forest was supposed to be her refuge, her happy place. Instead, here she was, her anxiety spiking with each shadowy movement in the trees. The traumas of her past seemed to cling to the shadows, stalking her like a predator.

She'd never escape it, would she?

The man who had kidnapped her was long dead, but he'd left his black mark on her soul, a wound that ran deeper than those he'd inflicted on her body. He'd wormed his way into the roots of all she loved, turning her sanctuary into something to be feared.

She clenched her jaw, pushing down the bitter bile of anger that threatened to choke her. She wished he wasn't dead. She wished she'd had the opportunity to face him in court, to see him trapped for life like she'd been trapped in that cave.

"Hey," Sawyer said softly, breaking through her thoughts. "You okay?"

She willed herself to relax before answering, opening her mouth a couple times to relieve the tension in her jaw. "Yeah," she lied, forcing a smile she didn't feel. "Just plotting our next move."

Sawyer's head tilted in the way it did when he was listening intently, a gesture that made her chest tighten. She wondered if he knew she was lying. Probably. The man may be down a sense, but he was the most perceptive person she'd ever met. He didn't say anything, but he didn't have to. He'd already said it back on the ridge before they'd heard Maya's calls for help.

"Lean on me. Let me take some of that weight."

And now she realized how badly she wanted to, how badly she needed the support.

"Sawyer," she began, her voice cracking with emotion. "I'm..." She trailed off, unsure how she was going to finish the thought. Scared? Damaged? Madly, deeply in lust with him? All of those things were true, but none of them felt right to voice. Instead, she opted for a simple honesty. "I'm tired."

"I know." His hand found hers, his fingers lacing through hers in a warm, firm grip. A simple gesture, but it held the power of an embrace and the promise of comfort she so desperately needed.

It was strange how much she craved the sound of his voice, taking comfort in its steadiness. How the touch of his hand acted as an anchor, grounding her in reality, keeping her from getting lost in her own dark thoughts.

It was okay to falter, she reminded herself. A part of healing was admitting that you're hurt in the first place.

As they neared the camp and she spotted the others huddled together, their faces pale and drawn, Lucy released his hand and locked all of her vulnerability away again. "How's Maya?"

Bea straightened. "Unconscious," she reported in her no-nonsense way. She eyed the two of them, and then her gaze dropped to Zelda, and her lips flattened. "What happened?"

"A run-in with a sharp branch," Sawyer said before she could tell them the truth. She sent him a questioning sideways glance—which, of course, he couldn't see.

"But she's okay," he added with his easy smile back in place as he ruffled Zelda's ears. "My girl is tough."

"What did you find out there?" Theodore asked.

"Nothing, but Lucy spotted the tower. We're close." Another lie.

Lying to them didn't sit well with her, but as she watched a collective sigh of relief move through the group, she understood why he chose to in that moment. They didn't need more fear and uncertainty right now. They needed reassurance and hope.

"So we're still going to the tower?" Joel asked, pulling himself up onto his one good leg with the help of the hiking pole Sawyer had loaned him.

She eyed the kid, assessed the group, then did some quick mental calculations. If they were where she thought they were, they could still reach the tower before complete darkness set in. And they'd be safer there than out in the open, and it was the best chance they had of getting a signal out to rescuers."

Finally, she nodded.

"Yes," she said firmly, steeling herself. "We're still going to the tower."

She felt Sawyer's approving nod beside her, and she had to squash the urge to lean into his solid presence. Instead, she pushed past it and focused on rallying the group.

"We're not too far off, and if we move together in a line, we can make it before nightfall. Stick close. Watch each other's backs."

A murmur of assent rippled through them, their faces reflecting a mix of determination and wariness. Lucy ignored the leaden weight in her stomach as she glanced around at them.

She moved to Maya, taking hold of one end of the stretcher as Bea moved to the other end. Her hands were shaking ever so slightly as she lifted the injured woman— from fear or anger, she couldn't tell. Maybe both. It didn't matter, though. What mattered was that they made it to the tower tonight.

They had to.

chapter
six

THE BLUE MOUNTAIN fire tower sat on the precipice of the mountain that gave it its name, at nearly five thousand feet above sea level. The climb was more arduous than Lucy remembered, and her legs ached from the exertion. She couldn't imagine how her hikers felt.

Especially poor Joel. He lagged behind, each step obviously agony for him, but he still kept moving. There was a determined set to his jaw that Lucy admired. The kid had grit. Far more than his father gave him credit for. Chuck also lagged, huffing and puffing like a steam engine. His gaze kept flashing toward his son, filled with a mixture of frustration and grudging respect.

They had traded off carrying Maya, but Lucy once again took over his end of the stretcher after he nearly dropped her. The man was a lot of bluster, but no stamina. He had been quick to boast about his athletic past at the beginning of the trip, but it was obvious that those glory days were far behind him.

Thankfully, Bea was holding up like a trooper, her sturdy frame bearing the brunt of the stretcher's weight. She was steady and uncomplaining, and Lucy appreciated her more than she could express.

Sawyer, Zelda, and Theodore flanked the stretcher on either side when the path was wide enough, and fell into single file behind it when the trail narrowed. Sawyer moved with a steady confidence that didn't falter, his trusty cane tapping out a reassuring rhythm on the rocky path. Theodore chatted quietly with Maya, even managing to pull a weak smile from her once or twice before she lost consciousness again.

Maya's face was ghost white. She had lost a lot of blood, and her breathing was becoming more ragged and shallower. Lucy checked the makeshift bandage around Maya's abdomen, but saw that it was soaked through with crimson. They needed to get her medical attention soon or she might not make it.

The trail snaked up the mountainside, dotted with loose rocks and tree roots that made the going treacherous. More than once, someone's foot slipped, or the stretcher tilted dangerously. But they kept on, determination and adrenaline fueling their ascent.

At last the fire tower came into view, a steel frame with a wraparound balcony perched atop a bald rock outcropping.

Finally.

Lucy wanted to sob with relief. She held it in—couldn't let the others know she'd been worried. What if she'd been wrong about the location? What if she'd misled them in the confusion after the landslide? What if the earthquake had destroyed the tower despite its fortifications? What if? What if? What if? She'd silently tortured herself with the questions and doubts throughout the entire hike.

But they were so close now. Just a little further, and they'd reach help.

Lucy carefully set Maya's stretcher down and cupped her hands around her mouth and called, "Hello!"

No response. But someone was up there. A light flicked in the windows.

"Hello? Please, we need help. We have injured hikers."

The door opened, and a man stepped out onto the balcony. His beard was scruffy, and he wore a faded green jacket with a Forest Service patch on the arm.

The man peered down at them from the balcony, his expression unreadable in the fading light. He didn't call out or wave, just watched as they struggled up the last bit of trail to the tower. He had a hunter's watchful gaze.

Lucy shifted anxiously as the seconds ticked by. Why wasn't he saying anything? Sawyer moved closer to her side. She liked having him there. Just like in that cave last year, his mere presence soothed her nerves.

"Who are you?" the man finally asked. His tone wasn't unfriendly, just direct.

Lucy stepped forward. "I'm Lucy Harper. I was leading a tour group when the earthquake hit. We have injured— a broken leg, a concussion, and possible internal bleeding. Do you have a working radio?"

The man studied them for another moment, then glanced over his shoulder at someone inside. He finally set the rifle down, leaning it against the balcony railing. "Name's Ethan Voss. I'm the fire lookout here. Radio's nothing but static since the quake."

Her gut clenched at his words. She'd been counting on that radio. She needed to get a message to the Forest Service or, even better, Redwood Coast Rescue. They were better equipped to handle a rescue operation of this magnitude.

She swallowed the knot in her throat and forced a nod, pushing back the mounting panic. "Look, Ethan, can we come up? We really need help. There's a girl here —Maya." She gestured toward the unconscious woman on the makeshift stretcher. "She's in bad shape."

Ethan's gaze shifted to Maya, then flicked back to the room behind him. "Not a lot of room up here."

"But we'll make do." A new voice drifted down from above, followed by the face of another man. He was younger than Ethan, with a severe gaze and a grim line to his mouth. He had a bandage on the side of his head, the middle of the white gauze dark with blood. "We can't leave them out here. Let 'em come up."

Relief loosened the knot in her chest, letting her breathe again. "Thank you."

Ethan grunted something about a lack of supplies, but made his way down the zigzagging steps to the ground. He moved fast and sure-footed, despite the dimming light. Whatever reservations he had about letting them up, at least he seemed willing to help.

As Ethan reached ground level, his gaze flicked over their haggard group and settled on Maya. His jaw hardened, but it wasn't out of indifference—there was a flicker of something else in those watchful eyes.

Without any further talk, Ethan lifted one end of Maya's stretcher. The younger man with the bandage was already down from the tower, striding towards them in long, hurried steps. He picked up the other end and, together, they lifted Maya up the narrow stairs. Joel followed, leaning heavily on his dad and Bea. Theodore brought up the rear, hands out like he could catch them if they fell.

She felt Sawyer lingering nearby like a static charge along her nerve endings.

"Go on," she told him. "The stairs are right in front of you."

He moved forward until his cane hit the bottom step, then shifted to look back in her direction. "Not coming up with us, Harper?"

She flashed him a smile that felt brittle on her lips. Lucky for her, he couldn't see how unconvincing it was. "In a moment. I just need to..."

What?

She didn't know. Stand here for a minute and just breathe? Maybe breakdown and let out all of the fear and anxiety swirling inside her? No, she couldn't do that, but she could take a moment alone to be Lucy and not Ranger Harper.

Sawyer nodded, understanding flashing in his pale

blue eyes. "Take your time," he said softly, then started up the stairs, Zelda by his side.

Lucy watched them disappear into the tower before finally allowing herself to crumple onto a nearby stump. Her knees were shaking so hard they could barely hold her weight, and her chest felt like it was being crushed under the weight of all their problems. Buried beneath the concern for her group was terror for herself. The memories of her own trauma were still too fresh, nightmares that often woke her in a cold sweat.

The Shadow Stalker.

No matter how hard she tried, she couldn't shake the memory of his cold laughter echoing off the cave walls as he left her to die. But she wasn't dead. She was alive and she had people depending on her. She had to be strong for them.

With a determined swallow, she stood from the stump and ascended the stairs to the tower.

Ethan wasn't lying about not having much room. The cabin was one room filled with a wood-burning stove, several mismatched chairs, and a single bed in the corner. Maps of the surrounding forest were pinned to the walls, and a radio setup took up most of one table. It was tight quarters, but it was shelter, and right now, that was more important than anything else.

Maya was placed gently on the bed while Joel settled into one of the chairs, his bloody leg propped up on an ottoman. The rest of their group squeezed themselves into remaining spaces, their faces etched with exhaustion and worry. Ethan hunched over the radio, his brow furrowed in intense concentration as he attempted to hail rescue. The occasional crackle of static was the only response he got.

The younger man crouched beside Maya, his fingers resting on her wrist as he looked at his watch.

Lucy crossed to him. After a moment, he gently placed Maya's arm back on the bed and covered her with a fraying quilt. His eyes said what Lucy already knew—Maya wasn't going to make it.

"Are you a doctor?" she asked.

He shook his head. "Army medic."

So he probably had a bit more medical training than her EMT certification, but not necessarily the extensive experience of the seasoned trauma surgeon that Maya needed.

"Is there anything more we can do for her?"

"Not without proper medical equipment and supplies. We can keep her comfortable. That's about it." He held out a hand over the bed. "Grant Clarke. I was hiking through when the quake hit. Got knocked out, woke up here with the grumpy Mr. Voss taking care of me."

She accepted his handshake. "Lucy Harper. I'm a park ranger here."

"Figured as much from the uniform." Grant smiled briefly, his gaze still on Maya. After a moment of silence, he rose and grimly surveyed the room. "We'll need more water," he said to no one in particular and moved toward the stack of water jugs along one wall. He picked one up, hefting it in his grip as he measured the remaining contents with a critical eye. His gaze drifted once more to Maya, taking in her ashen complexion and her uneven breaths before landing back on Lucy.

"I'll walk down to the nearest spring and bring back what I can." He looked at Ethan. "If I remember correctly, it's not far."

Ethan grunted but didn't lift his attention from the radio as he fiddled with the dial. "Half a mile to the east."

"Finally someone's taking control of this situation," Chuck said.

Bea scowled. "What do you mean, *finally*? Ranger Harper got us here, didn't she?"

Grant shot the man a look, clearly unimpressed, then hefted two empty jugs up on his shoulders. "You all should get some rest. I'll be back soon."

Lucy made sure Maya was firmly tucked in, then watched Grant disappear down the stairs. The door closed, leaving them in silence save for the crackle of the radio and Maya's labored breathing.

Stepping back from Maya's bed, she assessed the room. Theodore was already dosing with his head on Bea's shoulder, and Bea looked just as exhausted. Chuck's face was still an unhealthy red from the hike up to the tower, while Joel's was a sweat-slicked mask of pain. She moved over to where he sat in one of the mismatched chairs, his leg propped up on an ottoman. One look told her his leg was swelling despite the makeshift splint she had applied earlier.

"Joel, we need to elevate your leg higher." She shooed

Chuck out of the other chair and grabbed the cushion, sliding it gently beneath his leg.

Joel grimaced. "Thanks," he said through gritted teeth. The adrenaline rush was wearing off, and the pain was setting in full force.

The kid was so much stronger than his father gave him credit for.

"So what's the plan now?" Bea asked, startling her husband out of his doze. She laid a hand on his shoulder to keep him from jumping through the roof.

"We wait," Lucy answered simply.

"Wait for what?" Theodore asked, the panic clear in his voice.

"Rescue."

"And what if they don't come?" Chuck demanded. "What then? My boy can't walk off this mountain in his state."

"Dad..." Joel protested.

"They'll come." It was Sawyer who spoke this time. "I know my team. They'll come."

"But they don't know where we are," Joel pointed out.

"They'll figure it out."

"But how long will it take?" Theodore's gaze darted nervously behind his glasses. "How long do we just sit here?"

Lucy looked at Sawyer, seeing in him the calm she wished she could feel.

"As long as we need to," he answered.

"Easy for you to say," Chuck muttered under his breath.

Bea shot him a reproachful look. "What about food? We didn't bring much more than snacks. We were only supposed to be gone for six hours."

Lucy glanced toward Ethan's stockpile of canned food on the shelves of the tiny kitchenette. If this went on longer than a couple of days, it wouldn't nearly be enough for nine people. "All right, listen. We're not going to solve anything by staying awake through the night. We have shelter, and people *are* looking for us. In the morning, we'll figure out our supply situation, but for now, we all need sleep."

"But what about Maya?" Joel asked, worry creasing his forehead.

"That's out of our hands now. What she needs is rest, and so do you," Lucy said, laying her hand gently on Joel's shoulder.

The others settled down, using their backpacks as makeshift pillows and curling up in whatever available floor space remained. Sawyer guided Zelda over to a spot near the door. After making sure everyone was settled, she crossed to him and sat on the floor next to him.

"Gonna be a long night," Sawyer murmured.

A chill crept up her spine, icy fingers tracing her vertebrae one by one. No radio, dwindling supplies, no way off this peak until help arrived... if it arrived.

"Yes. It is." She exhaled hard and ran her hands over her face. Only then did she realize they were caked in mud and blood. She couldn't help the small, distressed sound that escaped her as she tried to rub it off.

A hand gently covered her own, and she looked up to see Sawyer's face, his eyes focused somewhere over her shoulder. He was so calm, so steady, even in the face of utter uncertainty. He gently moved his fingers over the dried blood and grime, tracing every scrape and bruise.

"It's going to be all right, Luce," he said softly.

She swallowed thickly, her heart pounding in her chest as she met his unfocused gaze. This was not the time for this, but the warmth of his touch, the familiar comfort of his presence, was something she desperately needed.

She had so many conflicting emotions when it came to this man—relief that he was here by her side again, anger that he had disappeared without a word, and an undeniable draw to him that both frightened and excited her.

"Why did you leave?" she whispered, unable to stop herself from voicing the question that had haunted her for a year.

Sawyer's brow furrowed. He opened his mouth but hesitated.

"You didn't need me anymore," he said finally.

"What?"

"You were healing, and I thought if I stayed around..." He shrugged one shoulder. "I didn't want to be a reminder of what happened to you."

Lucy blinked in surprise. "Sawyer, you were the reason I survived. If you hadn't found me..." She trailed off, unable to voice what would have happened if he hadn't shown up when he did.

He was silent, head bowed. She studied his profile, taking in the strong line of his jaw and the furrow between his brows.

"I know I was a mess afterward," she continued, finding her voice again. "The panic attacks, the nightmares... but I wouldn't have gotten through that without you. And then, when I finally started to feel like myself again, you were just gone."

Sawyer turned his face toward her, pale eyes glistening. "I thought it was for the best. I didn't want to hold you back."

"You should have let me decide that. I needed—" She stopped short, emotion closing her throat.

You.

God had she needed him. His quiet strength. His gentle understanding. His optimism. His jokes. During those long days in the hospital, he had been her rock. And when he disappeared from her life, she'd felt as if her anchor had been ripped away, leaving her adrift.

Lucy looked down at her lap, blinking back tears. She had needed him so much back then. And if she was being honest with herself, she still needed him now. The old anxiety was creeping through her like a cancer, bringing with it the hypervigilance and bone-deep fear that had plagued her for so long after the attack.

She looked up at him again, opened her mouth to tell him all of that, but a loud thump sounded from the stairs, startling her.

They both turned toward the sounds as Grant pushed through the door, arms laden with full water jugs. Ethan jumped up to help him haul them over to the counter.

"That should be enough to get us through tomorrow at least," Grant said.

Lucy pressed her lips together. Their conversation would have to wait. She stood, legs stiff from sitting still after such a strenuous hike, and went to check on Maya. The woman's breathing seemed a little less labored now, her face not quite so pale.

Small miracles.

Maybe she still had a fighting chance.

Maybe they would all make it out of here in one piece.

chapter
seven

THE MURMUR of voices woke Sawyer from a restless sleep. He opened his eyes, but it was too dark to even see his usual splashes of light and shadow.

He closed his eyes again and focused on the sounds, the muffled voices too indistinct to tell whether they were male or female. Boots creaked over the old wood floor. A thunk. Something that sounded like... a strangled shout? A thump. Zelda growled deep in her chest. It was a strange sound and he put his hand on her head to comfort her. His girl almost never growled.

Crash.

Everyone came awake as glass broke and a cool breeze swirled into the cabin. Sawyer thrust himself upwards, heart pounding with a sudden surge of adrenaline. "Lucy!"

"I'm here." Her hand closed around his. She was still by his side. "Everyone's okay." She sounded like she was trying to assure herself as much as everyone else. "It's just another storm rolling through. The wind broke a window."

He could feel the wind, damp and cool, on his face. Hear it howling through the opening like a ghostly wail.

"I got it," Ethan said. "Someone grab that plywood over there."

"Got it," Grant said.

Sawyer heard them shuffling around, wrestling the plywood sheet over the broken window, heard the hammer of nails going into wood. Everyone breathed a sigh of relief. And then it was quiet again.

Too quiet.

Something was wrong.

There weren't enough breath sounds for the number of people in the room.

"I don't hear Maya's breathing." He shoved to his feet, fumbled for his cane and tapped his way over to the cot. He found Maya's arm with his hand. Her skin was unnaturally cold. He traced up her arm to her chest—no movement.

A chill of dread seeped into his bones as he slowly drew back. His hand was wet. He raised it to his nose and sniffed. Blood. It was cold and slightly gummy between his fingers. Coagulating.

"Oh, no," Lucy said, horror in her voice. "Grant! Help! Maya's not breathing."

Sawyer caught her before she could launch a rescue. "Luce. She's already gone."

"No. No, that can't be." Lucy's hand slipped from

his, and he heard the rustle of her movements as she leaned over Maya. "We need to try CPR."

"I'm sorry." He reached out but found only air. "She's cold. She's been gone for a while."

"She's dead?" Joel said faintly.

"It was a long shot," Bea muttered and then cleared her throat. "We all knew it when we dug her out from under that tree."

"No tree did this," Ethan said gruffly. "Unless trees have started carrying knives. She was stabbed."

"What?" Lucy demanded. "Show me."

There was a flurry of movement, a cacophony of voices, curses, exclamations of surprise. Sawyer stood in the middle of it all, his hands clenched into fists at his sides. He thought he'd come to terms with his blindness. He'd thought all the years of therapy and soul-searching hikes had helped him adapt, reclaim his independence, and find peace with his limitations. But in this moment, he felt the stark edges of his disability—unable to see the blood on his hands, unable to see Maya's lifeless body, and worst of all, unable to see the danger before it struck.

What if it were Lucy lying cold on that cot? He wouldn't have been able to stop it. Wouldn't have been able to protect her any more than he'd been able to protect Maya.

A light flickered on, and finally Sawyer could see the usual blobs of colors and shadows. The vise around his chest loosened and he sucked in a sharp breath.

"Who the fuck stabbed her in *my* house?" Ethan's boots thumped loudly on the wooden floorboards as he paced. Sawyer followed his movement, catching glimpses of a bushy head of hair and a bushier beard. He looked like a growling bear disturbed from its hibernation.

Another figure moved to the center of the room and held up his hands. Sawyer got an impression of a younger man, mid-to-late twenties, tall and fit, with a white bandage wrapped around his head, but then the guy stopped moving and disappeared back into the blur before he could make out any more details. That had to be Grant, he decided, which was confirmed when the guy spoke:

"She was fine when I checked on her before we all went to sleep. I think she was going to pull through."

"An accident," Joel whispered. "It has to be, right? Just some kind of..."

"Accident?" Ethan scoffed. "Kid, you don't *accidentally* stab someone in their sleep."

"Which of you bastards did it?" Bea's voice was quiet, yet it somehow filled the room and silenced everyone else. "And why? Why would you kill *her*? She was helpless."

Lucy's breath hitched, and Sawyer could hear her choking back a sob. An alarming surge of emotion threatened to overtake him, but he forced it down and tapped his cane on the floor to get everyone's attention. "Okay, we need to stay calm," he said, trying to bring back some order in the chaotic room. "Let's all—"

Joel spoke over him, his voice cracking with fear: "One of you did it. One of you killed her."

"Damn it all to hell," Ethan spat, his footfalls abruptly halting. "Get out. All of you." He paused.

"'Cept the kid. He's the only one I know for sure didn't do this. I'll protect him until help arrives, but the rest of you aren't welcome here anymore."

"Joel stays, I stay," Chuck said, and there was genuine concern behind the bluster. "I'm his father, and there's no fucking way I'm leaving him here alone with you."

The guy was a grade-A asshole, but he truly cared about his son, and for that, at least, Sawyer had to give him a modicum of respect.

"No one's leaving," Lucy said. "It's dark outside, it's storming, and if one of us is a murderer—*if*," she stressed when someone made a grumble of protest, "then we're safer as a group. One person can't take us all on."

"Wasn't safer for Maya," Chuck muttered.

And there went that tiny bit of respect right out the window. Sawyer glowered in his direction. "You know, you're always so fast with a snarky comment, but I never hear you offering any solutions."

"At least I'm not pretending to be the goddamn hero in all this. What are you gonna do when we catch the guy, Sawyer? Whack him with your stick? Sic that doe-eyed dog on him? Why don't you sit down and shut up and let the normal people handle this?"

Normal.

Sawyer kept his back straight, refusing to let the word hurt him. When he woke up in the hospital in Germany and realized he'd never be normal again, he'd succumbed to a bitterness so potent, it had threatened to ruin him. But he wasn't that broken soldier anymore. He'd found his worth again, first in Zelda and then in Redwood

Coast Rescue. And he would not let this angry little man take that away from him.

Zelda growled, a low rumble that echoed through the room.

Sawyer tilted his head and smirked. "Zelda doesn't like your tone, Chuck."

"No one does," Bea said.

Chuck moved then, backing up a step, allowing Sawyer to zero in on his location. He took a confident step forward without help from the cane and stared at the man. He knew people found the pale blue of his eyes intimidating, and used to use it to his advantage. At one time, all it took for a wayward Marine to fall back into line was a hard stare from Staff Sergeant Murphy.

"Zelda's trained to protect me at all costs, so don't underestimate her because she's cute. And as for my stick?" He swung it and Chuck flinched, which gave him the target he needed. He stopped short of actually hitting him, instead resting the tip against Chuck's shoulder. "It's specially made, reinforced with steel. I whack someone with this, it will do damage."

"Whoa, okay, let's all take a breath!" Lucy set a hand on his arm. "Sawyer," she said more softly. "Lower the cane."

After another moment, he relented, choking up his grip on the cane until his hand rested back on the handle. He stroked Zelda's head, and she stopped growling. Chuck's relief when they turned away was palpable, and he sorely wished he could see the guy's bravado deflate like a slowly leaking balloon.

He'd always hated bullies.

Lucy, however, didn't let it go. Her voice was sharp as she confronted Chuck. "We're all scared. We're all paranoid and on edge, and rightfully so. But lashing out at each other won't help. It will only make things worse."

Chuck grumbled something unintelligible under his breath, but Sawyer caught two words: "...not blind..."

"I'm sorry, what was that?"

"I said you're not blind," Chuck snapped, his bravado returning. "You all saw the way he looked at me just now. He's lying. Maybe *he* killed Maya."

Every gaze in the room turned to him. He felt the stares like the hairy legs of a spider skittering down the back of his neck. "Blindness is a spectrum, asshole. It's not all or nothing. I can see colors and vague shapes and shadows. My eyes are fine; the problem is my brain can't interpret the information it receives from them because a sniper tried to blow my head off in Afghanistan. But movement helps— so, yes, I can see you reaching for whatever it is you're about to throw at me, and, yes, I can catch it."

Chuck's hand paused in mid-air.

"Chuck." Lucy stepped between them. "Let's be civilized. Put down the bottle. You'll just waste water that we can't afford to lose."

For a long moment, the standoff continued, each man stiff with defiance. Finally, Chuck harrumphed, and the plastic bottle crackled as he set it back onto the table. He didn't apologize, but Sawyer wasn't expecting him to.

An uneasy silence filled the room, until Theodore finally broke it:

"If one of us is dead, and we're all stuck here together, how long before the rest of us follow?"

"Well, damn, Theo," Bea muttered. "That's a cheerful thought."

"It's a legitimate concern, isn't it? I mean..." He trailed off and didn't finish the thought.

Sawyer sensed Lucy tense beside him, and he gently touched her arm, offering what little comfort he could. Paranoia seeped into the room like an insidious gas, filling every corner and twisting every shadow into something monstrous.

"We're not animals," Lucy said finally. "We're not going to start tearing each other apart."

"How do you know?" Joel asked.

Sawyer grimaced. The kid had grown up with Chuck as a father. It had to be difficult to see past the ugly parts of human nature when that was all you were exposed to. Still, Sawyer thought, he should try to offer some hope.

"I know because I've seen what happens when people turn on each other." He motioned toward his eyes. "I barely survived it. But I've also seen what people are capable of when they are stronger than fear. We're only animals if we choose to be. If we stick together and have each other's backs until rescue arrives, no one else will die."

Chuck snorted. "I don't trust any fucking one of you."

Before Sawyer could answer, a sudden gust rattled

the windows. Sawyer put his hand on Zelda's head to calm her, feeling her fur prickle against his palm. His sweet, laid-back girl was just as on edge as everyone else in the small room.

"Storm's picking up." Grant's voice cut through the tense silence. "No one's going anywhere tonight."

"We'll sleep in three-hour shifts," Lucy added. "Grant, Sawyer, and I will take the first watch."

Again, Chuck gave a derisive snort.

Sawyer hated that the man's snide remarks bothered him. He'd dealt with worse. Hell, his own father had been a verbal bulldozer, always quick to tear down anyone in his path. Sawyer had built up a thick skin from an early age and learned to wield self-deprecating humor like a weapon to deflect the worst of the barbs, but something about Chuck's dismissive attitude rubbed him raw. Maybe it was the parallels he saw between Chuck and Joel's strained relationship and his own fractured relationship with his father, or maybe it was the way Chuck's words were like splinters under the skin of the group's already fragile unity.

He bit back a sharp retort, reminding himself that his role was to maintain harmony, not stoke conflict. He needed to keep the peace, for everyone's sake. He couldn't let Chuck's toxic attitude poison their survival efforts.

"It's eleven now," Lucy continued as if Chuck hadn't made a sound. "At two, Bea and Theodore, are you good to take over?" They must have nodded their consent because she finished, "Then at five, Ethan, Chuck, and

Joel will finish out the night. Once we've all had some rest, we can figure out our next steps, okay?"

There was a murmur of agreement and a reluctant grumble from Chuck. Tension still crackled in the air as everyone returned to their makeshift bunks, but it was less like an imminent lightning strike now and more like static electricity.

Grant moved toward them, his form taking shape from the white noise of Sawyer's vision. He looked worried, his brows drawn together, a deep frown on his face. Then he stopped moving and disappeared again.

"This has the potential to go sideways fast," he said, keeping his voice low. "Chuck is a wild card. Maybe he's all talk, but I'm not so sure. He's pissed and scared, and that makes him dangerous."

"I know," Lucy replied, and she sounded exhausted.

Sawyer reached out until he found her back and rubbed in soothing circles.

She sighed and leaned into him. "But right now, I'm just concerned with getting us through the night."

chapter
eight

GOD.

The mountain was half gone. Lucy gripped the balcony railing and stared out over the ruined landscape. It looked like an angry god had reached down and sheared off the east slope with a sharp blade. Large patches of the land were still scarred from a rampant wildfire two summers ago, and now with this new damage, it looked barren and alien. The national park service was going to have a hell of a time cleaning up this mess.

She exhaled a long breath. She had known the earthquake was bad, but she hadn't realized the full scope of the damage it had done. She looked toward the valley below and worried about how the towns there had fared.

No wonder they couldn't reach anyone on the radio.

She turned her gaze to the unscarred wilderness, the vast expanse of trees that stretched out below the tower, dark and foreboding as the light of dawn hadn't broken over the tops of the mountains yet. The forest was deathly silent, the normal sounds of nature waking up conspicuously absent. A chill ran down her spine that had nothing to do with the cooler temperatures the storms had left in their wake. She shuddered and drew her blanket closer around herself.

A board creaked behind her, but she didn't jump. She instinctively knew who it was. She always knew, and smiled a little as Zelda nuzzled her neck below her ear.

"Hi, girl," she murmured and kissed the dog's cold nose.

Sawyer lowered himself to sit beside her, using the balcony railing to guide him down. "Couldn't sleep?"

"No."

"Yeah, me either." His lips thinned into a hard line as he slid his legs under the railing to dangle over the edge next to hers. "I don't trust Chuck to watch my six while I'm sleeping."

"Ethan wouldn't let him do anything."

"Ethan wanted to kick us out in a storm last night," he reminded dryly. "Don't really trust him, either."

She closed her eyes and leaned her forehead against the cold metal railing. "Trust is a commodity we're sorely lacking."

He bumped her shoulder with his. "I guess we'll just have to rely on each other." He laughed softly as Zelda wiggled between them. "And Zelda, of course."

She liked his laugh. Always had. Despite all he'd been through, and despite their current dire situation, there was a lightness to it that never failed to make her smile.

"Of course." She ruffled the dog's furry ears. "Zelda's the only one making any sense right now."

"That's because she's smarter than most of us humans."

"I believe it." She shifted to study him, half assessing, half admiring. Other than tired, he looked okay. If his concussion was troubling him, he didn't let it show. His profile was in shadows from the pre-dawn gloom. His golden hair, unruly and a bit longer than she remembered, gleamed with the first touch of sunlight. It struck her how beautiful he was, just sitting there wrapped in a blanket, his gaze directed toward the horizon he couldn't see.

His face was calm, the lines of tension that had been there earlier relaxed. Even though he carried burdens that would have crushed a less resilient man, he seemed almost untouchable in his tranquility, his peace extending outward like a buffer against the chaos around them.

She wanted a little of that peace for herself.

Lucy scooted closer, sliding her arm through his. They fit together easily, as if they were two parts of a puzzle. She rested her head on his shoulder, and let herself wonder, for just a moment, if they would fit together as easily in other, more intimate ways. She hoped someday she could find out.

He leaned his head against hers. "I wish I could see it," he said softly, drawing her out of her thoughts.

She looked toward the mountain again. "What, the earthquake damage?"

"No." His lips curved into a smile as they brushed her temple. "My Lucy. Always so pragmatic."

Warmth curled through her belly. Had he just claimed her as his?

"No, I meant the sunrise. Describe it for me?"

She looked toward the east. "It's still mostly dark out here, but there's this warm promise of light just at the edge of the mountains. The clouds are like... wisps of cotton candy, all pink and orange and purple."

He groaned. "Jesus, I'd give a body part for some cotton candy right now."

"Sweet tooth, huh?" She'd never have guessed it. From the hard lines of his body, she'd pegged him for a health food fanatic. The kind of guy who bought dry-as-dirt granola and tried to convince you it was as good as a candy bar. She'd dated more than her share of that type.

He grinned. "Sugar is my kryptonite. But don't tell anyone and ruin my rugged, man-of-the-wilderness facade."

"Oh I wouldn't dream of it." She took a deep breath, the pine-scented air filling her lungs. "The trees are still in shadows, but they're beginning to take on different shades of green, from the deepest emerald to a light sage. And the sunlight... it's like melted gold, pouring over everything slowly, lighting up the world bit by bit."

His fingers brushed against hers. "Sounds beautiful."

"It is."

"You love it these mountains. I can hear it in your voice."

"I do. I'm from Ohio originally, but my parents

brought me out here to see the redwoods when I was about ten, and I fell in love. I wrapped my little arms around the biggest tree I could find and knew right then I wanted to work here."

His lips curved into a smile at her temple. "This place... it has a way of captivating people."

"It does. I've seen it time and again. And until last year, I always felt most at peace in the woods. Most at home. There's an honesty in nature that people lack. It's raw and beautiful and..."

"Unforgiving," he finished.

She turned to look at him. His face was cast in the early morning light now, his blue eyes reflecting the sunrise he couldn't see.

"Yes," she agreed softly. "It can be unforgiving and brutal, but nature doesn't kill just because it can. Not like people." She realized he was looking at her instead of out at the horizon. Well, not exactly at her, but in her direction. His expression was quiet, contemplative.

"I wish you didn't have to know that firsthand."

"Me too." She glanced down at Zelda who lay patiently between them with her head resting on Sawyer's thigh, brown eyes soft and tail wagging.

"The Shadow Stalker is dead, Lucy." He said it softly, gently, as if worried the name might trigger her. His fingers tracing over the back of her hand. "He can't hurt you anymore."

She cleared away the sudden knot in her throat. "I know that, but..."

"But," he finished when she trailed off, "the fear

doesn't just disappear because the threat is gone. I get it. After what happened to me, I had nightmares for years. Still do sometimes, honestly. I saw his face all the time—the sniper who shot me. Of course, I never actually saw his real face, but my fucked-up brain decided to fill in the blanks. One of the other fun side effects of an occipital lobe injury is hallucinations. They've mostly disappeared now, but for a while I saw that sniper everywhere. He was the only thing I could see. Just a blur of light and color and then there he was, crystal clear. I thought he was real, and I was afraid of every shadow, every unexpected sound. It took a lot of therapy and time to feel safe again. But there are still moments when I feel on edge, when all the progress I've made seems to vanish."

God, what he'd gone through. Her heart ached for him. And, really, her experience, as awful as it was, paled in comparison. Why couldn't she just suck it up and move on like he had?

But...

"I have nightmares all the time. I close my eyes and I'm back in that damn cave, shot and bleeding. Cold. Alone." The thought made her sick, and she had to swallow back the bile rising in her throat.

"Hey, come here." He traced his hand up her arm to curl around her waist. He pulled her into his side, and she let herself be pulled, sinking into the warmth and security he offered. Zelda shifted back to make room, and Lucy curled up against Sawyer, nestling into his side. His other arm slid around her, too, until he was completely encompassing her.

"You weren't alone in that cave," he murmured into her hair. "You had me. And you have me now."

The words seemed to hang in the air between them for a moment, charged with something she didn't dare name. And then he was gently tilting her chin up. It felt like the world narrowed down to just this moment, everything else forgotten.

His thumb brushed back and forth over her lips, a quiet, almost reverent touch as if he were memorizing their shape. A jolt of electricity sizzled down her spine, lighting her body on fire in a way she hadn't experienced in a very long time. She found herself leaning into him. Their noses brushed against each other's in a feather-like touch before Sawyer's lips found hers in the gentlest of kisses.

Her heart pounded wildly as Sawyer's hand moved up to cup her face, his thumb stroking her cheek. It was disarming and sweet, the gesture so full of care that it brought tears to her eyes. She'd missed him more than she ever admitted to herself. She'd spent the last year worrying that the connection they'd shared had been nothing more than a trauma response, a fleeting, desperate grasp at humanity during a nightmarish ordeal. But this...

The emotions swirling through her now were just as potent, if not more so. This was real. He was real, and so was their connection. And if his desperate grip on her was anything to go by, she wasn't the only one who felt it.

The kiss deepened, taking on a life of its own as Sawyer's fingers slid into her hair, cradling her head. Her body trembled in response as his lips moved languidly over hers, his tongue seeking hers with a gentle urgency that left no room for doubt about his feelings or intentions. It was a slow dance of desire and intimacy that sent waves of delicious heat pulsing through her body.

Finally pulling away, he rested his forehead against hers, breath mingling with hers in the early morning air. "I've wanted to do that for a long time."

"Why didn't you?"

He was quiet for a moment, a small frown furrowing his brow as he seemed to gather his thoughts. "Because you were in pain, Lucy. You were hurting and traumatized, and the last thing you needed was me complicating things. And..." He exhaled a soft, sad laugh, his fingers absently tracing circles on her back. "I thought you could do better than me. I don't exactly have a lot to offer a woman like you."

She sat back, pulling away enough to look into his face. His features were soft in the growing light, but there was a deep sadness in his pale blue eyes.

She reached up to cup his face in her hands. She wanted to tell him that he was wrong. She wanted to tell him that he was enough, more than enough for her. He was one of the strongest, kindest, most beautiful people she had ever known, tonya she didn't want better. She wanted him.

But the words stuck in her throat. All she could manage was his name.

"Sawyer," she said softly.

"Yeah?" His voice was a low rasp that sent shivers down her spine.

"I…"

"Lucy, it's okay," he interrupted before she could push out the confession. He brushed a thumb against her cheekbone in a comforting stroke. "We've got time."

But they didn't. Not with Mother Nature trying to kill them at every turn. And not with a killer among their ragtag group of survivors.

They could both die up here.

She should tell him how she felt and make sure he knew how special he was. She should kiss him again, kiss him like there was no tomorrow because there very well might not be.

She opened her mouth to speak, but a voice cut her off.

"Hey, Lucy? Sawyer?"

They broke apart abruptly and turned toward Grant. The guy stood in the open doorway of the tower, the lamplight from inside making his silhouette fuzzy. "Sorry to interrupt," he said sheepishly, scratching the back of his head. "But I found something you'll want to see."

Lucy tamped down a surge of annoyance at the interruption. She had no right to be annoyed. She and Sawyer weren't alone up here, and this wasn't the ideal place for… whatever that was.

She got to her feet and grabbed the blanket that had slipped off her shoulders during the kiss. Funny, she hadn't even felt the cool morning air until that moment.

Sawyer also stood slowly, his expression unreadable as he made his way toward Grant using the rail of the balcony as a guide. "What is it?"

Grant hesitated a beat, then held out a wallet.

Lucy took it and turned it over in her hands. It was thin, made to hold only a few cards. The soft leather was a pale peach color. Definitely feminine.

"What is it?" Sawyer asked again.

"A wallet." She flipped it open and pulled out the first card she found. A credit card in the name of Amaya Thomas. "Wait. Is this Maya's?"

Grant nodded and glanced over his shoulder, back inside the cabin. Everyone was sleeping except for Ethan, but the grumpy man was at the radio again, trying to get it to work, and not paying them any attention.

Still, Grant moved further out onto the balcony and swung the door shut behind him. "I found it in her backpack. I was looking to see if she had any contact numbers for emergencies... and I found that stuck inside the lining of the bag like she wanted to hide it."

Lucy pulled out another card— a California driver's license in the same name as the credit card. "Didn't she tell us her last name was Thompson?"

"She did," Sawyer confirmed.

"Her ID says her name is Amaya Thomas, not Maya Thompson. Why would she lie about that?"

"She was in shock," Grant said. "She'd lost a lot of blood. Maybe she was confused."

Lucy picked out another card and held it up so he

could see it. "She lied about her profession, too. She told us she was a photographer, but this sure as hell looks like a military ID. She was active duty."

"Okay, I'll play devil's advocate," Sawyer said. "Photography could've been a hobby. The biggest, baddest Marine I knew was into birdwatching. *Weirdly* into it, you ask me, but I'd still want him to have my six in any pucker situation. Being military doesn't mean you can't have hobbies."

"But why lie about it?" She kept coming back to that one sticking point. There was no reason for Maya—or Amaya? —to hide her military background unless she was also hiding something else.

Lucy frowned, turning the ID over in her hand. The picture matched Maya's pretty face, but the blue uniform she wore, the rigid posture, and the stern expression were a far cry from the scared girl they'd found trapped under a tree.

Had she been running from something?

Or someone?

And, if so, was that person among their group? It made sense since Maya had ended up with a knife wound in her chest. But she couldn't see how any of her hikers were involved. Chuck was all bark and no bite, and Joel was just a kid. Bea was tough and ex-military, but underneath that toughness was a caring soul. She wouldn't kill a helpless woman. Theodore wouldn't either. He was too gentle, too kind, too meek. That left...

She looked at the two men standing in front of her.

Not Sawyer. He'd been by her side all night—she was sure of it. And he'd been the one to raise the alarm that Maya wasn't breathing.

She eyed Grant. She knew very little about him and Ethan, but it made the most sense that one of them was the killer.

But why would either of them kill an injured, unarmed woman?

Grant glanced over his shoulder, again checking to make sure nobody inside was paying them any attention. "Listen, I don't want to sound callous, but Maya's dead and her reasons for lying died with her. Right now, we have bigger problems and need to make some decisions. Like what to do with her body. The last forecast I saw said it was going to be hot today. By this evening, she's going to start..."

He didn't finish the sentence. He didn't need to. They all understood the implications.

Lucy's stomach roiled at the thought. She had seen death before—too much of it. People died all the time in national parks and part of her job was to clean up the sometimes horrific messes made by those deaths. But the natural, inevitable decay that followed death was something she had yet to get used to.

Ethan appeared in the doorway, moving silent as a ghost for such a big man. "Got that damn radio to work for a minute," he grumbled, ignoring the way they all stiffened at his interruption. "Didn't get anything out, but caught a few garbled transmissions. Sounds like every town up and down the coast is a mess and San Francisco is in chaos. We're on our own."

"Fuck." Sawyer took a step back, rubbing his temples as if warding off an impending headache. Zelda moved closer, nudging her head against his leg in an attempt to comfort him. He gave her a small smile and a loving stroke before turning back to the group. "All right, so we're on our own. We'll bury Maya as best we can, and mark her grave so we can comeback for her once we're safe. Then we need to figure out what we have for food and water and how long it will last us."

Ethan crossed his thick arms over his chest. "The kid's gotta get off this mountain if he wants to keep that leg. Infection's already set in."

Lucy closed her eyes. Everything in her trembled with a raw, primal fear at the news.

God, she couldn't do this.

She didn't want to be the one in charge, to have to make all the decisions.

Breathe, she reminded herself. *Just breathe.*

"I'm going to hike down to the nearest ranger station." The words popped out of her mouth before she fully registered that was her plan.

"What?" Grant and Sawyer said at the same time.

Ethan shook his head. "It's twenty miles through rugged, unstable terrain. It'll take you at least two days, if you make it at all."

"Hey, weren't you the one that wanted to kick us all out last night?" Grant muttered. "Thought you'd be happy to get rid of some of us."

Ethan glowered, his bushy brows slamming together over his navy blue eyes. "I was pissed. That girl may have been lying about who she was, but she didn't deserve to go out like that."

So Ethan had been paying attention to their conversation after all.

Grant dismissed him with a scowl and turned to Lucy. "I'll go with you."

"No," she said at the same time Sawyer said, "Hell no."

Grant's scowl only deepened. "Who else do you suggest? Ethan?"

Ethan grunted. "I'm not leaving my tower."

"Okay, well, Chuck's not an option. Neither is Joel. Bea could do it, but she won't go anywhere without Theodore, and he's all but useless. And you can't go with her either, Sawyer. You'll just slow her down more."

Sawyer straightened, his usual good-natured calm shattering. Fury snapped in his eyes. He obviously wanted to deny it, but he couldn't. He could do a lot despite his blindness, but the disability made him a slow hiking partner. And speed was critical.

Lucy saw the muscles along his jaw work as he ground his teeth together. She touched his arm, felt the corded muscles tense under her fingers.

"He's right, Sawyer," she murmured. "I'm going alone. I know the terrain better than any of you, and I'm the fastest."

His head jerked in her direction, his pale eyes blazing with disbelief. He looked like a man about to spring into a fight. But instead, he let out a long sigh and nodded, accepting defeat.

"I don't like it." He paused, rubbing at his forehead again. He definitely had a headache he was trying to hide. "But we can't sit around waiting for rescue, and you're the best one to go."

chapter
nine

THEY WERE RUNNING out of room.

Rylan Cross studied the packed community center at Redwood Coast Rescue. In the hours after the quake, he'd helped Zak and Anna set up cots in neat rows and prepared to receive those displaced by the disaster. Now, every inch of the place was filled with a mix of locals and tourists, all seeking shelter, medical aid, or news from loved ones. Men and women with cuts and bruises, some with broken bones wrapped in makeshift casts, huddled together. The air buzzed with low murmurs of conversation, the strain of worry audible in every tone. The hum of anxiety was a living, breathing thing in the crowded space. It was like a war zone.

And there were still more survivors pouring in.

Rylan moved through the center, providing what comfort he could to the injured and scared, directing the flow of traffic to try to keep some semblance of order.

"Over here, folks." He waved the newcomers through

the door. Everyone looked exhausted, their faces ashen with dust and shock. Some staggered, relying on the support of friends or strangers to stay upright. "We don't have any cots left, but there is plenty of food and blankets to your right. If you're injured, we have medics set up in the back. If you're missing a loved one, there's a sheriff deputy stationed in the office down the hall taking reports."

He'd given up his office space so Deputy Isabella Delgado had a quiet place to record missing person reports.

He didn't envy her task.

Every hour or so, she emerged, her pretty face grim as she shared the growing list of the missing with her boss. Even from across the room, Rylan could see the deep creases in Sheriff Ash Rawlings' forehead. Ash was a stern, taciturn man, a workaholic who had gotten only slightly better about taking time off after marrying his wife, Rose, last year. Ash was known for his unshakeable stoicism, but even he looked overwhelmed by the magnitude of the disaster.

Just then, Rylan's cell phone buzzed in his pocket, pulling him from his thoughts. Surprised that the cell network was still functional, he dug it out and saw his dad's name. Guilt stabbed through him. He should've known his folks would be worried. He should've tried to contact them before now.

He started to answer, but a soft tug on his prosthetic arm distracted him. Looking down, he saw a small girl, maybe four years old, with tear-stained cheeks. She wore a Disney princess dress and had a grimy teddy bear clutched tight in her tiny fist. She tugged on his arm again, her gaze locked onto his with an intensity that went straight to his heart.

He slid the phone back into his pocket without answering and knelt down to her level. "Hey there, princess. That's a cute teddy bear. What can I do for you?"

"I lost my doggie," she whispered and there was so much fear and sorrow in those four words that his heart ached for her.

"I'm so sorry to hear that. What's your dog's name?"

"Bo. He's really big and fluffy and he's scared of thunder."

"Tell you what— I know just the people to help you find Bo." Rylan scooped the girl up onto his hip and scanned the crowd. He didn't see a frantic mother looking for a child, and dread settled like a rock in his gut. Maybe the girl was missing more than just her dog. He spotted Anna Hendricks' red hair in the crowd and weaved through the rows of cots toward her. As a co-founder of Redwood Coast Rescue and a mother herself, Anna was undoubtedly the best person suited for the task of finding Lily's family.

"Anna," he called, raising his voice above the drone of hushed conversation and the occasional wail of a baby. She and her teenage daughter, Bella, both turned, their faces pale and drawn. But at the sight of the little girl in Rylan's arms, Anna's expression softened, and she moved to their side swiftly.

"We've got a missing pup," Rylan said, shifting the little girl on his hip. "Bo— big, fluffy, scared of thunder. And maybe a missing mom," he added in a lower voice so the girl wouldn't hear.

Anna briefly closed her eyes as if asking for strength from some unseen power. Then she opened them again and smiled at the girl. "What's your name, sweetheart?"

The girl buried her face in Rylan's neck. He felt her hot tears seeping through his shirt collar.

"Lily." Her tiny voice was muffled against his shoulder.

Anna's gaze flicked up to him in silent question. He gave a tiny shake of his head. No, he hadn't seen any other family around her.

"Hi, Lily. I'm Anna and this is my daughter, Bella."

"Hi, Lily," Bella said gently. "Where's your mom?"

Lily sniffled. "She went to get Bo. He ran away when the shaking started."

"All right," Anna said and gently extracted the girl from her death grip on his neck. "We're going to do everything we can to find your Bo, okay? And we're going to help you find your mom, too. Can you go with Bella now?"

Bella held out a hand. "Hey, Lily. Come meet my sister, Poppy, and the other kids. I see you like Disney. We have a movie going in this room over here. Do you like Frozen?"

After a beat of hesitation, Lily nodded and set her tiny hand in Bella's.

Rylan watched them walk away. He only knew some

of the teenager's history from what little Zak mentioned of it during the team's therapy sessions. It wasn't pretty. Zak and Anna had adopted her and Poppy out of a horrible situation, but she seemed remarkably well adjusted. "She's good with kids."

"Yes, she is," Anna said with a small smile, watching as Bella introduced Lily to Poppy and the other parentless kids they'd gathered in a small room off the main lobby. Music from the Frozen soundtrack faintly echoed down the hallway, a surreal counterpoint to the grim reality they were facing.

"She's all set to go to college in the fall?" Rylan asked. Somehow, the small talk seemed important in that moment. Anna just looked like she needed the break.

"Yes, she is. She wants to study special effects makeup."

"That's very cool." Of course he already knew all of this. Zak had told him as much during one of their sessions. He was worried that Bella wasn't ready to leave the only stable home she'd ever had, was worried that she'd chosen such a difficult field to make a living in, but Anna didn't seem to share those reservations.

Anna laughed softly. Pride radiated off her. "She's way cooler than I could have ever hoped to be. Her and Poppy both."

Rylan glanced back at the crowded hallway and then returned his gaze to Anna, "You and Zak... you've done a hell of a job with those girls."

"I wish I could take all the credit, but that's mostly Bella's doing. But thank you." Anna set a hand on his arm. "For the compliment and the moment of distraction."

He set his hand over hers and gave it a squeeze.

Just then, a wail cut through the air. It was a sound Rylan knew too well— the raw, unfiltered scream of someone learning their world had just been torn apart.

Anna withdrew her hand from his arm and inhaled sharply. "I'd better check in with Bella, see if she got a description of Lily's mom, then get it out to Zak and the search teams."

"Is there anything—" Rylan's phone buzzed again in his pocket, and he silently cursed himself as he dug it out. His father's name blinked on the screen, persistent and demanding attention. "Sorry, I have to take this."

He excused himself, stepping down the hallway toward his office, out of the flow of people and noise. Only then did he answer.

"Hey, Pa. I'm okay."

He heard an explosive exhale of relief. "Jesus on a crutch, Ry. Why didn't you call your mama? You scared the shit out of her. The news said the quake was centered right near you."

"The news was right for once." His gaze strayed back to the main room where Anna was directing a fresh wave of newcomers. "We got hit pretty hard."

"You shoulda called sooner, boy." His father's reproach was softened by concern. "Your ma's been worried sick."

Translation: *I* was worried sick.

Rylan smiled faintly at that. Clayton Cross was a

good old southern boy from the top of his receding hair-line to the soles of his worn-out work boots, and he wouldn't admit to fear even if a black bear was gnawing on his leg.

"I know, Pa. I'm sorry. It's been chaos here."

"He's okay," Clayton called away from the phone. "Delia, I got through. They're okay."

A second later, his mother's voice, as sweet as a glass of iced tea on a hot summer day, rushed through the line. "Oh, Rylan, thank the Lord you're okay. We saw what happened on the news and I just about died from worry. How are you? Is your sister all right? Let me talk to her."

Rylan pulled the phone away from his ear and frowned.

His sister?

Rhiannon wasn't supposed to be here for another week. He'd cleared a long weekend off from his duties with Redwood Coast Rescue so they could spend time together.

He put the phone back to his ear. "What are you talking about, Ma? Rhia isn't here. She's still in Japan until next week."

Silence echoed through the line for a moment before his mother replied. "What do you mean she's not there? She was coming early to surprise you."

Ice trickled down his spine.

Had Rhiannon been in Steam Valley during the earthquake?

"When?" he demanded, his voice coming out harsher than he intended. "When did she get here?"

"She landed in San Francisco yesterday and rented a car. She was going to take a few days driving up the coast. She should have arrived at your place this afternoon."

Fear clawed its way up his throat, choking off his words for a moment. His little sister, his Rhia, looked at the world with wide green eyes and chose to see the good in it, even when the darkness threatened to swallow her whole.

She could be anywhere. Buried under rubble or trapped, alone and scared. If she lost her hearing aids, she'd be unable to hear rescuers calling out for survivors.

She could be hurt. Worse, she could— No. He wouldn't let his mind go there.

His grip tightened on the phone. "I'll find her," he croaked out, struggling to keep his voice steady.

A muffled sob sounded from his mother on the other end of the line followed by soft, fervent prayer whispered by his father. He wished he could take away their fear. He'd already put them through so much—the endless hospital visits, the worry in their eyes when he spiraled into PTSD and depression, the murmured reassurances that he was okay, even though they all knew it was a lie.

After all that, he couldn't, wouldn't, let them lose Rhiannon.

"Go, son," Clayton said firmly. "We'll be praying for you both."

His parents' faith was unshakeable in moments like these. His? Not so much. He'd been raised a good Southern boy, attending church every Sunday and reciting his prayers dutifully every night. But after that

FUBAR mission where he'd lost his arm, most of his team, and his sanity, after all the nights filled with terror and cold sweats, he'd learned that sometimes life kicked you down and kept you there, regardless of how hard you prayed. If there was a God, He didn't give one hot damn about what was happening here on Earth.

But now...

Now, he wished he could borrow a bit of his parents' unwavering belief.

"I *will* find her," he promised again. "I love you both." He hung up before his parents could say anything else. His world had just narrowed down to one single mission: finding Rhiannon.

As if on autopilot, he barreled toward his office, where Deputy Delgado had just finished with another tearful family.

She looked up as he burst through the door. "Oh. Rylan. Did you need your office—" She broke off, her dark eyes widening when she saw his face. "What's wrong?"

"My sister." Was that his voice, all hollow and broken? He couldn't recognize it. "She was on her way here. She was... she's missing."

"THIS IS EVERYTHING WE HAVE," Grant said, dumping the last of the backpacks onto the table.

Lucy catalogued the meager pile of supplies.

Food: trail mix, jerky, granola bars, and the six packages of ready-to-eat meals she'd packed for the weekend.

Multiple First Aid kits of various sizes.

Four flashlights.

Climbing gear from Grant.

Three canisters of bear spray—one from her, one from Sawyer, and one from Ethan.

Three boxes of electrolyte drink mix from her, Sawyer, and Grant.

She sighed. Her hikers definitely hadn't followed her packing list for the trip, or they'd have a lot more.

A single, sad-looking compass with a cracked face sat in the middle of it all. She picked it up, turning it over in her hand as if hoping to find some hidden source of strength or direction. Its needle spun aimlessly, pointing nowhere.

After a moment, she set the compass back down on the table and straightened, shrugging the weariness from her shoulders. There wasn't time for self-doubt, not now.

Sawyer's pack also contained dog food and treats, and she separated that out for Zelda.

"Take the electrolyte drink." Sawyer reached out until he found the stack of slightly crushed boxes. He pushed them toward her. "We have water here."

"Take the jerky, too, for protein. We'll be okay without it." Ethan tilted his head toward the kitchenette. "I have a freezer full of meat that has to be eaten before the generator runs out of fuel."

"How much fuel do you have?" Grant asked.

Ethan grunted. "Not enough. Maybe another day's worth, tops. I was due to go into town for supplies."

"Enough for the ATV I saw outside?"

"Wait," Sawyer said. "There's an ATV? Why the hell haven't we already sent someone down on it?"

Ethan scowled. "Because the damn thing doesn't work."

Grant stared at him. "So how do you get off the mountain for supplies?"

"Same way you got up the mountain. Walk."

Lucy cut a hand through the air between them. She'd had enough of their dick swinging. "Enough. Even if it worked, I wouldn't take it. It can't navigate over downed trees."

"You're leaving?" Joel spoke up from his seat and she

turned to look at the kid. He was pale and shaking, his face wet with sweat, his eyes glassy. She moved across the room to him and crouched beside his chair, testing his forehead with her hand. He was burning up, which only solidified why she had to go in her mind.

"Yeah, Joel, I'm going to get us some help, okay? You need to hang on until I get back."

"I don't want you to go."

She squeezed his hand, finding it cold and clammy. "I'll be back in no time with a rescue team."

Chuck, sitting on Joel's other side, met her gaze. There was doubt in his eyes, but also torment as he looked back down at his son. He said nothing, which was probably for the best.

She straightened and turned back to the table, grabbing her pack from the floor.

She organized her supplies— electrolyte drink mix, jerky, first aid kit, flashlight, bear spray, and the poor excuse for a compass—stuffing them into various compartments. She attached the rope and carabiners from Grant's climbing gear to the outside of her pack. She was about to zip the bag closed when Sawyer's hand appeared on hers.

"Is anyone watching?" he murmured.

She glanced around the room. Ethan had gone back to the radio. Grant was talking softly to Bea and Theodore. Chuck was staring worriedly at his son. "No. Nobody's paying attention."

"Then I have something you should take." He slid a

gun from under his shirt and pressed it into her palm, his big hand covering hers.

She stared at him. "Where did you get this?"

"I always have it with me. Blind man hiking alone in the woods? Seemed like a good idea. Still does." His hand tightened over hers. "Take it, Lucy."

She looked at the other members of their group again. One of them was most likely a killer, and Sawyer wanted her to take his only weapon?

But she couldn't deny it felt good in her hand, weighty and solid. She'd carried a gun everywhere since The Shadow Stalker took her, but she'd lost hers in the landslide and had been feeling vulnerable without it.

"Sawyer..." she began, but he cut her off.

"If I have it, and I don't have you here to watch my back, more likely than not, it will be used against me."

He was right, as much as she wished he wasn't. She nodded, tucking the weapon into her bag. "Keep Zelda close. She'll keep you safe."

A smile flickered over his mouth. "My girl always does."

She slung the bag over her shoulders and took a deep breath. "All right," she said to the room. "Wish me luck."

"Here." Grant shoved a roll of duct tape at her. "Always handy to have."

She took it without a word and stuffed it into one of the outer pockets of her backpack. She glanced around the room one last time at everyone who was now looking at her, some with hope, others with suspicion or stark fear. Sawyer was the only one not staring at her, his pale blue eyes fixed on the wall behind her.

She turned away, made it out the door and to the top of the tower's stairs before a hand grabbed hers and dragged her back into a hard body. Sawyer kissed her, hard, his mouth demanding and rough. It was a collision of lips and teeth, a crash of emotions that sent her heart reeling. His hands were strong on her waist, pulling her closer until there was no space left between them.

"I still don't like this," he whispered fiercely against her lips when they finally broke apart. "You better fucking come back, Lucy Harper. I have plans for you."

She was scared. Sawyer could taste the nerves in her kiss, smell the salty tang of fear. But there was also determination. This woman was nothing if not tenacious, and it was that fiery will that had drawn him to her in the first place.

They clung to each other for a moment longer, their bodies pressed close, their breaths intermingling.

Finally, she pulled away, patting his chest lightly. "I'll be back with help," she promised. "Then I'd like to know more about that plan of yours."

"It doesn't include clothes."

She made a small sound that was part needy groan, part laugh. He liked it. He wanted to know what other sounds she'd make when he had her underneath him, his cock stretching her, her body surrendering to his. He'd spent too many lonely nights over the last year fantasizing about her, and now he was kicking himself for not acting on the desire sooner. He could've spent the last twelve months making her come every night instead of staying away and pining after her in some misguided attempt at chivalry.

He pulled her closer again. "It's a damn good plan. Trust me."

"Down, boy." Her fingers brushed against his roughened cheek before she stepped back. "I'll see you soon."

He nodded, not trusting himself to speak as he let her go. It felt like his heart was lodged somewhere around his Adam's apple. He listened as her footfalls echoed down the stairwell. Zelda nudged her nose against his hand, and he reached down automatically to stroke her furry head.

"You're going to have to keep everyone sane until she gets back, baby girl."

The dog gave an acknowledging whine and pushed her snout deeper into his palm.

The moments ticked by as he stood at the top of the stairs, listening to the fading echo of Lucy's footfalls. Soon, all was quiet, save for the hushed whispers of the people inside the tower.

A knot formed in his stomach as he navigated his way back inside and heard Ethan's frustrated voice.

"This fucking piece of junk! Why won't it work?"

The radio again.

Sawyer sighed. Lucy was gone, and the responsibility

to keep everyone safe had fallen squarely on his shoulders. He moved toward Ethan.

"Let me have a look at it," he said, extending his hand.

Ethan grumbled but gave up his seat and guided Sawyer's hand to it.

Sawyer sank into the chair and ran his hands over the old radio as Zelda settled under the table, her head resting protectively on his foot. Years of working with components like this during his time in the military came flooding back. He used to fix machinery when it was pitch black— for this one thing, blindness had never been an obstacle for him. He frowned at the odd combination of wires that seemed out of place in the radio's guts. His fingers worked on instinct, mapping the layout of the circuitry. He could picture it all in his head—the diodes and capacitors, the intricate mesh of resistors, each individual solder point—all requiring careful inspection and adjustment.

As he worked, he felt the tension radiating from Ethan and the others. The room was heavy with fear and suspicion. He could almost taste it in the air— a bitter tang on his tongue.

"Damn thing's been a piece of shit from the start," Ethan mumbled beside him, radiating impatience.

"Here's your problem." He held up a wire that was frayed at the end. "This needs to be replaced. Do you have any spare parts or an old radio I can pull apart?"

Ethan was silent for a moment. "I might have an old walkie-talkie somewhere," he finally said. "Will that do?"

"It's worth a shot," Sawyer replied, keeping his tone neutral. He didn't want to give Ethan too much hope—there was always the chance that the parts wouldn't be compatible.

With a muttered curse, Ethan left to search for the walkie-talkie, leaving Sawyer alone with the damaged radio. He picked up the frayed wire again, running his fingers over its brittle plastic coating thoughtfully. It was always damage like this— small, yet devastatingly effective— that caused the most trouble. The analogy wasn't lost on him— in a group of people, it was often one person who could fray the sense of unity and trust, causing everything to fall apart.

How the hell was he supposed to keep this group together when they didn't trust him, and he didn't trust them?

He frowned as his fingers ran over the wire again. This wasn't from normal wear and tear. The insulation of the wire was cleanly cut as if by a knife.

A knot of suspicion hardened in his gut.

Ethan was the only one who had touched the radio since they arrived. But why would he sabotage it?

"Here," Ethan's gruff voice interrupted his thoughts, and something plastic was pushed into his hands.

"Thanks." He studied the walkie-talkie by touch, noting its size and weight. It was larger than most modern ones, which meant it held promise for what he needed. He set it down on the table and began to systematically dismantle it.

As he suspected, the walkie-talkie had similar components to the radio— old technology often shared common design elements. His fingers moved with practiced ease, locating the compatible wire and disconnecting it from the motherboard.

With a fine-tuned precision that left Ethan grumbling with what could only be begrudging admiration, Sawyer spliced the wire into the radio's circuit. As he worked, the anxious chatter in the room faded to a tense silence that prickled at the back of his neck.

"Just need to connect this here..." he muttered under his breath as he reattached the new wire. After a couple of failed attempts, a surge of triumph coursed through him as he finally managed to secure the connection.

"All right, let's see if she'll turn on now." He flicked the switch and held his breath.

A crackle of static filled the room.

Sawyer exhaled, adjusted a few dials, and pressed down on the talk button. "This is Blue Mountain Fire Tower calling for any available assistance. Does anyone copy?"

More static.

"Great," Chuck muttered. "He broke it."

Sawyer ignored the comment, adjusting the frequency dial before trying again. "This is Blue Mountain Fire Tower calling for any available assistance. Does anyone copy?"

The radio hissed and whined, but slowly, another sound emerged – a faint crackle and then a voice so low it was almost drowned out by the static.

"...Blue Mountain..."

The voice faded into static again.

"That was a reply!" Theodore said. "He got through!"

A ripple of excitement went through the group, and he felt them all crowding around him. It made the back of his neck prickle, but he tried to block them out and turned up the volume dial. "Bad copy. Repeat your last transmission."

Static popped and crackled.

He changed channels and tried again.

Still nothing.

Sawyer growled, frustration burning through him. He was so close. It was a delicate dance of tuning and adjusting, one he had performed countless times before in his military days. The radio was his lifeline, the only connection to the outside world they had. Failure wasn't an option.

As seconds ticked by into minutes, the excitement in the room slowly started to ebb away, replaced by a stifling dread. Ethan's pacing grew more frantic, Chuck's muttered curses louder, and a low whimper from Joel spiked tension even higher. Sawyer ignored them all, his attention solely on the radio in front of him.

"Fuck this," Ethan growled, pushing past Sawyer. "Let me—"

"Back off," Sawyer snapped, his tone icy. "I've got this."

Ethan snarled something under his breath but backed off.

Another adjustment.

Another call for help into the void.

More static.

Until finally— faintly— a voice came over the airwaves.

"...-peat your las—...break up...Fire Tower...come in..."

Sawyer exhaled sharp and fast; that was Ash Rawlings' voice. He pressed the transmit button. "Ash, it's Sawyer. We have eight people stranded at Blue Mountain and need help."

No response.

"They heard us," Sawyer said aloud, more to himself than anyone else. He adjusted the dial minutely left, then right, as he waited for Ash's voice to cut through the static once more.

It didn't come.

"All right," Grant finally said. "Sawyer, keep at it. Everyone else, grab a shovel. We need to bury Maya."

chapter
eleven

SAWYER TRIED for hours to get another response on the radio, pausing only long enough to feed Zelda when she got antsy. Nothing worked. Eventually, his lack of sleep caught up to him. He was getting sloppy, his brain fuzzy. His head ached, and his back protested the long hours he'd spent hunched over the radio. He needed to close his eyes for a few minutes, but the prospect of sleeping now without Lucy here to watch his six felt dangerous.

God, he hoped she was having better luck than him.

Sawyer sat back in his chair, rubbing the bridge of his nose with a weary sigh.

The radio sat silently on the table before him. He had done everything possible to get it working again— everything that his knowledge and instincts told him to do— but it seemed the old machine had given up its last breaths for that one fleeting connection.

Maybe it was enough. Maybe Ash had already mobilized Redwood Coast Rescue, and his team was on its way.

He gave a bitter chuckle, running a hand over the rough stubble on his jaw. Wishful thinking. Too bad that never saved anyone.

Fuck, he really needed to sleep.

He laid his head back against the headrest and let his heavy lids drift shut...

The prick of pain at his neck startled him awake. Adrenaline surged through his veins, blasting away any traces of fatigue.

His hand instinctively shot up to his neck and found the point of a blade digging into the soft flesh over his jugular. His breath hitched in his chest as he processed the situation. Assailant—unknown. Weapon— knife. Objective—unclear. Chances of getting out unscathed? His weary brain couldn't calculate.

A hand snaked out of the dark, clamping down on his arm. Its grip like a vise, cold and impersonal. "Where is Pierce St. James?"

Pierce?

What the hell?

He didn't recognize the harsh whisper and couldn't even tell if it belonged to a male or female. The blade dug deeper, drawing blood. The metallic tang filled his nostrils.

Oh, God.

Zelda!

He still felt her weight on his foot. She hadn't moved.

Why wasn't she reacting?

"I asked you a goddamn question," the voice hissed.

He willed himself to stay calm. "I don't know."

The knife pressed down harder. "Liars bleed, Murphy. Just ask Maya. Now tell me where Pierce is."

What the hell did Maya have to do with Pierce?

"I don't fucking know," he spat out, the pain making it hard to control his breathing. The blade's pressure eased against his skin, and he exhaled in a rush.

"Bullshit," the voice whispered. "You're his best buddy, aren't you?"

"I am," Sawyer replied evenly, the sharp edge of the knife making his words come out more like a huff than actual speech. "But I haven't seen him."

There was a pause, then a soft, barely audible chuckle that made Sawyer's stomach twist. "Funny. You're a funny guy. You haven't *seen* anyone in years."

The grip on his arm slackened just a fraction. He took the chance, jerking free and lunging for the assailant even as pain ripped through his neck.

Everything was still for a moment, as if time itself was holding its breath. Then, without a word, his attacker withdrew the blade and vanished as abruptly and silently as they had appeared.

Darkness was everything and everywhere as Sawyer grappled with the shadowy figure. His fingers gripped onto a narrow wrist, the pulse beneath his fingertips erratic and thrumming. He was rewarded with a hissed intake of breath, and the figure recoiled, working to regain their balance on the uneven cabin floor.

Sawyer used it to his advantage, shoving hard against

them, launching himself towards the table where he knew there were still two cans of bear spray. His hand slapped onto a canister just as a body hit him full force from behind.

The impact sent a jolt of pain through his already battered body, but he held tight to the bear spray. His vision was a useless morass of color and shadow, but his hearing, amplified by adrenaline, could pick up on the ragged breathing of his assailant. He twisted, aiming for where he thought they were, and pressed down hard on the canister's trigger. The spray burst forth in a cloud of pressurized liquid, and Sawyer prayed it hit its mark.

A guttural cry followed by violent coughing confirmed that it had.

"What the hell?" Joel wheezed between coughs. "Why did you spray that shit in here?"

Wait.

Joel?

No. The kid couldn't walk. There was no way he'd be able to attack a full-grown man twice his size.

Sawyer scrambled to his feet, his own eyes burning from the spray. "Did you see anyone just now?"

Joel coughed hard. "What? No! I heard you crashing around and woke up to find you spraying bear repellant like it was air freshener."

"Someone was just in here." He winced as pain radiated through his back. Fuck. He definitely pulled something. He raised a hand to check his neck and could feel the sticky warmth of blood smearing across his fingertips, but the wound didn't seem to be too deep.

Joel let out another violent cough. "Oh my God. Are you sure it wasn't just a bad dream?"

He held up his bloody hand. "When was the last time a dream made you bleed, kid?"

Footsteps pounded outside, and a second later, Chuck burst in. "What the fuck did you do to my boy?"

"I-I'm fine, Dad," Joel managed, still choking on the residual spray. "Sawyer just... he didn't know what he had in his hand. It was an accident."

Sawyer clenched his jaw and pulled off his T-shirt to press it to his bleeding neck. The kid was making him sound crazy. Or, worse, incompetent. Still, he kept his mouth shut. He didn't trust Chuck. Hell, for all he knew, the bastard had been the one to attack him.

Sawyer felt Chuck's glower, and, for a moment, he seemed like he was going to say something, but instead, his footsteps moved around Sawyer and went to Joel.

"Jesus Christ," Chuck muttered. "Your eyes. Let's get you cleaned up."

"I'm fine," Joel repeated, still coughing a little. "I told you it was an accident."

Two more sets of boots pounded up the tower's stairs. "What's going on in here?" Ethan asked from the doorway.

Chuck growled. "Sawyer's a fucking menace, that's what. He sprayed my boy with bear spray."

Guilt stabbed through him. Maybe it had been a nightmare. It had all seemed so real, but the nightmares he'd experienced right after he was blinded had been vividly real, too. For a long time, he hadn't been able to tell the difference between dreams and reality. "Joel, I'm sorry. I didn't mean to—"

"Just fucking stop," Chuck said. "Stop trying to act like you're normal. You're going to get us all killed."

The words hit like a physical blow.

Sawyer let out a bitter laugh. "Trust me. I know better than anyone that I'm not normal."

"Okay," Grant said, drawing the word out. "Let's all take a breath. Fighting isn't going to help. Let's get Joel outside into the fresh air."

There was movement, Grant and Chuck lifting Joel from his seat. Sawyer watched as their blurry figures limped toward the door, then scrubbed his hands over his face. "Fuck."

"You're bleeding," Ethan pointed out unnecessarily.

He jumped. He'd forgotten the guy was in the room. "Thanks for the newsflash," he said dryly.

"We need to clean that. It could get infected."

"I'll take care of it." He felt his way back toward the desk and crouched, reaching out for Zelda. She still hadn't moved.

What was wrong with her?

When he felt her chest expand, he let out the breath caught in his lungs. At least she was still breathing.

He felt Ethan close in behind him, and dread trickled down his spine. He was pretty sure his attacker had been a man. It could've been Ethan.

"The dog okay?" Ethan asked.

"I don't know." His voice came out strangled, and he cleared his throat. "She won't wake up."

Ethan grunted but said nothing for a handful of beats. "You didn't spray that shit accidentally. I know a good soldier when I see one. Blind or not, you're a good soldier."

"Marine." He stroked his girl's soft fur and silently willed her to be okay.

Ethan made a sound that might have passed for a laugh. "Jarhead. Should've figured."

"You were military?"

"Army Ranger. Long time ago. Another lifetime."

"I have a friend who was a Ranger." He thought of Zak Hendricks and hoped like hell the guy was mobilizing a rescue operation.

If his S.O.S. call got through to Ash.

If there was even a team left to mobilize. What if they were all injured? Or tied up with other rescues?

Too many ifs.

Adrenaline began to ebb, replaced by a dizzying exhaustion that threatened to pull him under. He leaned his back against the desk and dragged his girl onto his lap. He wasn't moving until she woke up.

chapter
twelve

LUCY WAS NOT HAVING BETTER luck.

Every path she tried to take down the mountain ended in an abrupt drop or some other impossible-to-scale obstacle.

Her heart pounded in her chest, and her breath came out in ragged gasps as she climbed a steep ridge. Every rustle of leaves, every snap of a twig, amplified her paranoia. She had desperately hoped to stumble across some sign of civilization by now—a cabin, a trail marker, anything—but so far, she had found nothing.

She paused at the top of the ridge, squinting into the distance. The dense forest stretched out before her, an unending wilderness painted in the ominous shadows of twilight. Somewhere out there were other people—help —but right now, it felt like she was standing at the edge of the world.

God.

She wasn't going to make it off the mountain. She had to turn back.

As the realization sank in, Lucy's shoulders slumped in defeat. All her energy ebbed away at once, leaving her knees weak and shaky. She sank to the mossy ground, hugging herself against the chilling breeze.

A lump formed in her throat, the weight of defeat making it hard to swallow. For a moment, she let herself wallow, let herself feel the all-consuming dread. Her gaze drifted over the vast expanse of wilderness, heart aching for the familiar sights and sounds of civilization.

But then, there was a glint—a metallic flash in the distance that caught her attention. Lucy squinted against the dimming light, straining her eyes to focus on whatever had sparked that fleeting glimmer. A sudden gust of wind shifted the branches, revealing a thin, vertical shape slightly swaying in the distance—a structure that seemed out of place amidst nature's chaos.

A cell tower.

Her heart leaped in her chest as a jolt of hope sparked through her veins. Finally, something tangible to hold onto. She scrambled to her feet, ignoring the protests of her weary muscles and retrieved her cell phone from her pocket. It was an old, battered thing, the screen cracked and chipped in too many places, damn near a relic.

With trembling fingers, she switched it on. The screen flickered to life, feeble in the encroaching darkness. Holding her breath, she watched as the tiny icon in the top corner blinked in and out of existence—a cruel tease of a signal.

"Come on," she muttered under her breath. "Just one bar."

She moved around, holding the phone up high as if offering it as a sacrifice to the gods. Up the ridge, down again, even scrambling up onto a tall boulder that offered a better vantage point. Every so often, she caught a glimmer—a flicker of a signal—that sent waves of anticipation through her. She quickly composed an S.O.S. text with the fire tower's coordinates and sent it out in a blast to anyone who might be able to help—911, the sheriff, Redwood Coast Rescue, her boss with the National Park Service, fellow park rangers. She stared at the little bubble, willing a response to appear, but the screen remained stubbornly silent. Her text just hung there in limbo. Then—

Message not sent.

A growl of frustration clawed its way out of her throat as she shoved the phone back in her pocket, the glimmer of hope snuffed out as quickly as it had sparked.

She had to get back to the fire tower.

They needed a different plan.

As she retraced her steps, the mountain seemed more hostile than before. Rocks that had been sturdy underfoot now shifted precariously. Branches seemed to reach out and snag at her clothes. The temperature was dropping rapidly as the sun set, and Lucy buttoned her jacket higher to ward off the chill. Sweat dried on her skin, leaving her colder still.

Still at least a mile from the tower, she rounded a bend and found Sawyer standing rigidly against a tree, his eyes closed. He didn't seem to notice her until she was standing in front of him.

"Sawyer," she managed to say, breathless from both the climb and the sight of him.

He jumped slightly, his pale blue eyes flicking toward her voice. "Jesus, Lucy. You could have made some noise."

"I'm sorry." She glanced around but saw no sign of anyone else. "What are you doing out here? Where's Zelda?"

His throat worked, his Adam's apple bobbing as he swallowed hard. "She's sick. Someone poisoned her. I was looking for Milk Thistle. Ethan said it can help protect her liver from the toxin, but we're too high up. It doesn't grow up here."

She noticed the raw, angry wound on the side of his neck and touched his cheek, turning his head to the side to get a better look at it. "What happened?"

He flinched away from her touch, grimacing. "I don't know. I thought—" He broke off and shook his head. He looked so sad, so lost, and her heart ached. This was not the same man who had promised to do naughty things to her when she got back. She took hold of his hand and pulled him over to sit on a nearby log, then took her pack off to find her first aid kit.

"Sawyer, this is a knife wound. Were you attacked?"

His jaw tightened as she dabbed the wound with an antiseptic pad. "I could've done it to myself."

"What?"

"Nobody saw the attacker. They think I was having a nightmare and hurt myself."

"Oh, c'mon. That's ridiculous."

His pale eyes shifted toward her. "I've done it before. When I was hallucinating. I hurt myself and others."

Her heart gave one hard thump. "Did you poison your dog, too?"

He flinched, and she realized the question had come out harsher than she'd intended. "Even if you had somehow cut yourself in a PTSD-induced nightmare, you wouldn't hurt her. Not in a million years." She peeled open a bandage and gently placed it over the wound. "Tell me what happened."

Sawyer sucked in a deep breath. "I was working on the radio. I got through to Ash for a second, but I don't know if it was enough. I kept trying to get him back, and I must've drifted to sleep because the next thing I remember is someone shoving a knife into my throat and demanding to know where Pierce is."

"Pierce?" That was not what she'd expected him to say.

"Yeah. They also said something about Maya and Pierce and—" He leaned forward, pressing his hands over his eyes. "Jesus, saying it out loud, it sounds crazy. It's entirely possible I dreamed it. I'm worried about Pierce. I'm upset about what happened to Maya, and it all just swirled together in my head."

Lucy rested her hand on his back, feeling the muscles under his shirt tense then slowly relax beneath her touch. "That still doesn't explain Zelda."

He dropped his hands to his lap. "I need to get back to her. I trusted Ethan to watch her, and maybe that was a mistake. Maybe he was the one to—fuck, I don't know anymore. I wish I could fucking see."

"Hey." She hugged him, and after a tense moment, his arms circled her, tugging her close. He buried his face in her hair and exhaled hard. He was shaking. "Zelda will be okay. We'll find Pierce, and we'll get off this mountain."

"I appreciate you trying to comfort me, but the fact that you're sitting here right now doesn't bode well." He released her and stood. "You couldn't find a way down, could you?"

"No," she admitted with a heavy heart. "But we have other options."

"Options?" He gave a bitter laugh and rubbed the back of his neck, wincing as his fingers brushed against the bandage. "We tried the radio. We tried to hike down. What other options do we have?"

"A cell tower. I saw one still standing in the distance and tried to send some SOS messages but... nothing. The signal comes and goes."

He frowned in thought. "Think it would work if we got closer?"

"It's worth a shot."

"How far away is it?"

"Maybe... ten miles. It was hard to tell. But we only need to get close enough for a phone to pick up the signal. So maybe half that distance?"

"If it's a 4 or 5G tower, we'll have to get within three miles."

She shrugged. "So more than half. I can do it, but I'll have to take everyone's phones with me. The more I have, the better chance I'll have at getting a signal."

"Yeah, okay," he said after a beat. "What do we have to lose? But you're not going alone this time."

"Sawyer, you don't have Zelda—"

He turned away and started up the path toward the fire tower. No dog, no hiking pole, but he moved confidently like he was sighted. "I promise I won't slow you down."

Lucy sighed. She didn't like that note of bitterness in his voice. This wasn't her Sawyer—the man who held her when she cried, who made her laugh when she'd forgotten how. the one who quipped and flirted with reckless abandon. This was a wounded, desperate man bent on proving his worth to himself and the world.

And it frightened her.

"There you are!" Bea's voice boomed from the tower as Sawyer and Lucy emerged from the trees. "Your girl's coming around. I think she's going to be okay."

Sawyer cursed himself for not bringing his cane. He couldn't move as fast as he wanted to without risking falling on his face, but once he reached the bottom step of the tower, he raced up. "Zelda's okay?"

Bea grabbed his shoulder in a reassuring squeeze. "Yeah, she's all right. Woozy, but seems to be in good health."

Sawyer felt his way through the cabin to find Zelda exactly where he'd left her on the floor in front of the radio. He ran a hand over her. She was awake with her head raised and gave a happy whimper when she saw him. Her tail thunk dully on the floor.

He exhaled a shaky breath and hugged her. She was still alive, and that was all he needed. "You had me scared there, girl."

"Looks like she was just drugged," Ethan said. "I found some empty packets of Benadryl stuffed in the trash bin right after you left, and there's a bit of pink powder mixed in with her kibble."

Which he wouldn't have noticed when he fed her. And now that he thought about it, she had seemed reluctant to eat, but he'd chalked it up to the stress of their situation.

"Who would do that?" Bea asked.

"I imagine it was the same person who stuck a knife to Sawyer's neck," Lucy said from the doorway.

"You're back! Is help coming?" Joel's voice was full of hope.

Sawyer lifted his head from Zelda as he felt all the attention in the room turned toward her. He imagined her standing there in the doorway, tall and strong, her brown hair pulled back in that practical ponytail of hers.

"Not yet," she said, her voice steady, but Sawyer could hear an undercurrent of frustration. "But I saw a cell phone tower not too far from here. It's intact, but we're too far away to pick up a signal from it. At first light tomorrow, Sawyer and I are going to hike closer and try to get a call out."

"You're taking *him*?" Chuck's disgust was evident in the way he stressed the word him. "Why not take someone who can actually help you? Like Grant or Ethan."

Sawyer clenched his teeth. He really disliked the guy.

"Shut up, Chuck." There was no heat in Lucy's statement. "I'm taking him because he has connections that could expedite a rescue. I'm also taking him because someone here just tried to kill him and his dog."

A chorus of protests rose up from the group, which Lucy cut off with a sharp "Enough!" She stalked into the room, her boots thudding on the wooden floor. "The fact is, we have a potential killer in our group, and frankly, Sawyer is the only one of you I fully trust right now. So, yes, he's coming with me."

The silence that followed was electric. Sawyer sat, Zelda curled beside him, absorbing the charge of suspicion and fear in the room. Resentment simmered, radiating from Chuck's direction, but he said nothing.

"And," Lucy added, "we'll need to take your phones with us."

That caused another explosion of protests.

"Everyone, quiet!" Bea thundered, and the room fell into silence again. She moved across the room toward Lucy, and Sawyer tensed, but the woman just handed over something that had to be her phone. "It's common sense. The more phones they have, the more chance at picking up a signal."

Slowly, one by one, the others began to follow suit. Sawyer heard the shuffling of bodies and the soft clinks of phones being deposited into what he presumed was a bag. He heard Lucy's soft words of thanks and felt a swell of gratitude for her leadership.

She was strong—so much stronger than she gave herself credit for. She'd get them out of this.

"And what if you don't get a signal?" Chuck asked.

Lucy paused, and then said coolly, "Then we try again. Until we succeed."

chapter
thirteen

LUCY WASN'T SURPRISED to see Sawyer awake before dawn the following morning. She'd stayed by his side all night and he'd slept restlessly.

In truth, so had she.

He sat out on the balcony again, his face lifted toward the warmth of the rising sun, his eyes closed. Zelda lay beside him, her eyes now bright and alert.

Lucy wrapped the blanket around her shoulders and padded out onto the balcony, careful not to disturb the others.

"Can't sleep either, huh?" Sawyer asked without opening his eyes.

"Too many thoughts," she admitted, running her fingers through her ponytail. "How's Zelda?"

"She's better," he answered, scratching behind the dog's ears. "She doesn't seem to have any lingering effects."

"That's good." She moved to sit down beside him. "Can I ask you something?"

"Sure."

"How do you always know it's me approaching before I speak?"

A slight smile curved his mouth. "I know your footsteps and your smell."

She made a face. "Ugh, what I wouldn't give for a bath right now." The bath wipes she always packed with her hiking gear weren't cutting it anymore. She was covered in too much grime and blood, and who knew what else.

"I'd settle for a plain old shower," Sawyer said. "But, hey, at least we all still have toothbrushes and minty fresh breath."

"Thankfully." She stared out over the horizon as dawn speared through the sky, chasing away the darkness. The morning was still, the world holding its breath as if waiting for something. "Sorry if I stink."

"No, it's not like that," he chuckled, still not opening his eyes. "I mean, you have a... distinct scent. Hard to describe. A mix of pine and wildflowers and something else I can't place..." He broke off, frowning slightly as if trying to find the right words. "Like the air after it rains. Sweet and earthy."

Lucy blinked, taken aback. Slowly she turned her gaze from the rising sun to Sawyer. She studied his face. He was so pretty, though he'd probably hate being called that. Something fluttered in her chest, and she took a deep breath to steady herself.

"Well," she said, attempting to keep her voice light. "You smell like dog."

He chuckled at that, the sound surprising a laugh out of her as well. It felt good to laugh.

"That's an insult to dogs," he said. "I reek. I don't know how you can stand sitting beside me right now. I can barely stand it."

"Well, it's either sit here with you or stay in there with Chuck, and I'd pick you over his BO any day."

"Jesus, it's so bad, right? I thought I was the only one who noticed. It's like dirty socks and onions."

She wrinkled her nose. "He's one of the most unpleasant people I've ever met, both personality-wise and scent-wise. I feel bad for Joel."

Sawyer was silent for a beat. "My dad's a lot like him."

Surprised by the admission, she turned to look at Sawyer. "Really?"

"Yeah," Sawyer said, opening his eyes and turning to face her. "Always had to be the biggest, toughest, loudest guy in the room. Thought it made him strong."

Lucy could see the hurt in his posture—the rigid set of his shoulders, the tight clench of his jaw. She knew what it was like to carry that sort of ache around, the one that burrowed its way into your bones and made you feel alone even in a crowded room. "That's not strength."

"No, it's not. He's an obnoxious bully." He exhaled a long, slow breath. "He's why I joined the military, you know. 'Be a man,' he'd always say. He was so proud when I enlisted, and for the first time in my life, I felt like I had a relationship with him. But that was when I could still see." He paused, and a frown tugged down the corners of his mouth. "But now he acts like I'm a disappointment. Like it was my choice to be blind and fuck up my life. I haven't talked to him in years. I think that's why I have no patience for Chuck. The guy reminds me too much of him."

Lucy felt an unexpected surge of anger at his father for ever making him feel like a disappointment. He was the most incredible person she had ever met. Kind, loyal, strong. He wasn't a disappointment... he was an inspiration.

She reached out and gently touched his hand, all too aware that any physical contact ran the risk of conveying more than she was ready to admit. But the warmth of his skin against hers provided an odd sense of comfort, grounding her in a way that nothing else could at that moment.

"I'm sorry, Sawyer," she said softly. "You didn't deserve to be treated like that. Your blindness doesn't make you any less of a man."

He flipped his palm upward to hold hers. "Thank you."

For a heartbeat, they sat in silence, their hands entwined. He didn't say anything more. He didn't have to.

Then she remembered something she'd seen on the trail yesterday and got an idea. She stood, pulling him up with her. "How about a change of scenery?"

He hesitated. "Shouldn't we head out to the cell tower?"

"It can wait another hour until the sun's up. Come on."

Sawyer heard the rush of the water and felt the cold spray of it on his face. He smiled. His Lucy was full of surprises. "A waterfall?"

"It's really more of a trickle than a fall. I found it yesterday when I was trying to find a trail down." She released his hand, and he heard the rustle of clothes. "C'mon. It's not a hot bath, but it will get us clean."

"Are you proposing we skinny dip together, Ranger Harper?" He gave an exaggerated gasp of mock outrage. "My God. If I had pearls, I'd be clutching them."

"You're an ass," Lucy said with a laugh and smacked his shoulder. "I didn't bring you here for some cheesy romantic moment. We smell bad, and this will help. Also... it's beautiful."

"I'll have to take your word for it on the beautiful part." He heard her clothes drop into a pile, and his breath caught in his suddenly tight chest. He imagined her body— the curve of her waist, the fullness of her breasts, the roundness of her hips, the strength in her shoulders. He pictured her standing there, the shadows of the trees dappling her skin, the spray of the waterfall dampening her hair. He had no way to know if his imagination was close to reality, but he liked the picture it painted in his head.

"Are you naked right now, Lucy?" His voice came out in a low rumble.

"You'll have to catch me to find out." She swept past him, her footsteps slapping softly on the rocks. Then he heard a gentle splash as she entered the water.... followed by another splash, much less graceful than the first.

Lucy laughed. "See? Even Zelda thinks it's a great idea."

"She loves to swim." He tugged off his shirt and peeled his pants and underwear down his legs, feeling a pang of nerves as he stood bare to the world.

Bare to Lucy.

He wasn't usually self-conscious about his body. He spent many hours in the gym or on the trail to make up for all the hours he sat stationed in front of a computer. His muscles were hard and well-worked, his stomach was flat and rippled with abs. His cock was on the bigger side or normal. He'd never before had anything to feel self-conscious about...

But this was different. This was Lucy—driven, independent, beautiful Lucy—the woman who'd crawled into his heart and set up camp there, whether he liked it or not.

He wanted her to like what she saw.

And he suddenly, fiercely regretted that he'd never be able to see her naked. He'd never be able to see her face flush with arousal or light up with laughter, never watch her eyes darken with desire or sparkle with mischief.

God, he wanted to see her.

The sharp pain of that longing surprised him.

"Are you okay?" Her words echoed strangely off the rocks and water, rippling back toward him. He realized he'd been standing still for too long, exposed and silent.

"Yeah," he replied, his throat tight. He fumbled his way over the rocks toward the sound of splashing water and found himself at the edge of the pool formed by the waterfall. He dipped a toe in and was taken aback by the temperature. "Fuck, that's cold."

"You'll get used to it." Suddenly, she was right beside him, her hand sliding into his. He could feel her warmth, smell that sweet, earthy scent that was uniquely hers.

He took a step and then another, and with each one, the water rose higher and higher, swallowing him up to his waist. The cold really wasn't that bad once he was in, and the water was a balm to his aching muscles, washing away the sweat and grime of the past few days. It was reviving, invigorating.

"Soooo....?" Lucy said. Her voice came from his right, closer than he expected. Her fingers nudged against his under the water.

"What?"

"Are you gonna get in all the way or just stand there?"

A smile tugged at his lips. "Depends."

"On?"

"If you're gonna drown me or not."

"No promises." Her laughter bounced around him. It was a sound he could get lost in, a sound that made him forget for a moment the dangerous situation they were stuck in.

Jesus, he'd needed this.

And somehow she'd known it.

"All right then." He inhaled deeply and dunked himself into the cold pool, gasping as he resurfaced, his skin tingling from the shock of it.

Zelda barked from somewhere nearby and there was another splash. After the scare yesterday, he loved hearing her joyful energy. It was infectious and he found himself laughing along with Lucy.

"She's found a rock to jump off," Lucy told him, a grin in her voice. "It's hilarious. She jumps and all four of her legs start paddling before she hits the water."

He was about to say something, to crack a joke, when he felt Lucy move closer. Her fingers brushed his chest, and all of his remaining sense sparked to painful life. He inhaled sharply as she slid her hand up his torso, tracing the line of his shoulder with a soft touch that made him shiver. Suddenly, the water wasn't cold at all. His skin felt tight and hot, his blood like fire coursing through his veins.

"You mentioned something about a plan for me when I got back," she murmured, her hand curling around the nape of his neck. "If I remember correctly, it didn't include clothes."

"Lucy..." His voice sounded strange, breathless.

"I know this isn't the moment. I just... I needed this." She took a deep, shaky breath. "I needed to feel this connection. Needed to feel... normal again."

Her words echoed in his head as he wrapped his arms around her, pulling her close. He could feel her heart thudding against his chest, her body trembling under his touch. The sound of the waterfall was a distant buzz in his ears as he focused solely on Lucy.

"You're not normal, Ranger Harper," he told her, stroking a hand down the sleek curve of her back. "You're extraordinary."

He felt her laugh against his neck, low and warm. "Flattery will get you everywhere."

"Good to know. I'll store that information for future use." As he said it, Sawyer realized he meant every word. He wanted a future where he could learn all the things that pleased Lucy Harper.

Her body was hot against his in the chilly water, and even without sight, he could envision the toned lines of her body, the slope of her breasts, the curve of her hips.

"I want to touch you." He found himself leaning in, burying his nose in her hair, inhaling the scent of waterfall and Lucy.

Her arms tightened around him, holding him closer. "Then touch me."

He gave a rueful laugh. "We don't have time. Not for the way I want to, at least." His voice was rough and low as he traced his fingers back up her spine. "I want to taste every inch of you. I want to map the shape of your body with my hands and mouth until you're trembling and begging for release. I want to hear your sweet, throaty moans as you come undone beneath me, Lucy." His hand cupped the back of her head, his fingers tangling in her wet hair. "I want to hear you say my name like it's a prayer and a curse all at once. Like it's the only word you know."

"Sawyer," she whispered on a shaky exhale, and her nails bit into his shoulders.

"Yeah, just like that." He traced his lips up the curve of her jaw to her ear. "I want you as desperate for me as I am for you."

Her arms tightened around him, and the hard peaks of her breasts scraped against his chest. "Maybe I'm already desperate."

A thrill shot through him, and he growled low in his throat as his cock hardened to the point of pain. Jesus, he wanted this woman in all the ways a man could want. He'd wanted to protect her the first time they met in the cave. He'd wanted to comfort her in the hospital. And now, the deep, primal part of him wanted to claim her.

He cradled her face between his hands, thumb brushing softly over the curve of her cheek to her lips. He could feel every breath she took, each one shuddering and unsure. He leaned in, tilting his head and closing the small distance between them. Every muscle in his body coiled in anticipation as their lips brushed. It was barely a touch, just a whisper of warmth and wetness. But it sent a jolt of electricity rocketing through him.

With a low growl, he pulled her hard against him and kissed her properly. Her mouth opened beneath his with a soft sigh that he swallowed down like a starving man. God, she tasted sweet, like ripe berries and fresh water, like everything he'd ever craved but never knew he needed.

Her arms wound tightly around his neck as she kissed him back with equal fervor, her tongue tangling with his in a slow dance of shared desire. Every stroke fanned the flames within him higher and higher until they consumed all thought, all reason.

Lucy moaned into his mouth, a low sound that vibrated right through him and shot straight to his cock. He pressed up against her instinctively as heat pooled low in his belly.

"Fuck," he muttered against her lips as his cock nudged up against her bare stomach. His senses were on fire; every touch was amplified tenfold because he couldn't see where it was coming from or predict where it would land next.

Zelda barked.

Lucy jerked away and sucked in a deep, shuddering breath, flattening her hands on his chest and pushing until he released her. Cold water flooded between them as she moved back.

His blood pounded through his body, the taste of her still on his lips as he tried to figure out what had caused the abrupt ending. "What's wrong?"

"We should go. We have a long hike ahead of us." Her voice sounded weird, strained.

He reached out for her, intending to draw her back to him, but found only air.

"Lucy?" he called out, his hand stretching out further, grazing the water's surface in search of her. The only response was the distant sound of splashing as she made her way toward the bank.

With a frustrated sigh, he raked a hand through his wet hair, trying to regain some semblance of control. He had been so close, so damn close to something real, something raw and beautiful with Lucy.

He swore under his breath and swam after her. Despite his best intentions to take it slow, he had pushed her too hard, too fast.

SHE WASN'T IGNORING HIM...

Exactly.

Lucy just needed space. Space to breathe, space to think. Because God, did she need to think. The intensity of her desire for Sawyer was like a physical force, dragging her under its relentless wave. He made her feel things she didn't understand, things she had never felt before. Things she wasn't sure she wanted to feel.

As they trudged through the dense forest toward the cell tower, she kept her eyes on the path in front of her, refusing to look at Sawyer. She didn't trust herself not to turn around and throw herself into his waiting arms.

The ground beneath her was uneven, the foliage thick. She could hear the distant rush of water, a river or a stream, perhaps. She could hear him and Zelda, too, their steady footfalls just calmly following behind her. The silence was heavy, taut like a wire on the verge of snapping.

Dammit, she was a coward.

She was usually the kind of woman who faced everything head-on. She'd learned in the hardest possible way that the only person who would always stand up for her was her. She didn't hide or run away from her problems... unless they involved a six-foot-two blind tech genius with the body of a Greek god and a penchant for innuendos and pushing buttons. Apparently.

Damn Sawyer Murphy and his ability to get under her skin. She'd sworn off men a long time ago, and they were in the middle of a life-or-death situation. The last thing she should be doing was entertaining fantasies about that sexy body of his and the long, hard cock she'd felt pressed up against her belly in that pool. But here she was, all but whimpering at the memory of it, her panties soaked with want, her skin flushing hot.

If not for Zelda's well-timed interruption, she would've begged him to fill the empty ache between her legs and fuck the nightmares and fears away. She would've lost herself completely in him, and, God, she wasn't ready for that. She wasn't ready for the cracks in her armor it would cause, or the breach in her heart Sawyer seemed so determined to make.

The silence between them was deafening, the tension almost palpable. She wanted to break it, to say something —anything—just to fill the void. But words, it seemed, had abandoned her.

Sawyer broke the silence first. "Lucy, talk to me." His voice was soft, pleading. The undercurrent of worry was unmistakable. "What happened back there?"

"I..." Her voice caught in her throat. She couldn't let him know about the whirlwind of emotions raging through her. Couldn't let him see her vulnerability, her uncertainty. So, she settled for a diversion. "We've gone a couple of miles. We should check the phones. Maybe we're close enough for a signal."

Sawyer's silence was loud in her ears. She didn't have to look at him to know he was angry and confused and maybe a little bit hurt.

But instead of responding with fury or frustration, he replied with a calm, "Sure, it's worth a try."

Sawyer reached into his pocket and pulled out a phone. He extended his arm, waiting for her to take it. She crossed the few steps between them to collect the device from his outstretched hand. As her fingers brushed against his, the brief touch was like a spark of electricity shooting through her.

She quickly pulled away and examined the screen, looking for any sign of bars indicating network reception. She swiped her thumb across the glass surface, but no matter how hard she willed it, the No Service indication wouldn't go away. She tried her phone next and got more of the same. None of the phones they had were working.

"No signal yet." She tried to keep the disappointment from edging into her voice. "Let's keep moving."

Sawyer nodded, his jaw tight. "Right," he said, his tone flat and distant.

Suddenly, the ground beneath them began to tremble, a rumbling sound resonating from deep inside the earth. Her heart slammed against her ribs as she realized what was happening.

Aftershock.

"Get down!" Sawyer called. "Shield your head."

She crouched down... and the ground opened up under her feet. She was falling before she had a chance to scream, the world around her blurring as she descended into darkness. She hit the bottom of the hole hard, the air rushing out of her lungs in a painful whoosh. She gasped for breath as the world spun around her. She tried to blink away spots from her vision.

"Lucy!" Sawyer's voice echoed down to her. She could see him leaning through the hole way overhead, his ear turned toward her, listening. "Jesus. Lucy! Answer me!"

She opened her mouth to tell him that she was fine even though every fiber of her body protested against the idea. She was not fine. She was in pain. She was in the dark, with only a small shaft of light filtering down through the hole. And she was scared.

Just like the cave.

Except she wasn't in a cave.

And the Shadow Stalker was dead.

"I'm... I'm here," she managed to croak out between labored breaths. She bit down hard on her bottom lip, struggling to push herself upright despite the wave of pain that radiated through her. "I'm in some kind of... sinkhole."

"Are you okay?"

She forced a laugh, painful as it was. "Define okay."

"Can you move?"

She tested her limbs. "Yeah, I can."

He exhaled hard like he'd been holding his breath. "Hold on. I'm coming down."

"No!" Panic burst through her in a white-hot rush, drowning out the pain. There was no way a sighted person could climb down without risking a potentially fatal fall, much less a blind one. The last thing they needed was for him to get injured, too. "Sawyer, please, stay there. It's too dangerous. I'll find a way back up to you."

"The hell I will. You're hurt. I can hear it in your voice."

It was typical of him, she thought, to try and be the hero even when he was at a clear disadvantage. It was in his nature to be protective, to rush into danger without a second thought for himself. "We don't need you hurt, too."

"Would you just trust me for once?" There was a note of frustration in Sawyer's voice that she rarely heard. "I'm not helpless."

"I never said you were. But—"

"Do you trust me or not?"

Lucy sucked in a painful breath. The shadows felt like they were creeping in around her, and panic sizzled through her. She was back in the cave, the damp walls closing in around her. Trapped. Alone. Helpless. The memory of the Shadow Stalker's cruel laugh as he left her to die echoed in her ears.

No, she wasn't alone. Sawyer was there. He was always there when she needed him.

"Lucy?"

She swallowed back the fear. "I trust you."

"Good. Because I need you to stay calm and guide me down to you."

There was a rustling noise from above, then rocks tumbled through the hole. She instinctively covered her head with her arms as pebbles pelted down around her. There was a loud grunt and then a thud followed by a stream of soft profanities.

She still couldn't see him.

"Sawyer?" she called, struggling to push herself into a seated position. Ignoring the throbbing pain in her side and the threatening darkness at the edges of her vision, she strained her ears for his response.

"I'm fine," he grunted. "Just a small... hiccup."

Then there he was, his body blocking out the sunlight for a moment as he lowered himself through the hole. A warm wave of reassurance washed over her at his nearness. His dogged obstinance might have been infuriating, but it was also comforting.

She could always count on Sawyer to be Sawyer.

Suddenly, the sound of a soft thump echoed through the cavern.

"Shit," he muttered, his voice now much closer than before. Then something fell and landed in a heap a few feet away from her. There was silence, and for a heart-stopping moment, Lucy thought he had fallen.

"Sawyer!"

"Hang on, hang on. I hit a ledge. Jesus. Did you hit this thing in the fall?"

She honestly had no idea—it all happened so fast—but going by the aches and pains blooming all over her body, she wouldn't doubt it. "Please be careful."

More cursing. Then he appeared over the edge of the rock overhang above her, rappelling down while strapped into the climbing harness Grant had given her. Her breath rushed out of her in relief. He wasn't climbing blindly down to her, after all. She'd completely forgotten about the harness and ropes attached to her pack.

"Keep talking," he said. "I need to hear where you are."

She shifted and winced as pain lanced through her side again. "What do you want me to say?"

"Well, you could start by telling me why you pulled away earlier at the waterfall. You were running so hot. You wanted me as much as I want you. What made you suddenly turn so cold?"

He would go there right now. "No."

"Are you going to make me guess?"

"I don't want to talk about it."

"Was it because of The Shadow Stalker? Do I remind you of what he did?"

Just the mention of the name sent a chill scraping down her spine. "Please. I can't do this. Not right now."

"I will get you to open up to me, Luce," he said and continued descending carefully, his boots scraping against the rock every time he pushed off the wall. "And we *are* going to finish what we started at the waterfall."

She couldn't tell if that was a warning or a promise. She didn't know which she wanted it to be.

"Okay, fine," he said when she remained silent. "Then tell me about your first kiss. No, wait. I don't want to hear about that. Your favorite color. Your favorite food. Your favorite holiday. When did you know you wanted to be a park ranger? Tell me everything about you. Just keep talking."

This, she could handle. She opened her mouth to tell him her favorite color was green, and she'd decided she wanted to be a park ranger when she was ten after visiting the redwoods during one of the few vacations she'd taken before her parents divorced. They'd fought the entire time, but for once, she hadn't cared because the trees had captured her imagination. For a girl who had grown up in the flat farmlands of Ohio, they'd seemed almost magical, and she'd wanted to stay among them forever.

But instead of any of that, she blurted, "I was married once."

Sawyer's steady descent halted abruptly, his body swaying slightly in the air, blocking out the small shaft of light from above. Even though she couldn't see his face, she imagined the surprise registering in his pale blue eyes.

"You were... what?" His voice echoed off the rocky walls.

"I was married." The words tasted strange in her mouth, foreign and uncomfortable. They were true, but they were also a secret she'd buried deep within herself, tangled up with guilt and regret.

There was a pause before he started moving again. "What happened?"

God, why had she opened her mouth?

"Lucy," he said softly. "I need you to talk to me."

"I was young and naive," she began, hating the vulnerability and pain she heard in her voice. "He was older and said all the right things. I thought I was in love. I guess I didn't really understand what that meant. I put all of my dreams on hold for him, gave up a lot of myself. I didn't realize until it was too late what kind of man he really was, and by then, I was trapped, couldn't get out. He hurt me. A lot." She exhaled in a shaky rush. "Seems like men are always trying to fucking trap me. In an abusive marriage. In a cave. I refuse to fall into yet another one."

Sawyer stilled again, suspended above her like a rugged angel in the darkness. "Lucy, I'm not a trap. I would never cage you. If I could, I'd give you wings and watch you soar. You deserve it."

"You say that now, but the moment I sleep with you, that will change." She regretted her harsh tone as soon as the words left her mouth. She felt vulnerable and raw in a way she hadn't felt for a long time, and he didn't deserve to have it taken out on him. "I'm... I'm sorry. That came out wrong."

It felt like an eternity before he responded. "You've got this shield around you, and now I get why. But, someday, I hope you'll trust me enough to let it down. Just a little." Suddenly, he was there beside her in the dark, his hands tracing over her body before cupping her face. "I will *never* hurt you. I'd rather die than cause you a second's pain. And while I can't promise that I won't ever fuck up, I can promise you this: I will fight for you and protect you with everything I have." He wiped away her tears with his thumbs. She hadn't even realized she was crying until that moment. "If you give me a chance."

She said nothing, couldn't squeeze any words past the lump in her throat, and leaned into his touch. There was a comfort to his presence, a warmth that she couldn't ignore. But it also felt like Collins all over again—he'd been full of sweet words and charming smiles, and all of it had been nothing but empty promises.

Yet, she couldn't deny there was something different about Sawyer. A genuineness that radiated from him. He'd been there once before when she needed help.

But if she gave him her heart, could she trust him not to hurt her? Trust him to keep his promise?

"You don't have to say anything or make any decisions now," he said, releasing his hold on her face and shifting away slightly to pull something off his back. "We've got more pressing things to handle at the moment."

She almost laughed at that. How could he so easily compartmentalize things? One moment, he was baring his soul to her, and the next, he was back to problem-solving mode. But then again, that was Sawyer. Steady as a rock, unflinching in the face of danger, and fiercely protective. He made her feel like she mattered, like she was someone worth fighting for. And that was something her ex-husband never did. He'd never cared enough to fight for her.

So why was she measuring Sawyer against that bastard?

Right. She wasn't going to figure this out now. They had a tower to get to, and she had a hole to climb out of.

"All right," she said, her voice steadier than she felt. "Let's get out of here."

chapter
fifteen

SAWYER RAN his hands over her, checking for blood or broken bones. His heart was still lodged in his throat. He'd seen her fall. The moment the ground collapsed under her, his damaged brain had decided to kick into gear, and he'd seen the stark terror on her face. He'd seen her reach out a hand toward him. He'd lunged for her, but she was gone, and he couldn't see shit again. He'd heard her scream, a sound quickly swallowed by the rumbling earth. Then, silence.

Jesus, the silence had been excruciating.

His hands were trembling, but he managed to keep his voice steady. "Is anything broken?"

She hissed out a breath. "No, I don't think so."

He felt a warm wetness on the right side of the small of her back. Blood. She was bleeding, and something sharp jutted from her skin there. He ran a hand over her hip and belly, relief flooding him when he found nothing but soft, warm, unbroken skin.

Okay, so she hadn't been impaled, but whatever was sticking out of her back was going to be a problem. To get out of this hole, she needed to be able to wear the other harness.

Overhead, he heard Zelda's worried whine. "It's okay, girl," he called up to her. "Stay there. We're okay."

"She keeps looking through the hole," Lucy said. "Blocking out the light."

"Luckily, I don't need light to get us out of here." He tried to sound cheerful for her sake. "I'm like Batman. I do my best work in the dark."

Lucy snorted, then winced. "I'll just bet you do."

He could hear her smile in those words, and it eased his worry a fraction. "I could show you if you stopped denying how dynamite we'd be together in bed."

"Would you stop?" Her laugh echoed off the walls around them, bringing a small smile to his lips. "We're stuck in a pit, and you're still trying to flirt with me."

"Hey, if Batman can save Gotham while wooing women, I think I can do the same."

"Batman never really had time for women, though."

"Bruce Wayne did."

"Only to throw people off his scent so they wouldn't suspect him of being Batman. Bruce Wayne is the real mask."

He grinned. She really was his perfect woman. "I am so turned on right now."

"Your humor is seriously skewed, Murphy."

"That's why you love me."

There was a pause before she spoke again, this time

her voice softer, more vulnerable. "Am I that transparent?"

Hope fluttered in Sawyer's chest. "Only to me."

"I'm not—" She seemed to struggle for words. "I can't—go there yet with you. But I know there's something between us and it—it scares me."

"I know. It's okay." He couldn't stop his smile. It didn't matter that she wasn't ready. As long as she wasn't closing the door on him, he would patiently wait on the other side for her to step through and join him. "Why don't we focus on getting you out of here?"

"That sounds like a good plan."

He ran his hands carefully over her legs, feeling the hard, muscular planes of her calves and thighs, tensed with pain but thankfully whole. The only injury seemed to be the one on her back. "I need you to hold still while I check out that gash on your back."

"Feels like I've been stabbed." She hissed at his touch, and he felt her trying to squirm away from him.

"Easy," he soothed, drawing his hand back momentarily. He gently ran his fingers down her spine again, wincing when she gasped as he nudged the shard. "I think... it's a piece of a branch."

"Can you take it out?"

He hesitated. "I can try, but we don't have anything to clean the wound."

"I'll take my chances," she muttered. "Just get it out. Quick."

He nodded and reached for the shard, his heart pounding in his ears as he grasped it in his hand. With a quick jerk, he pulled it free, and Lucy cried out in pain. He quickly pressed his hand against the wound, trying to staunch the flood of blood.

"Fuck." He fumbled at his waist, unhooking the water bottle from his belt and unscrewing the cap. He splashed some of the water on the wound, and Lucy hissed.

"Sorry," he murmured, but his focus was on the injury. He needed to bandage it up somehow. "Hold on a second."

He unzipped his backpack and rummaged around until he found his spare shirt. It was clean, at least. He tore it into strips and pressed them against the wound. Lucy winced, her breath hitching in her chest, but she didn't say anything.

"All right," he said, his voice barely more than a murmur. "I need to tie this in place. Can you sit up?"

Lucy pushed herself up onto her knees with a groan, leaning heavily against him so he could wrap the makeshift bandage around her midsection. He worked as quickly as he could, trying to ignore the way her body shivered against his, the chemical scent of her fear mixing with the earthy smell of dirt and sweat.

He tucked in the ends of the shirt and sat back on his heels. "Done."

Lucy took a shaky breath and then another. "Thanks," she said after a moment. Her voice had taken on a husky quality that set off alarm bells in his head.

He wrapped his arms around her and could feel the

tension in her muscles, the way she was trying to keep herself from trembling. "You sure you're okay?"

"I'll live." She managed a small chuckle, grimacing as she shifted against him. "I'm not thrilled about the prospect of climbing out of here, though."

With a soft groan, she pushed herself to her feet. Her balance wavered momentarily, and Sawyer instinctively raised his hands to steady her. She flinched at his touch, sucking in a sharp breath through clenched teeth.

"Sorry." He lowered his hands, but stayed poised to catch her if she fell.

"I'm good," she replied far too quickly. "Just... give me a moment."

He wanted to give her forever. He'd spent the last few years sitting on the sidelines while each of his friends found love, and he'd always told himself that he was fine. He didn't need anything like the strong partnership of Zak and Anna, or the fireworks of Ash and Rose, or the sweet devotion of Donovan and Sasha, or the intimate camaraderie of Veronica and Connelly. He had Zelda and fulfilling work and he didn't need anything else.

But now he knew that was a lie.

When he found Lucy in that cave a year ago, something had shifted in him. He'd realized then he wanted what his friends had. He wanted someone to come home to, someone to laugh with, someone to hold onto at night when the nightmares became too much. And he wanted that someone to be Lucy. It was why he'd run from her all those months ago—he'd only told her a half-truth about his reason for leaving. Yes, he'd thought she needed to heal without the reminder of her ordeal hanging around, but he, too, had needed space. He'd cared too much, too fast for this brave, stubborn woman who could match him wit for wit and who saw through his bullshit better than anyone else ever had, and it had scared him.

But it didn't frighten him anymore.

He was done running, done denying himself.

Lucy Harper was his forever. He knew it with an unshakeable certainty that left him giddy.

But that definitely wasn't what she wanted to hear right now, so he backed up, giving her as much space as the cramped hole allowed, his ears tuned to any sign of distress from her. He could hear her breathing, rough and ragged, as she wrestled with the pain. He could only imagine how much it hurt and wished he could do more than just stand there and wait. But she didn't want him touching her, and until they were topside again, where the first aid kit waited in her bag, he couldn't do anything about the pain.

After what felt like an eternity, Lucy let out a shaky breath. "Okay. I think I can do this now."

He unclipped the second harness from his bag and held it out toward her voice. "This is going to hurt. The strap will rub right on the wound."

"Oh, goodie." She took the harness from him, her fingers brushing against his as she did so. Sawyer felt a jolt at the contact, and his instinct was to close his hand around hers, but he didn't. Right now, he needed to be strong for her, be her anchor in this chaos. He had to ignore the way his pulse raced and the way her touch made his heart thud in his chest.

"Just when I was thinking this wasn't quite painful enough." She let out a muffled groan as she slipped into the harness, clearly doing her best to smother the pain.

His hands closed around hers, helping her adjust the straps. He could feel her breath hitch, and he quickly withdrew his hands once more. They worked together, mostly in silence, as they secured the harnesses and prepared for the climb.

"Ready?"

Lucy shook her head. "No, but let's do this anyway."

They began their ascent with Sawyer leading the way. He reached out with his hand to feel for any stable footholds while Lucy followed closely behind. Every grunt, every gasp of pain made his heart clench.

She was magnificent. The strongest person he'd ever known.

He lost track of time as they climbed, each minute blending into the next, marked only by their ragged breaths. Finally, his fingers brushed against the cool dirt of the surface. He pulled himself up and over the edge, rolling onto his back and gasping for breath.

"Lucy?" he called out, reaching back over the edge, his hand finding hers.

"I'm... here," she panted. Her grip on his hand tightened as she hauled herself up, collapsing beside him. He heard a soft whimper escape her and he instinctively reached out, his hand finding hers. He gave it a reassuring squeeze, feeling her fingers close around his in response. They lay there for a few moments, both gasping for breath, the sun warm on their faces.

Zelda whined and bounded over to them, licking at their faces feverishly.

Sawyer laughed, pushing the excited dog away. "We're okay, girl. We're okay."

Beside him, Lucy let out a laugh, one of those raw, full-bodied laughs that comes after surviving something you weren't certain you'd survive. Despite her physical pain, there was joy in that sound. It was a victory cry of sorts. They'd made it out.

He rolled toward her, found her face with his hands, and crushed his lips to hers. Her lips parted in surprise, but she didn't push him away. Instead, she wound her arms around his neck and pulled him closer, her fingers threading through the hair at the nape of his neck. He could taste salt on her lips, could smell the scent of earth and sweat on her skin.

It was earth-shattering. It was life-affirming. It was everything he'd been denying himself for the past year.

When the kiss ended, they lay there for a while, foreheads pressed together, just breathing each other in.

"I'm glad you came for me," Lucy whispered.

"I always will."

With his hands still cupping her cheeks, he felt the smile curve her lips. "What? No sexual innuendo this time? I left you a perfect opening."

"I'm trying to be a gentleman here, Harper. I can stop if you want."

"No," she murmured. "I think I like this Sawyer, too."

He tightened his arms around her, pulling her closer against him until there was no space left between them. He could feel every inch of her, the heat of her seeping into him even through their clothes.

"And what about the Sawyer who loves you?" he asked softly, brushing a loose strand of hair from her face.

There was a moment of silence as Lucy stilled in his arms. He felt her stiffen and for one heart-stopping moment, he thought he might have pushed too far too soon.

His heart sank. She was going to protest. She'd tell him he couldn't possibly love her, tell him that it was just the adrenaline talking...

But instead, she let out a shaky breath and relaxed against him again. "I... I don't know how I feel about him yet," she admitted hesitantly. "But I think I'm willing to find out."

Zelda chose that moment to nose between them.

Sawyer sighed, patting the dog's head. "Zelda," he said with exaggerated seriousness, "you are the absolute worst third wheel."

"At least she's cute," Lucy said.

"That she is." He lifted himself to his hands and knees and pulled Lucy up to sit with him. He could feel her wince as she moved, but she didn't protest. Her fingers were trembling slightly when she brushed them against his cheek, and he thought of the pain she must be in and how bravely she was hiding it. "Let's find stable ground to make camp and get you properly bandaged up."

chapter
sixteen

AS THEY MOVED AWAY from the sinkhole and made camp on a flatter, more solid patch of land, the adrenaline started to wear off and the pain really set in.

Lucy tried to focus on her breathing, on Sawyer's steady presence beside her, on Zelda, who was scurrying around them like a puppy, sniffing at everything—on anything but the throbbing pain in her back. But it was hard. She was exhausted, physically and mentally, and the pain was relentless. It never stopped, only shifted from a dull, pulsing ache to sharp, stabbing jabs that took her breath away.

Sawyer was a quiet, solid presence beside her, his fingers careful as he unzipped her backpack and pulled out the first aid kit. She could hear the rustle of fabric, the crackle of the wrapper as he pulled out a fresh bandage. He took the time to clean his hands and then squirted sanitizer on them, and she was irrationally torn between gratitude for his gentleness and irritation at his efficiency. A part of her wanted to snap at him, to tell him to stop being so calm and competent when she was in pain. But she bit back the words before they could escape. She couldn't keep taking her bad tempers out on him.

"Okay," he murmured. "I'm going to need you to lean forward a bit."

She nodded, grimacing as she shifted her position. If it weren't for the pain, she might have enjoyed the feel of Sawyer's hands on her—strong, warm, and reassuring. It was getting harder and harder to ignore the feelings that were simmering inside her. She couldn't brush them off as mere gratitude or comfort-seeking anymore. Not when every laugh he shared, every touch, every quiet moment between them felt so intensely personal. So right.

Sawyer dabbed an antiseptic pad on the raw skin of her wound, and she hissed at the sting of it. Her thoughts immediately derailed.

"Sorry, sorry," he muttered quickly, his hands momentarily still against her back. "I'm trying to be as gentle as I can."

"I know," she said through gritted teeth, squeezing her eyes shut as another wave of pain washed over her. "It just... it fucking hurts."

She felt Sawyer's chest rise and fall against her back as he sighed quietly. "Just another minute, and I'll be done torturing you. And... there." He smoothed a fresh bandage over the wound, then handed her a packet of ibuprofen. "It's the best I can do, but we should head back at first light so Grant can take a look at it."

She winced at the suggestion and swallowed the pills, washing them down with a swig from his canteen. "I don't trust him."

"I don't trust any of them," Sawyer said flatly and leaned against the trunk of a tree, pulling her back against his chest. "But he was a medic."

She relaxed into him. "We should keep going toward the cell tower. Unless you think you can get the radio working...?"

His chin was resting on her shoulder, and she felt his jaw tighten in frustration. "No. It's fried."

"Then trying to get a signal on the phones is still our best bet."

Sawyer drew a breath, then let it out in a whoosh. "Dammit, I don't like it. I'd rather get you back to someone who can actually look at that wound... but you're right."

Sawyer's arms tightened around her in a protective manner, an unspoken promise that he would do whatever it took to see her safe. She'd never had that before he came into her life. After escaping her ex, she'd thrown herself into becoming a park ranger, and then into her job. She'd taken care of others, but couldn't remember a time when anyone had taken care of her, not like this. Not like Sawyer.

She turned in his arms and snuggled closer to his chest. Beneath her ear, she felt the steady thud of his heartbeat.

Something warm curled in her chest, something that felt suspiciously like love. She turned her head to look at him, at his pale blue eyes hidden behind the golden strands of his hair. He was looking right back at her, his gaze steady and unblinking. She knew he couldn't see her, not physically, but it still felt like he was seeing right into her soul. It was a feeling that both terrified and comforted her. It was also a feeling that made her want to kiss him stupid.

And so she did.

She slid her hands up his chest, one resting on his heart, the other curling around the nape of his neck. She pulled him down and pressed her lips to his.

His reaction was immediate and electrifying. He met her kiss with a force that left her breathless, his hands tightening on her as if he was afraid she would pull away. But she wasn't going anywhere— not now, not when everything felt so impossibly right.

It was the kind of kiss that made the world fall away. It was just them in that moment, wrapped up in each other's arms and lost in the taste of each other's lips.

Pulling back just enough to catch her breath, Lucy stared up at Sawyer. His pale blue eyes reflected a world she longed for— a world without predators lurking in shadows or wounds aching deep within her soul. A world where there was just him and her. That was what she wanted. What she had always wanted, even before she knew who Sawyer Murphy was.

She opened her mouth to tell him all of that...

Zelda nudged between them, dropping a wet tennis ball on their laps.

Sawyer groaned. "You really do have the absolute worst timing, girl."

Zelda sat and panted happily, her eyes flicking from the ball to Sawyer.

The dog looked so unapologetically hopeful, Lucy couldn't help but laugh. "Where did she find that?"

"My bag, probably." Sawyer picked up the ball and gave it a toss. Zelda launched after it. "I either knocked it out while looking for the ropes to pull you out of that hole, or she went digging for it."

Lucy looked over at his backpack. He'd propped it by a tree, but it now sat on his side with its contents strewn over the ground. "She definitely went digging for it."

"Crazy dog." Sawyer chuckled, ruffling Zelda's ears as she returned and dropped the ball again. He picked it up and lobbed it into the trees.

Zelda darted back and forth, the ball occasionally skittering out of her reach with every enthusiastic snap of her jaws. Sawyer leaned back against the tree and closed his eyes, listening to her play, his face creased in gentle amusement. Despite everything—despite the ache in her back and the uncertainty of their situation—a warmth spread through Lucy as she watched them.

After everything she'd been through, the simple act of a man and his dog playing fetch was almost unbearably sweet.

Neither of them spoke for a long while. The forest came alive with the night sounds as the sun sank beyond the horizon—the hoot of an owl, the rustling of leaves, and the distant howl of a coyote.

A chill crept over her skin as the air cooled. "I'm going to start a fire."

Sawyer's eyes popped open. He tilted his head in her direction, a small half-smile playing on his lips. "Do you need a hand?"

"No, I got it." There was an almost fierce pleasure in the task, in setting up the kindling just right and striking the flint until the spark grew into a flame. She fed it slowly, patiently, until it was a roaring fire that drove back the shadows and warmed away her aches. She pulled the MREs from her bag. She only had the a few packages, but she figured after the day they'd had, they deserved to splurge on a... well, if not good meal, at least a full one.

"Chicken burrito bowl or beef stew?" she asked.

"Whichever you're not eating."

"I have two packages of each."

"Then definitely the stew," he said. "It's the best."

She couldn't argue with that. As she heated enough stew for both of them, she realized she was feeling better. Still sore, but the pain wasn't as bad as before.

The first bite of stew had her nearly moaning. "I never thought I'd be saying this, but this doesn't taste half bad."

Sawyer chuckled softly and scooped up a spoonful of his own. "That's because you've been eating trail mix and beef jerky for the past two days."

They ate in comfortable silence. She watched the fire dance and crackle, enjoyed how the soft orange light played over Sawyer's face, accentuating his angular features. He really was a handsome man. Before his injury, she imagined he'd been quite the heartbreaker.

"Did you date a lot?" The question burst out of her before she could second guess it.

His eyebrow arched and he stopped with a spoonful of stew halfway to his mouth. "Date?"

Oh, God. It was a good thing he couldn't see her face. Going by the heat in her cheeks, it was probably flaming red. "I mean, before you were injured. You must have had women throwing themselves at you."

He set down his meal and looked in her direction, small smile pulling at his mouth. "Who says I still don't?"

"Oh." Could her face get any hotter? "I guess, the way you've talked, I assumed you haven't..."

Shut up, Lucy. You're just digging yourself a deeper hole.

She closed her mouth but couldn't help the little embarrassed sound that escaped her. "Forget I asked."

He chuckled and reached out until he found her hand. "No, it's okay. You can ask me anything." He gave her fingers a squeeze. "I didn't date that much before. I had a girlfriend for a while, thought I was going to marry her, but... well, it was difficult with the Marines always moving me around. She decided she didn't want that life. I don't blame her, don't hold any ill will toward her. She found a more stable guy and they got married, moved to the suburbs, had some kids. I didn't want that life. I liked what I was doing too much, so I'm happy she found what made her happy. And... you're right. I haven't really dated since I was injured. For the first few years after, I was too up in my own head, too fucked up. It's only recently I've started considering it again."

She blinked at him, feeling a lump lodge itself in her throat. "You... you've thought about it?"

He nodded. "Yeah, every year or so I think about joining an app or something, but it's a whole new territory. Not just the regular dating hurdles, but..." He trailed off, his face turning solemn. "Whenever a potential date finds out I'm blind, they start treating me differently. Either like I'm a kid or a fragile old man."

"That's because they don't know you," she said simply. "Anyone who can't see beyond your blindness is blind themselves."

He laughed softly and leaned back against the tree. "Dating is just..." He sighed heavily, then shrugged. "Never seemed worth it."

Lucy watched him in silence, her heart aching for him. She knew what it was like to be judged on something outside your control. To be seen as damaged and weak when you knew you were anything but. Her fellow rangers had been looking at her like she might break ever since she returned to work.

She looked down at their entwined hand. "Is there... anything that would change your mind?"

A slow smile spread over his lips, and he tugged on her hand, pulling her back into his lap. "Yeah, you. I've only started to consider it again since I met you."

chapter
seventeen

OH.

Oh.

Every nerve in her body tingled to life.

She was hyper-aware of the feel of his firm thighs under her, of the hand that still held hers, and the other that came to rest on her hip. His breath was warm against her neck, steady and reassuring. She swallowed, her heart pounding in her chest.

She was excited. And nervous. And... wasn't ready to go there yet.

"Can we... talk about something else?" Stupid of her to have brought it up in the first place.

He just kept smiling at her. "Sure. Like what?"

She scrambled for something... anything. "Can you... tell me what it's like being blind? If that's not rude to ask."

"It's not rude. I like when people ask questions instead of just assuming I can't see anything at all."

"What do you see?"

Sawyer was silent a moment, then held up the ball. "When you look at a tennis ball, you see a round, brightly colored object, and your brain tells you 'that's a tennis ball.' When I look at it, I can see something is there, but my brain can't interpret what it is because of the damage to my occipital lobe. Until it moves..." He threw the ball up and caught it. "Then my brain gets with the program again, and I can see. Just for a second, and it's not clear—nothing like how I used to be able to see. But it's enough that I can tell by sight what something is. When it stops moving, it's just a blur of light and shadows and color... and usually, it's not even the right color. Like this ball? I know it's bright green, but to me, it looks blue. Or sometimes it's green, but like a dark green. I have to use my other senses to fill in the blanks. Hearing. Smell. Touch." He dragged his fingers over the surface of the ball. "Taste—which obviously I'm not going to do because this has been in Zelda's mouth." He flashed a crooked smile, and she laughed. "But in this case, touch is enough to tell me this is a tennis ball. They feel different from a rubber ball or a baseball. They smell different, too, but I don't often go around sniffing things. That would be weird."

He handed the ball to her, and she dragged her fingers over the fuzzy felt, trying to imagine navigating the world the same way he did. It was fascinating. "Is it true your other senses are heightened now?"

He tilted his head in the approximation of a shrug. "Partially. I don't have superhero hearing now, but since I rely more on my hearing than other people, I've learned to pick up on cues that most people overlook."

"I hear you clicking your tongue when you're out on the trail."

He nodded. "I can tell by the way the sound bounces if there's a drop-off nearby or if something big is in my path. It doesn't always stop me from running into things, but it's enough to keep me from walking over a cliff."

The thought of finding him at the bottom of a cliff, twisted and broken, sent ice water splashing through Lucy's veins. She'd seen it time and again with careless hikers who disregarded the marked paths, who thought they were invincible against nature's wrath. One false step, one misplaced trust in the stability of a rock, and even familiar terrain could become fatally treacherous.

"Does that scare you?" she asked, trying to keep her voice steady.

"What? Falling off a cliff? I can't say it's high on my list of pleasant experiences," he joked, then grew serious. "I guess it does scare me. But living in fear isn't really living, is it?"

"No," she agreed, "I suppose it isn't."

The silence between them stretched, only broken by the distant hooting of an owl and the crackling of the fire. She watched as he leaned back against the rough bark of the redwood tree behind him and closed his eyes. Zelda set her head on his thigh, and his hand stroked over her brown fur.

"I wish I could see the stars again," he said softly.

Lucy looked up. Through the branches overhead, the

sky was ablaze with a multitude of stars, close enough to touch. The moon hung low, bathing the forest floor with an ethereal glow that caught on every leaf and twig.

"I wish you could see them too," she whispered, aching to somehow give him this sight. "They're beautiful tonight."

"Describe them for me?" he asked.

She hesitated for a second before speaking. "The sky's clear. Like black velvet strewn with diamond dust." Her eyes traced the constellations she knew by heart. "There's Orion. The hunter. And there." She pointed upwards. "Is Cassiopeia, the queen on her throne. The moon is full and yellow, hanging so low it feels like we could reach out and touch it."

His lips twisted into a wistful smile. "I've always loved the outdoors... The stars. It's strange to think that they're still there, but I can't find them anymore."

Emotion welled up inside her as she quietly listened to the nocturnal symphony of the surrounding forest. She glanced at Sawyer, his face warm in the flickering firelight, his hand still absently caressing Zelda's ear. Lucy's heart ached with a kind of fondness that was more than mere friendship.

God. She was falling for this man. This sweet, smart, nerdy man.

She swallowed back the sudden lump in her throat. "Sometimes I feel like we're just unimportant specks in this vast universe, spinning on this tiny planet under these infinite stars." She looked at him then, his face bathed in soft moonlight, his eyes closed as he listened to her describe what he could no longer see. "But when I'm with you... suddenly, it's not just me alone under these stars. It's us. And the universe doesn't seem so big anymore."

He turned his head toward her, his gaze hot. "I wish I could see you, Luce."

"Do you want to?" she asked softly. At his nod, she lifted his hand to her cheek. "My eyes are two different colors—one a light brown, like coffee with creamer, and one blue, like a clear summer sky. I've always liked that about myself. My hair is brown and wavy, always a bit messy from being outside all day. I usually keep it up in a ponytail or a braid, but when it's down, it brushes my collarbones. I'm not much for makeup. I wear it occasionally, but mostly just lip balm. My lips are kind of big."

His fingers moved down, tracing lightly over her lips, and a thrill of heat shot straight down her middle, tightening her nipples. "You have gorgeous lips."

She released a shaky exhale. "My mom always told me I had a Julia Roberts smile—big and playful and lights up a room."

"I bet you're more beautiful than any actress when you smile." His thumb slid down the indent in her chin. "You have a dimple."

"Yeah, I have a butt chin."

He gave a genuine laugh, and her heart did a funny little dance inside her chest. "I... um." She shook her head slightly, trying to regain her train of thought. "There's a small mole on my left shoulder blade, a scar on my right knee from when I fell off a bike as a kid. Another scar, just here." She guided his hand to touch the faded line on her forearm. "From wrestling with a thorny bush on one of my first ranger assignments."

She watched as his eyebrows furrowed in concentration. His fingertips pressed into the scar tissue before dropping down to trace the veins in her wrist. His touch was gentle, attentive, almost reverent.

"Another scar on my thigh from—"

He shook his head. "I don't want you reliving that."

Neither did she. She didn't want to think about the man who had shot her and left her for dead deep in a cave. Didn't want to think of the darkness, so absolute it had been like a living thing all on its own. Didn't want to think of the cold. The endless hours of fear. But she would never forget how it had felt to see the flashlight, and then Sawyer was there, and she wasn't alone anymore. Under normal circumstances—if they'd met in a bar—she would've thought him handsome, but when his sweaty, mud-streaked face appeared from a crevasse in the cave's wall, he was the most beautiful thing she'd ever seen.

She took a deep breath and shook off the haunting memories, focusing instead on his face in front of her.

"Do you want me to keep going?"

"Yes." His voice was rough. "Please."

Lucy let her hands fall into his, their fingers intertwining. "My hands are rough from working. I have calluses here." She pressed his thumb into the most worn spots. "And here."

His fingers were rough against hers. He had a strength in his grip that was comforting and frightening all at once, reminding her of the danger he was always so willing to walk into without hesitation.

"My hands aren't soft either." A ghost of a smile touched his lips as he held up his own hand, palm facing outwards so she could see the worn ridges and scars criss-crossing along his skin. "But I like your hands. They feel... strong. Capable."

Lucy smiled at that, her heart fluttering in her chest. "I suppose they are. I'm always climbing or handling various tools. My job demands it." She paused, trying to think of what else she could tell him. "I prefer jeans and a flannel shirt over dresses and heels. I'm tall for a woman and I've got broad shoulders from years of rowing. My legs are strong from hiking." She guided his hand over her arm muscles, then to her thigh. His touch sent sparks through her blood.

"And yet," he murmured, running his hand back up to rest on her waist, "you fit perfectly right here." His grip tightened slightly, drawing her closer until she was sitting on his lap.

"Sawyer," she whispered.

His name hung in the air between them, a quiet plea for something she didn't quite dare articulate.

"Lucy," he whispered back, his own voice thick with longing.

His fingers traced the curve of her waist, then upwards along the column of her spine, taking care around the bandage. Her body felt like a live wire, electricity humming through her veins.

"You have goosebumps," he murmured, his tone dancing between teasing and serious. "Cold?"

God, no. She was on fire, burning up with a desire she had been trying to ignore for months. But it was Sawyer. It was always Sawyer. From the moment he had saved her, she had felt an unparalleled connection to him, a bond that went beyond gratitude into something deeper, wilder, more intimate.

"No, not cold," she said, her voice barely louder than the crackle of the fire. She leaned in, her heart pounding in her chest. "Just... excited."

He froze for a second and then his touch moved again, tracing the line of her neck up to cup her face once more. He leaned in slowly until their lips were scant inches apart.

"Can I?" he asked softly.

chapter
eighteen

LIVING *in fear isn't really living, is it?*

His words echoed in her mind. She had been living in fear long before the Shadow Stalker took her. Fear of her past, fear of her future, fear of the unknown. She'd avoided anything that could potentially harm her, she'd avoided truly living.

She was tired of it.

She wanted to live.

She wanted him.

"Yes." The word was barely out of her mouth when he closed the distance between them, and their lips met in a kiss that shot fire through every nerve in her body.

The world disappeared in that instant and all she knew was Sawyer. She was acutely aware of every point where his body touched hers—the curve of his bicep under her fingers, the firm muscles of his abdomen against her own, his strong thighs beneath hers, the growing ridge of his erection. And always, there were his hands—mapping her face, tangling in her hair, tracing the curves of her body—as though he was committing every inch of her to memory.

Sawyer pulled back, but only slightly. "Wait. Lucy, you're injured." There was an urgency in his voice that matched the pounding of her own heart. "Are you sure you're okay for this?"

"Yes," she said again without hesitation.

His mouth reclaimed hers with an intensity that took her breath away. It was raw and full of a burning desire that ignited her from within. His hands roamed over her body, tracing the outline of her figure. The heat of his touch sent a tremor through her, making her arch closer into him.

His fingers laced through her hair, tilting her head back to give him better access. He traced a line down her throat with his lips, causing her to gasp and close her eyes. The sensation was irresistible—every touch from him was lighting her up like a sparkler.

"Sawyer," she breathed out, her voice shaky. Her fingers dug into his back as she clung to him, feeling completely and utterly consumed by the man.

"Tell me if you want to stop," he whispered against the shell of her ear. His hot breath caused a shiver to run down her spine.

"No," she choked out. "God, don't stop."

A growl of approval rumbled from his chest. "Good. I want to touch every inch of you. Taste every inch. Feel all of you." He shifted her, positioning himself so that his erection was impossible to ignore. There were too many fucking layers of clothes between them. She wanted to be skin-to-skin.

Still, she moved her hips experimentally and he groaned, his fingers clenching around her hips, guiding her. Their mouths met again in a heated clash of teeth and tongues. Hot, fast, desperate kisses. He tugged on her lower lip with his teeth before plunging his tongue back into her mouth.

His hands went to the hem of her shirt, fingers grazing the bare skin of her waist as they slipped underneath the material. The air between them crackled with anticipation as he slowly guided her shirt up and over her head, leaving her in her bra and hiking pants. He traced his fingers over her collarbones and down to the swell of her breasts, his touch light but sending a current of desire down her center.

She captured his mouth with hers again, desperate to feel him. She fumbled with the belt of his pants, then moved up to unbutton his shirt, revealing the strong muscles of his chest underneath. He had a tattoo on his pec of a compass rose, the intricate design drawn with such precision that she could almost feel the points of the compass.

She didn't know why that surprised her.

She traced it gently with her fingers, memorizing the texture and pattern under her fingertips. "When did you get this?"

"I told you how after I lost my sight, I was fucked up. I was lost for a long time." His voice was soft, a gentle rumble against her ear. "The compass was to remind myself that I can still find my way, even if I can't see the path." He groaned softly and dropped his lips to her bare shoulder. "Fuck, I wish I could see you right now."

Her heart ached at his words—the regret, the longing, the subtle undercurrent of frustration.

She cupped his face in her hands, her thumbs brushing over the stubble on his jawline. "I'm right here. I'm not going anywhere."

His brief smile told her he recognized those words. They were the same ones he'd said to her in that cave when he appeared out of the darkness to rescue her.

She kissed him deeply, tangling her fingers in his hair like she couldn't get close enough of him—and God, she couldn't. As their tongues danced together, she continued her exploration of him, feeling the hard ridges of his abs under her fingertips and the trail of hair that led tantalizingly below the waistband of his pants.

She shifted away from him enough to pull down his zipper. His cock strained against his boxers, thick and long, desperate for her touch. She obliged him, stroking him through the fabric until he let out a strangled groan, and his hands clamped around her wrist so tightly it almost hurt.

Lightning fast, he shifted so she was now underneath him, her legs wrapped around his hips. He pumped once against her.

Still too much fabric.

"God, Lucy..." he muttered, resting his forehead against hers as he caught his breath. "I want you."

She was wet with arousal, aching for him to fill her

up and complete her in ways she didn't even know she was missing. "Then take me."

"You're injured."

"I'm okay." To prove it, she lifted her hips, rubbing herself against his erection.

"Fuck, Luce," he groaned, his voice hoarse with desire. She could hear the internal battle in his voice, the war between lust and his overactive protective streak. "I don't want to hurt you."

She grinned up at him, her lips swollen from their intense kisses. "I promise I'm okay." Her hands found his face again, tracing the rough patches of his five o'clock shadow and messy hair. She tangled her fingers into the strands, pulling him down for another deep kiss. He groaned into it, his mouth opening wider to allow her tongue deeper access, as if he couldn't get enough of the taste of her. He spread her legs wider with his thighs, grinding against her entrance, sending shockwaves of pleasure through her entire body.

"Undress me," she whispered against his lips.

Right then, Zelda tried to nuzzle between them.

Sawyer growled in annoyance and pushed her away. "No," he said firmly. "Go lay down, Zelda. You're not invited."

Zelda whined softly but obediently padded away. She circled a couple times under a tree, then laid down in a huff with her back to them.

"Did she listen?" he asked.

Lucy laughed. "Yes. Poor girl's not happy about being left out."

Sawyer grinned, trailing his fingers along her collarbone. "She'll survive." His mouth followed his fingers, leaving a scalding trail over her skin. "I'm not stopping what we're doing for anything short of the apocalypse at this point. Now where were we?"

"I think you were about to undress me."

"Ah, yes." He lifted her enough to find the clasp of her bra, deftly unhooking it. He pulled it away, revealing her breasts to the cool night air. His calloused palms cupped the soft mounds, thumbs grazing over her pebbled nipples and eliciting a gasp from her.

"You're so soft," he murmured against her skin as he trailed open-mouthed kisses down her sternum. "So perfect."

Lucy arched into his touch, nails digging into his shoulders as jolts of electric desire shot straight to her core. Her hips rocked up, seeking friction against the impressive bulge straining his boxers.

Sawyer left a trail of scorching kisses down the valley between her breasts, his stubble scraping deliciously against her sensitive skin. His lips closed around one rosy peak, swirling his tongue and sucking gently, drawing a keening moan from deep in her throat. His hand palmed her other breast, pinching and rolling the nipple between his fingers until she was panting and writhing beneath him.

"Sawyer, please," she breathed, desperation coloring her voice. The ache between her thighs was becoming unbearable. She needed him, all of him, now.

He released her nipple with a wet pop, a wolfish grin

spreading across his face. "Please what, sweetheart? Tell me what you want."

She grabbed his wrist and guided his hand down her body to the waistband of her pants. "Touch me."

He popped open the button of her hiking pants and tugged down the zipper with deliberate slowness, his knuckles brushing against her lower belly and making her shiver with need. He hooked his fingers into the waistband and peeled them down. His hands caressed back up her legs, his calluses rasping deliciously along her sensitive flesh.

When he reached the apex of her thighs, he paused, his fingers hovering just shy of where she needed him most. "You're so wet for me. I can smell your arousal."

She whimpered as he rubbed her through the damp fabric, applying just enough pressure to drive her wild but not nearly enough to satisfy the ache building inside her.

He finally slipped a finger inside her slick folds, groaning at the feel of her. "Christ, Lucy. You're soaked."

She could only moan in response as he stroked her, his fingers mapping her most intimate places with devastating accuracy. He circled her clit, making her hips jerk up off the blanket.

"That's it," he murmured approvingly. "Let me make you feel good."

He slid a second finger into her tight channel, pumping slowly as his thumb kept up its maddening pressure on her clit. White hot pleasure lanced through her, coiling tighter with each thrust of his fingers. Her inner muscles clenched around him, trying to pull him deeper.

"Sawyer," she panted, her walls fluttering around his fingers as she climbed higher and higher. "I'm so close..."

He captured her mouth in a searing kiss, swallowing her cries of pleasure as he increased the speed of his fingers, curling them to stroke that sensitive spot inside her. His thumb circled her clit faster, tighter, sending her hurtling toward the edge.

"That's it, baby," he rasped against her lips. "Come for me."

His words were her undoing. Her orgasm slammed into her, pleasure crashing over her in wave after wave. She cried out his name, her body shaking with the force of her release.

Sawyer worked her through it, drawing out her pleasure until she was boneless and trembling beneath him. He pressed soft kisses to her face, her neck, her shoulder as she slowly floated back down to earth.

"You're so beautiful when you come," he murmured, nuzzling her neck. "The sounds you make, the way you feel... I could happily spend the rest of my life making you feel that good."

She could only hum in blissed out agreement, her body limp and sated. But she wasn't done with him yet. Not even close.

She wanted more, needed all of him. With trembling fingers, she reached for the waistband of his boxers and pushed them down over his hips, freeing his straining erection.

He was magnificent, thick and heavy in her palm as she wrapped her fingers around his length. Sawyer hissed in a breath at her touch, his hips flexing involuntarily.

"I need you inside me," she whispered, guiding him to her entrance. "Please, Sawyer. I want you."

He groaned, the blunt head of his cock nudging against her slick folds. "I don't have any condoms."

"I have a birth control implant. And I'm healthy. I haven't... not since before..." She swallowed hard and he captured her lips with his, kissing her gently.

"No thinking about the past. Focus on now. On us." The broad head of his cock nudged at her entrance and they both moaned at the contact. He rocked against her, coating himself in her slickness, but made no move to enter her yet. His hand slid down to where they were almost joined, his fingers stroking over her sensitive flesh before wrapping a hand around his base.

"I'm clean, too," he rasped and rested his forehead against hers, their ragged breaths mingling. "Tell me again, Lucy. Tell me you want this, want me."

With a flex of his hips, he pushed forward, the broad head of his cock breaching her entrance. He sank into her with agonizing slowness, letting her body adjust to the intrusion inch by delicious inch.

Lucy's head fell back on a moan as he stretched and filled her, the sensation both foreign and exquisite after so long.

"Fuck, you feel incredible," Sawyer groaned once he was fully seated inside her. He stilled, giving her time to accommodate his size. His arms trembled with the effort of holding himself above her. "So tight. So perfect."

She lifted her hips experimentally and they both gasped at the pleasure. "Move," she demanded breathlessly, wrapping her legs around his waist to pull him deeper. "Please, Sawyer."

He withdrew almost fully before surging back in, setting a slow, deep rhythm that had her seeing stars. Lucy met him thrust for thrust, her nails scoring down his back as she held on for dear life. The slick slide of him inside her, stretching her, filling her so completely, was exquisite torture.

"Harder," she panted, needing more, needing everything he could give her. "I won't break."

With a growl, he snapped his hips sharply, driving into her with more force. The change in angle had him hitting that perfect spot inside her with every thrust, sending sparks of electricity zinging under her skin. She could feel the tension coiling tighter low in her belly, her inner muscles starting to flutter and clench around him.

"I can feel you getting close," Sawyer rasped, his voice rough with strain. "You're squeezing me so tight." He dropped his head to her shoulder, his teeth grazing her skin as his hand snaked down to where they were joined. He circled her clit with the rough pad of his thumb, providing the perfect counterpoint to his deep, pounding thrusts. "Come for me again. Let me feel you."

His words, his voice, the delicious drag of him inside her, it was all too much. The coil inside her snapped. Her orgasm burst through her, stealing her breath and her vision in a blinding rush of ecstasy. She cried out his name as wave after wave of pleasure crashed over her, her body clenching rhythmically around his as it tried to pull him even deeper.

"Fuck, yes, just like that," he groaned, his hips moving erratically as he chased his own release. He thrust once, twice more before burying himself to the hilt, his body going rigid as his cock pulsed inside her. He emptied himself in long, hot spurts, her name falling from his lips like a prayer.

She held him close as he shuddered through the orgasm, her hands stroking soothingly over the sweat-slicked skin of his back. Slowly, he relaxed into her, his weight pressing her into the blanket and for the first time in over a year, the ever-present knot of fear and anxiety in her chest eased. Here in Sawyer's arms, she felt safe. Protected. Cherished. Like nothing and no one could touch her.

Finally, he shifted just enough to take some of his weight off her but made no move to separate their still-joined bodies. He nuzzled into her neck, pressing soft kisses to her damp skin. "Are you okay? I didn't hurt you?"

Hurt her? She laughed at that. She felt like she could conquer the world just then.

"I'm more than okay. That was..." She trailed off, unable to find words that could adequately describe the depth of emotion and pleasure she'd just experienced.

Sawyer lifted his head and grinned down at her. Even

disheveled and sweaty, he was the most gorgeous thing she'd ever seen.

"Fucking incredible," he finished for her, his voice still rough with lingering passion. "You're incredible."

He brushed a tender kiss across her mouth before carefully withdrawing from her body and rolling to the side. The loss of his warmth made her want to protest, but he gathered her close, tucking her against his chest. Lucy pillowed her head on his shoulder, her fingers idly tracing the compass tattoo over his heart while his trailed up and down her spine in a hypnotic caress that made her eyes droop.

The night air cooled her overheated skin, making her shiver. Sawyer must have felt it because he groped blindly for something to cover them with, finally coming up with his discarded shirt. He draped it over her shoulders before wrapping his arms around her and tugging her closer.

Her heart swelled until it felt like it would burst out of her chest. This man had saved her in every way a person could be saved. He made her feel whole again, like maybe the broken pieces of herself could be put back together...

Lucy drifted off to sleep, safe and sated in Sawyer's embrace. For the first time in over a year, no nightmares plagued her. She slept peacefully, her mind and body at ease.

She woke sometime later to Sawyer gently shaking her shoulder. "Lucy, sweetheart, wake up." His voice was soft but urgent.

She blinked up at him, momentarily disoriented. The first pale light of dawn was just starting to streak the sky. "What's wrong?"

He had already dressed and was holding out her clothes. "Zelda's alerting. I think she heard something."

That snapped her fully awake. She scrambled to her feet, ignoring the protest of sore muscles and the sharp stab of pain up her side from her wound, and quickly pulled on her clothes.

Zelda was standing rigidly at attention, her ears pricked forward and her nose twitching as she stared intently into the trees. A low growl rumbled in her chest.

Lucy's heart started to pound. She scanned the surrounding forest but saw nothing out of place in the gray predawn light. "What is it, girl? What do you hear?"

Zelda's growl deepened and the fur along her spine bristled. Sawyer reached out and rested a hand on the dog's head. "Easy," he murmured. "Luce, can you see anything?"

She shook her head before remembering he couldn't see the gesture. "No, nothing."

But the hairs on the back of her neck stood on end.

They weren't alone.

chapter
nineteen

SAWYER CURSED at himself as he dragged on his pants. He knew better than to let his guard down like that, especially out here in the wilderness with a killer on the loose. But being with Lucy, holding her, loving her, had driven every rational thought from his mind. All he'd been able to focus on was the feel of her skin against his, the sounds of her pleasure, the way she clenched so tightly around him as she came apart in his arms.

Now, cold dread trickled down his spine as Zelda's warning growl vibrated through him. He quickly buttoned his pants and reached for his boots, jamming his feet into them. He didn't know where his shirt was. Hopefully still draped over Lucy's shoulders, but he wasn't about to waste the time looking for it.

They needed to move.

Sawyer stood, every muscle tense and ready for action. Zelda pressed against his leg, a comforting weight grounding him as his other senses strained to pick up any sign of danger. The scent of pine and damp earth filled his nose, but underneath it was something else. Something that made his gut churn with unease. "We need to go. Now."

He heard the rustle of fabric as Lucy finished dressing. "I don't see anything," she whispered, fear making her voice tremble slightly. "But something feels... wrong."

"It's okay." He hoped he sounded more confident than he felt. "We're going to be fine. But we need to get moving."

He grabbed their packs and blankets, hastily stuffing everything inside. He slung his pack over his shoulders and handed Lucy hers before picking up his cane.

He gripped the cane tightly in one hand and reached for Lucy with the other. "Stay close to me."

He felt her small hand slip into his, her palm cool and slightly clammy. He gave it what he hoped was a reassuring squeeze as they set off into the dense forest, moving as quickly and quietly as possible over the uneven ground.

The only sounds were their ragged breathing and the crunch of pine needles beneath their feet. Sawyer strained his remaining senses, trying to pick up any indication of pursuit, but all he could hear was the thudding of his own heart.

They had only gone maybe a hundred yards when a sharp crack broke the stillness of the forest behind them, like the snap of a large branch. Or a gunshot.

Lucy gasped and stumbled, her grip on his hand

tightening to the point of pain. Zelda froze beside him, her entire body vibrating with tension.

"Fuck," Sawyer swore under his breath. "Run!"

He took off, trusting Zelda to guide him. He hated he had to let go of Lucy, but he needed both hands free for better balance or he was going to end up face-planting into a tree or sprawling over some unseen root. And they didn't have time for that.

Lucy kept pace beside him, her breathing coming in sharp, panicked pants. They crashed through the under-brush, branches whipping at their faces and snagging their clothes.

Another crack echoed through the trees, closer this time. Sawyer's heart seized in his chest. Definitely a gunshot.

Who the fuck was shooting at them?

"This way," Lucy gasped, tugging him sharply to the left. He followed her lead without question.

They barreled down a narrow game trail, the dense foliage providing a little cover from whoever was taking potshots at them. The terrain was treacherous, full of hidden roots and rocks that could easily trip them up. Sawyer stumbled more than once, and Lucy was right there by his side, pulling him up when he did.

"Fuck, fuck, fuck," she panted as they ran, repeating it like a mantra.

Another shot rang out then, closer still, followed by the sharp whizz of a bullet flying past them. Sawyer flinched instinctively, pushing Lucy further ahead of him. "Go!"

He'd be damned if he let anything happen to her because he was lagging.

"No." Her hand closed around his again. "We're staying together."

"Stubborn."

"Learned it from you." She guided him as they made a sharp turn, veering down a steep incline. The scent of water filled the air— a river.

Suddenly, Lucy let out a terrified yelp and vanished from his side, her hand tearing from his.

"Lucy!" he roared, spinning wildly on the spot.

"Sawyer!" Her shout was swallowed in the thunderous roar of rushing water. His heart slammed against his ribs as he lurched forward, cane probing the ground in front of him. Zelda whined at his side.

A gunshot cracked again, this time so close he could feel the air splitting apart near his head. A bullet whizzed past, punching a hole into a nearby tree with a soft *thwack*, sending splinters into his cheek.

Too close.

He had to find her and get out of here.

"Lucy!" he shouted again.

"I'm okay," she called from somewhere below him. "Get back from the ledge! The ground is very unstable there. I'll find a way back up to—Sawyer! Behind you!"

Even before her warning left her lips, he felt the other presence closing in behind him. He didn't think. He threw himself over the edge after Lucy. His shoulder connected with something hard and unyielding, and a shout of pain tore from his lungs. He bounced and rolled for what seemed like an eternity, then plunged into freezing water. He gasped and choked, flailing to keep his head above the surface.

Zelda.

Shit.

She would've followed him. She was trained to stay by his side.

He had just enough time to take a lungful of air before the fast current pushed him under again. A heavy weight knocked into him from behind— Zelda. He could feel her wet fur against his skin and grabbed onto her harness, kicking toward what he thought was the surface. He broke through the surface, sucking in a desperate breath. Zelda was paddling furiously beside him, her doggie instincts taking over.

"Lucy!" he shouted again.

"Over here!" Her voice echoed back to him from somewhere downstream. "There's a log jam. When you hit it, swim to your left, and you'll reach the bank."

He turned his body toward the sound, pulling Zelda along with him. "Keep talking!"

"Oh, don't you worry. I have *a lot* to say. You're a fucking idiot," she snapped. "Jumping off a fucking cliff."

"You jumped, too."

"I *fell*. It wasn't a choice. You know how many people I've peeled up from the bottom of a cliff? If you were just a little bit off, you wouldn't have hit the river. Oh my God. I can't decide if I want to kiss you or kill you when we get out of this."

"I'm a fan of the first option," he called back, smiling despite the pain radiating through his shoulder and the freezing cold water numbing his limbs.

She sounded close now. Just a little more, he told himself. Then he could grab Lucy and kiss her senseless, silencing that sharp tongue, reminding her that he may be an idiot, but he was her idiot.

The river was tossing him around like a rag doll, rocks and fallen logs looming out of nowhere. He could see most of them as they bobbed past him, and he did his best to avoid colliding into anything that could bruise or break bones. Suddenly, a wave crashed over his head, shoving him under, slamming him into a submerged boulder, and pain exploded in his ribs. He lost his grip on Zelda, lost all sense of direction as water filled his lungs. His chest burned. His body bucked against the frantic need to breathe, and he reached out for anything that could anchor him. But there was only the icy kiss of the river, the cruel lash of the current.

Air. He needed air.

He heard Lucy's panicked shouts growing nearer even through the murky underwater chaos. "Sawyer! Keep your head up!"

He kicked toward what he hoped was the surface, but his boots felt like they were filled with lead. His hand caught on something that felt like tangled roots and slippery rocks. Using all his strength, he pulled himself toward it. The surface came crashing back as he broke through, choking and spitting out water. He sucked in lungfuls of air, harsh and raw.

"Zelda!" His voice came out as a croak. His heart pounded at the terrifying thought of losing her. His girl.

"Sawyer! Sawyer, she's okay. I've got her," Lucy yelled from somewhere on his left. "Move to your left. You're almost there."

Another wave hit him, and he was pushed under again. But this time, he kept his grip on the log, holding on even as the river tried to tear him away.

He couldn't die here. Not like this. Not after everything he and Lucy had survived. Not after he'd finally broken through those tough walls of hers.

With all the strength he had left, Sawyer pulled himself along the log until his feet hit solid ground. Gritting his teeth against the cold, he clawed his way up the bank, slipping on the wet grass and mud. The world tilted sickeningly as he crawled onto flat ground, coughing and retching.

"Fuck..." He rolled onto his back, gasping for air, and realized he still somehow wore his backpack. He struggled out of it and laid back in the cold mud again. His whole body ached with an intensity that made him grimace.

The sound of frantic panting and scuffling approached. He reached out with a shaking hand and Zelda licked it. She flopped down on top of him, knocking the air from his lungs, and pushed her face against his, whimpering as her tail flew like a whip.

He didn't even care that it hurt and hugged her. "There's my good girl. She's the best, bravest girl."

Lucy threw herself down next to him, wrapping her

arms around both him and Zelda. "God damn it, Sawyer. You could have died."

"Hey now, you started this. Jumping off a cliff..." He managed to wheeze out a laugh between coughs. His whole body was shaking uncontrollably from the cold and adrenaline.

"Fell," she corrected faintly, but the fight had gone out of her voice. He felt a hot tear hit his cheek and gently nudged Zelda aside so he could pull Lucy into his arms.

She fit perfectly against him, her body molded to his despite the layers of wet clothing between them. She was shivering and burrowed deeper into his side, burying her face in the crook of his neck. He held her tighter, stroking her damp hair with trembling fingers.

"I was so scared," she whispered. "I thought... I thought you were going to die."

"I didn't," he said gruffly, smoothing a hand over her back in comforting circles. "I'm here. We're okay." When she gave a soft sob, his heart all but shattered. "Shh, sweetheart. We're okay."

He pressed a kiss on her forehead, his chapped lips lingering on her cold skin. She was crying quietly, her body shaking with silent sobs. He was freezing, and as the adrenaline faded, bone-deep exhaustion set in, but he didn't care. All he cared about was the woman in his arms, the woman who meant everything to him.

Finally, Lucy shifted against him and lifted her head. "We can't stay here. Whoever was shooting at us could still be out there. It will take him time to cross the river, but we're wasting our head start."

There she was. His strong, brave park ranger was back, taking control of the situation. Relief unfurled in his chest, loosening the knotted muscles around his shoulders. He never would've said it out loud, but he'd been worried there for a moment as she clung to him, terrified the stress of the last few days had finally broken her. Hell, she hadn't even sobbed like that in the cave after the Shadow Stalker left her for dead. But he should've known his Lucy was made of stronger stuff than that.

He slowly sat up, grimacing as his battered body protested the movement. Every-fucking-thing hurt. "Right now, I'm more concerned with getting dry and warm. You're shaking like a leaf."

"S-so are you," she said through chattering teeth.

Thankfully, the sun was coming up. He could feel it burning away the dampness of the night and it promised to be a hot one. They needed to find shelter, let their clothes dry out, and then keep going toward the—

Fuck.

Cell phones.

His stomach dropped as the thought struck. He groped around for his backpack and dug a hand in one of the pockets for the phones. When he pulled them out, they were all dripping.

"Oh, shit," Lucy muttered, and he heard her digging through her bag. "Mine are soaked, too."

"Do any of them turn on?" He picked through them

until he found his phone in its rugged case. He hit the button to turn it on, then raised it to his ear to listen for the tones indicating it was starting up. Nothing. He pried it out of the case and shook water off it, then tried powering it up again.

"Come on. Come on."

The stupid thing was supposed to be waterproof.

"Nothing," Lucy said after a long moment. "They're all dead."

No phones meant no way to call for help, no lifeline to the outside world. And a killer was out there somewhere, hunting them.

He shoved the phones back into his bag and pushed himself to his feet, gritting his teeth against the pain that lanced through his shoulder and ribs. Zelda pressed against his leg, and he reached down to stroke the wet fur of her ear. It steadied him. "Let's stick to the plan. Find a safe place to dry off, and I'll see if I can get one of the phones working again."

chapter
twenty

HE WAS HURTING.

Lucy could see it in the stiff way he walked, but he didn't make a sound of complaint as they trudged through the dense underbrush. Since he lost his cane in the river, he kept one hand on Zelda's harness, and Lucy stayed close by his side, ready to steady him if he stumbled. Her hand brushed his every few steps. She told herself it was to let him know she was still at his side, but that was only partially true. She needed the physical reassurance that he was still there with her. The icy river water had leached the heat from her body, and her muscles ached with cold and fatigue. But it was the chilling fear that squeezed her heart that made each breath a struggle.

If she had lost him...

A shudder ripped through her that had nothing to do with the cold, and dread sat like a stone in her stomach.

Someone had shot at them.

Someone wanted to kill them.

And that person was still out there somewhere, possibly tracking them at this very moment.

She shook her head, trying to dislodge the terrifying thought, but questions kept running on a loop through her mind.

Was it the same someone who had killed Maya and attacked Sawyer? The same person who had sabotaged the radio? Were they trying to stop her and Sawyer from calling for help?

But why?

She wished she could check in with Blue Mountain Tower, make sure her hikers were all safe, and see if anyone had disappeared from the group. Maybe then she would finally have some answers, some clue as to who was doing this.

But with the phones dead and no working radios, they were cut off.

Alone.

So she needed to stop wondering about the hypotheticals and focus on their immediate problems—getting dry, getting warm, and finding a safe place to hole up and regroup.

A branch snapped nearby, and she nearly jumped out of her skin, heart slamming against her ribs. Sawyer froze beside her, his head cocked as he listened intently. Zelda's ears perked up with interest, but she didn't seem too concerned. That had to be a good sign, right? If the dog wasn't worried, there was probably nothing to worry about.

Still, Lucy held her breath, straining to hear over the pounding of her pulse in her ears.

A squirrel scampered across their path, disappearing into the underbrush with an irritated chitter. Zelda trembled with excitement, watching the squirrel with rapt fascination, but she didn't leave Sawyer's side. She really was the best dog ever.

Sawyer squeezed her hand. "What was it? Rabbit?"

Lucy let out the breath she'd been holding in a shaky exhale, some of the tension draining from her shoulders. "Squirrel."

Just a squirrel. Not a crazed killer with a gun.

She tried to inject some lightness into her tone. "Looks like Zelda wants to chase it."

He shook his head, and a smile—his first since they climbed out of the river—flitted over his lips. "No, she wants to cuddle it. She thinks everything should love her as much as she loves it. She doesn't understand when small animals are afraid of her."

Lucy let out a small laugh, surprising herself. "She's not wrong, though. Everyone should love her. She's the best girl."

Zelda's tail wagged at the praise, and she looked up at them with a doggy grin, tongue lolling. Lucy's heart melted. She reached down to pat Zelda's damp head.

Sawyer's fingers tightened around hers. "Both my girls are pretty amazing."

His girl.

A few days ago, having any man claim her would've sent her running for the hills. But coming from Sawyer, the words sent a warm glow spreading through her chest, momentarily chasing away the chill. Being his felt right. Safe.

And also still terrifying.

Ugh. Why were her feelings for him so messy and complicated?

She squeezed his hand back, leaning into his solid strength. "We make a good team."

His thumb rubbed soothing circles over her abraded knuckles. "The best."

They walked a little farther until Lucy spotted a lean-to. It looked like it had been there a long time, the roof covered in moss. "There's a shelter here."

She led Sawyer and Zelda over to it, eyeing the slanted roof dubiously. It wasn't much, but it would at least help hide them from anyone nearby.

Sawyer ran his hand along the rough-hewn logs forming the wall. "Feels solid. Good spot to hole up for a while." He ducked inside, Zelda padding after him.

Lucy followed them in, having to hunch over in the low space. The earthen floor was hard-packed and dry. Sawyer sank down against the back wall with a groan, stretching his right leg out in front of him and rubbing at his thigh.

"Your leg bothering you?" she asked and knelt beside him.

He shook his head. "It's fine."

"Oh, of course. I always limp when my leg's fine, too."

He exhaled, long and slow. "Okay, yeah. It's bothering me. I jammed my knee on something in the river. And my ribs. And my shoulder. And... every other part of me. But I will be okay. I just need to rest for a bit."

"Then let's get you out of these wet clothes." She helped him shrug out of his jacket. The thin material of his T-shirt clung to his chest and back, outlining the sculpted planes of muscle. Her fingers itched to trace them, to feel the warm, living heat of his skin...

But she resisted the urge, instead focusing on wringing out the excess water from his jacket. "Take off your shirt."

"This is not how I wanted you to get me naked again." He winced as he pulled off the T-shirt, and her heart lodged in her throat. His back and shoulder were an ugly patchwork of purple and blue.

"Jesus, Sawyer." She reached out, fingertips hovering over the mottled skin, afraid to touch him and cause more pain. "Why didn't you say something?"

He shrugged, then winced. "What could you do about it except worry? I'll be fine."

She bit her lip, unconvinced. Those contusions looked serious. He could have other internal injuries. He needed a doctor, x-rays, pain meds. Things she couldn't give him stuck out here in the middle of nowhere.

Pushing to her feet, she grabbed his wet clothes and draped them over branches outside the shelter. She peeled off her own wet shirt and pants, teeth chattering as the breeze hit her damp skin. Goosebumps erupted across her flesh, and her nipples pebbled against the thin fabric of her bra. She draped her clothes next to Sawyer's, hoping the summer breeze would dry them quickly.

Ducking back into the lean-to, she found Sawyer struggling to unlace his boots, his face pinched with pain. While she was gone, he'd laid out the phones on a rock to dry, but she doubted that would do much to improve their functionality.

She knelt beside him again, gently nudging his hands away. "Let me."

She made quick work of the knots, easing the boots off his feet. His socks squished when she peeled them off. She set them in the sun with the rest of their clothes, then turned her attention to his soaked pants.

He sucked in a sharp breath when she reached for his fly, his abdominal muscles contracting as her fingers brushed against his stomach. She paused, looking up at him through her lashes. His pale blue eyes were heavy-lidded, his lips parted.

Desire, hot and fierce, lanced through her. She wanted to press her mouth to his, to taste him, to feel his naked skin against hers again.

"Easy, Luce," he murmured, voice strained, and wrapped a hand around her burrist. "You can't look at me like that. It's torture."

"How am I looking at you?"

"Like you want to lick me like a popsicle."

She did want to lick him. She wanted to wrap her mouth around his big cock and suck until he was writhing with a mix of pain and pleasure. The mental image made her pulse throb, heat curling low in her belly, her panties going damp.

"How do you know that?" she asked a little too breathlessly.

"Your breathing changed. Your touch changed." His voice dropped to a husky whisper, fingers tightening on her wrist. "And as much as I would love for you to have your way with me, I'm not exactly in fighting shape at the moment."

He was right. Now wasn't the time. They needed to focus on survival, not sex, but it was difficult with the memories of last night so fresh in her mind.

Dragging in an unsteady breath, she lowered her gaze and finished unzipping his pants, all business. "I'm not trying to turn you on. I'm trying to help, and these need to come off. You can't get warm with wet clothes on. Lift your hips."

He braced his hands on the ground and pushed up with a low grunt of pain. Together, they worked the wet cargo pants down his legs, which were almost as bruised as his back. The fabric clung to his muscular thighs and calves, and she had to tug to get them off.

Finally, he was naked except for a pair of black boxer briefs. She tried not to stare at the impressive outline of his cock straining against the thin, wet fabric. He was beautiful, even battered and bruised. She swallowed hard and averted her gaze, draping his pants over a branch outside before ducking back into the shelter.

Sawyer had his eyes closed, head tipped back against

the wall. His chest rose and fell with shallow breaths. Zelda curled up at his side, her head resting on his thigh. Her heart clenched. He looked so vulnerable, so human. Not the cocky, self-assured charmer he pretended to be. Seeing him like this, stripped bare in more ways than one, made her want to wrap herself around him and never let go.

"Some second date, huh?" His voice rumbled in his chest, laced with exhaustion and pain he couldn't quite hide.

"Oh, come on, this is at least our third."

His brow wrinkled, but he didn't open his eyes. "What are you counting as the first?"

"When you pulled me out of that cave."

He frowned fiercely. "So far, our dates suck. I need to take you on a real date. Something that doesn't involve near-death experiences or hypothermia."

She grabbed the emergency blanket from her pack and shook off the water. Thankfully, it was still sealed, so the blanket itself should still be dry. "Oh yeah? So what does a real date with Sawyer Murphy entail?"

She sat beside him, shoulder to shoulder, thigh to thigh. Opening the blanket with a crinkle of mylar, she draped it over both of them, cocooning them in silver. She wrapped an arm around Sawyer's waist, careful to avoid his bruises, and guided his head down to her shoulder. He came willingly, melting into her with a sigh. His arm snaked around her back, palm splaying across her hip. Skin to skin. The heat of him seeped into her, thawing her from the inside out.

"Well, first, I'll pick you up on my motorcycle." His voice was a low rumble, his breath warm against her collarbone. "We'd take the scenic route along the coast. Stop at a secluded cove I know. Spread out a blanket, pop open some wine, feed each other fancy cheese, and discuss the meaning of life while the sun sets over the ocean."

She let out a soft snort. "*You* have a motorcycle?"

"No, but I will for our date."

A smile tugged at the corner of her mouth. She could indulge in this fantasy for a few moments. "Okay. Then what?"

His thumb traced idle patterns on the bare skin of her hip as he considered. "Then, once the stars come out, I'll build us a bonfire on the beach."

She hummed, the sound vibrating through her chest. "I do love a bonfire."

"I'll grab a guitar and serenade you with off-key renditions of every love song I know until you can't take it anymore and kiss me just to shut me up."

A laugh bubbled out of her. "You play guitar too, huh?"

"Not even a little bit." His lips curved against her shoulder before he placed a soft kiss there.

She huffed out another laugh. How did he do that? Even cold, wet, and injured, he could still make her laugh, could make her believe—if only for a moment— that everything would be okay.

"Sounds like a pretty epic date. Might be worth sticking around to see if you can make it happen."

He lifted his head from her shoulder. "Yeah?"

There was a vulnerability in that single word that squeezed her heart. He was always so confident, so self-assured. It was easy to forget that he had his own doubts and insecurities. That maybe he needed reassurance just as much as she did.

Cupping his stubbled jaw in her palm, she leaned in and brushed her lips softly over his. "Yeah. I'm willing to see where this thing between us goes."

He let out a shuddering breath and rested his head against hers. "Good. That's good."

They sat like that for a long while, huddled together, listening to the forest sounds filtering in from outside their little shelter—the rustle of leaves, the chirping of birds, the skittering of small creatures in the underbrush. Gradually, Sawyer's shivering eased, and his breathing deepened. His body grew heavier against hers.

"Sawyer?" she whispered, but he didn't respond. He was out, his face relaxed in sleep, the lines of pain around his eyes and mouth eased. She didn't have the heart to wake him. She suspected he hadn't slept last night when she did, instead staying awake, listening for signs of danger, protecting her. He needed the rest.

Carefully, so as not to jostle him, she eased him down until his head rested in her lap. He murmured something unintelligible but didn't wake.

Zelda repositioned as well, curling up tighter against Sawyer's side, her head on his hip. Lucy absently stroked the dog's soft ears as she studied Sawyer's face in the filtered daylight seeping in through the cracks in the lean-to roof. Even in sleep, a furrow remained between his brows, as if he couldn't fully relax. Not that she blamed him. It wasn't exactly a restful situation.

Her gaze traced over the hard planes and angles of his face, committing every detail to memory. The faint scar on his chin. The golden stubble shadowing his jaw. The surprisingly long lashes fanning over his cheekbones. He looked younger in sleep. More vulnerable. Her heart squeezed with a fierce protectiveness.

He was so strong, always pushing forward no matter how much he was hurting, no matter how bleak things seemed. But everyone had their breaking point. Even Sawyer Murphy. And she couldn't help but wonder how close he was to his.

She leaned her head back against the rough wall, blinking against the stinging in her eyes. Exhaustion pulled at her, but she resisted the siren call of sleep. One of them needed to keep watch. She wouldn't let them be taken by surprise again. But it was hard to stay alert when her body felt leaden. Her eyelids fluttered shut, and she let herself drift, not quite asleep but not fully awake either. Time stretched and warped in the warm cocoon of the emergency blanket, Sawyer's steady breathing and the distant birdsong lulling her into a doze.

She floated in that hazy place between dreaming and waking, her thoughts wandering aimlessly. Snippets of memories and anxieties churned together—flashes of the river, the echo of a gunshot, Sawyer's broken body in her arms...

chapter
twenty-one

LUCY STARTLED AWAKE, heart pounding. She hadn't meant to fall asleep. The lean-to was dim, the light outside fading to dusk.

How long had they been out?

Hours at least.

Panic clawed at her throat. She'd left them vulnerable, defenseless against whoever was hunting them.

Sawyer still slept, his head heavy in her lap, face pale and pinched with pain even in slumber. Dark purple smudges underscored his eyes. He looked utterly wrecked. Guilt chewed at her insides. She should have kept watch, made sure they were safe.

Zelda lifted her head from Sawyer's hip and let out a soft whine, her hazel eyes fixed on something outside the shelter. Lucy tensed, following the dog's gaze. The lean-to's entrance yawned like an open mouth, shadows gathering in the corners as night crept in. She held her breath, straining to hear over the pounding of her pulse in her ears.

But there were only the normal sounds of the forest settling in for the evening—the hoot of an owl, the chirp of crickets, the rustle of nocturnal creatures beginning their nightly foraging. No snapping twigs or crunching footsteps to indicate they weren't alone. Still, the hairs on the back of her neck prickled with unease. They couldn't stay here, exposed and unprotected. They needed to find real shelter, and she needed to check the phones.

She stood and stretched, working out the kinks. A shiver raced through her as the evening breeze kissed her bare skin. Goosebumps erupted over her arms and legs.

Their clothes were dry, if a bit stiff and wrinkled. She tugged on her T-shirt and cargo pants, the fabric rough against her skin. Then, gently, she roused Sawyer. His hand shot out and gripped her wrist tightly, eyes flying open in alarm.

"It's okay," she murmured soothingly, the words catching in her throat as she met his gaze. "We're safe."

He blinked slowly, disoriented, before his grip on her slackened and he groaned. "Shit." He scrubbed his hands over his face. "I feel like I was hit by an entire highway full of trucks. Don't suppose there's any coffee?"

"Sorry, fresh out of Starbucks."

A grunt came from Sawyer as he pushed himself into a sitting position. His face turned a shade paler at the movement, but he didn't protest.

Lucy watched, teeth worrying her lower lip, as Sawyer got to his feet. He wavered slightly, a hand shooting out to steady himself against the rough logs of the lean-to.

"How's the leg?" she asked.

"Still attached."

"I didn't figure it fell off overnight," she said dryly.

Despite the pain etched on his face, he gave her a wan smile. "Ready to move?" he asked, voice hoarse as he took a limping step forward.

She frowned down at his legs. His knee looked painfully swollen. "Yes, but you don't look ready."

"I'm fine."

"Sawyer—"

He scowled. "You're so worried about me, but I'm not the one who was impaled by a stick yesterday."

God, with everything else that had happened, she'd forgotten about the wound. She touched her lower back and found the bandage was miraculously still there. She could only imagine how disgusting it was now. She should probably have Sawyer change it. "Maybe we should stay the night here and rest."

He shook his head. "It's too risky. We need to keep moving." He looked down toward Zelda, a faint smile curling his lips as he reached out to pat her head. "And I think someone needs a walk."

Zelda's tail thumped against the ground, and she lifted her head, nuzzling into Sawyer's hand. He stroked her, fingers digging into her fur. If she hadn't known better, she might have thought he was drawing strength from the contact.

She frowned at him. His face was drawn, skin almost

translucent in the dimming light. And yet, there he stood, ready to soldier on.

Goddamn stubborn man.

"All right," she said, sighing. "But we take it slow, and we stop when it gets dark."

He nodded, not arguing this time.

They gathered their belongings and exited the lean-to. The forest was shrouded in deep shadows. The blanket of dusk that felt both ominous and protective. At least if they couldn't see, then the shooter couldn't see them.

Zelda led the way, her nose to the ground. Sawyer kept his hand on her harness, the two of them moving as one. Lucy followed, watching as he navigated the uneven terrain with confidence. He trusted Zelda implicitly, and it was heartwarming to see their bond in action.

Despite their slow pace, they managed to cover a significant distance before the need for a break became apparent. Both she and Sawyer were gasping by the time they found a decent spot—an ancient redwood as wide as a large truck, its hollowed-out trunk offering a sheltered place to rest that wasn't readily apparent to anyone who might wander by. They crawled inside, the cool dampness of the mossy floor seeping into their clothes.

Sawyer rested his back against the tree, eyes closed, face pinched with pain, chest rising and falling as he caught his breath. Zelda lay down beside him, resting her head on his thigh. His hand absently stroked her fur.

"I'll check the phones," she said, breaking the silence.

Hopefully, by some miracle, they'd be dried out and working again.

She took the waterlogged phones from her bag, her heart a heavy stone in her chest. She turned on her phone first. Nothing. Dead.

Her heart sank further.

She lifted Sawyer's phone, flicking the power button with a trembling finger. Nothing.

She tried the other phones and got more dead screens. Bea's phone flickered on, but there was no signal.

"Shit," she muttered under her breath, regret and helplessness washing through her as she stuffed the phones back into her bag and sank down beside Sawyer.

His hand sought hers, his fingers warm and reassuring against her cold skin. "We knew it was a long shot."

"Without the phones, there's no sense in us continuing. We should go back to the fire lookout. We'll be safer there."

Sawyer was silent for a heartbeat. "Except there's a killer back there."

She groaned and squeezed her eyes shut. "So 'safer' wasn't the best choice of words. But someone in the forest service will eventually remember that Ethan is stationed there and send a rescue team for him. We need to be there when they do. Without the phones, it's our only option now."

He didn't respond immediately, his fingers still idly tracing circles on the back of her hand. She watched as he mulled over her words, his eyes staring blankly ahead as his forehead creased with worry. She could practically see the gears in his head turning.

"Okay," he finally conceded, voice barely a whisper in the enclosing darkness. His grip on her hand tightened ever so slightly. "Okay. We go back."

Lucy felt an unexpected wave of relief at his agreement. But that relief was short-lived as reality crashed in. Going back meant potentially crossing paths with the shooter. And if they somehow miraculously survived to make it back, there was still the problem of Maya's killer —if it wasn't the same person.

"We'll rest here for tonight," she decided. "We need to regain our strength before we can attempt the trek back. We've pushed ourselves enough."

She was careful to keep using "we" rather than "you." The last thing she wanted to do was tap into that stubborn streak of his. He needed to rest. The fact that he was too exhausted to argue or crack a joke told her just how close to his limit he really was.

"Sounds like a plan," Sawyer murmured, voice raspy with fatigue. Zelda let out a soft whine and nuzzled her head into Sawyer's lap. He responded by laying down and wrapping an arm around the dog's body, pulling her closer against his side.

The quietness of the forest felt thick and heavy, pressing in on them from all sides. Lucy listened to the rhythm of their breathing as it filled the silence— Sawyer's shallow gasps gradually slowing to match the steady rise and fall of Zelda's flank.

Eventually, exhaustion tugged Lucy down into a

fitful sleep. Even in her dreams, the image of the shooter loomed over her like a specter—faceless, nameless, but very real.

She burst awake from the nightmares before dawn and automatically rolled over to check on Sawyer.

He wasn't beside her anymore.

Her heart lurched in her chest, a frantic wave of fear washing over her. She shot up, glancing around the hollowed-out trunk. It was empty. Zelda, too, was missing.

"Sawyer?" she whispered.

There was no response.

The pit of dread in her stomach deepened. She scrambled to her feet, wincing at the sharp, shooting pain that traveled up from the wound on her back.

"Sawyer!"

Louder this time, but there was no response but the rustling of foliage in the early morning breeze.

A sob stuck in her throat as she frantically scanned their surroundings, but there was no sign of either Sawyer or Zelda. The early morning fog was thick and soupy, making it nearly impossible to see anything beyond a few feet ahead.

She stumbled forward, eyes darting around the dark forest, every rustling leaf and groaning branch making her jump. He wouldn't have left without saying anything. Something must have happened.

Crackling leaves underfoot made her freeze, hand clenching into a fist. A shadow moved in the fog—Zelda.

The dog emerged from the underbrush, gaze focused and serious.

"Zelda," Lucy breathed out in relief before her worry returned in full force. "Where's Sawyer?"

The dog whined, moving to nudge against Lucy's knee before turning around and heading back into the underbrush. Lucy followed without hesitation, fear knotting her stomach tight.

Zelda led her off their makeshift path into denser woods. The faint light that barely seeped through the thick fog had an eerie, haunting quality to it.

Don't trip. Don't stumble.

Zelda was a few feet ahead of her, her tail wagging anxiously.

"Sawyer?" She called again, heart pounding in her chest as she finally broke through the dense foliage.

He stood on a ridge overhead, bathed in the soft, ethereal glow of the early morning light that cut through the fog. His hair looked wilder than usual, sticking up in every direction as if he'd been running his hand through it incessantly.

And he was way too close to the edge.

Fear was a living beast inside her, choking her. She scrambled up the incline. It was steeper than it looked from the ground. How the hell had he climbed up here with a bum knee?

"Sawyer! Don't move!"

He turned toward her voice...

And the crazy man was grinning. He held up a phone. "I got a signal!"

part two
healing

They say that love is blind, but it's trauma that's blind. Love sees what is.
Neil Strauss

chapter
twenty-two

SAWYER SAW her running toward him, her momentum enough to kick his brain into gear. She was all wide, panicked eyes and loose flying hair, and still, she was the most beautiful thing he'd ever seen. He braced for the impact, but instead of throwing herself into his arms as he thought, she grabbed him by the shirt and yanked him away from the edge.

He stumbled backward, caught off guard by her force.

"Are you fucking insane?" she gasped out, clutching tightly to his shirt.

Shocked, he could only blink at her. "I... uh..."

"You could've slipped. You could've fallen. You're already a giant bruise. You want to add broken bones to your list of injuries? God!" She grabbed his face and pulled him down for a kiss. It was hard and fast and tasted of relief and fear. And it was over too fast, leaving him breathless and mute.

"Don't scare me like that again." She hugged him fiercely then, as if afraid he'd disappear, and he felt tears soaking into his shirt.

He momentarily forgot about the phone and wrapped his arms around her, burying his face in her hair. "Hey, I'm okay."

She smacked his chest. "What are you doing up here?"

"I got a signal."

She made a surprised sound and jerked back. He imagined she was staring at him in disbelief. "You... what?"

He grinned and held the phone up again. "I couldn't sleep, and I heard one of the phones beep. When I figured out which one it was, I tinkered with it and... I got a signal."

She grabbed it from him. "This is Bea's phone." Then, after an extended silence, she whispered, "Holy shit. We have four bars."

The phone spoke in a fast, robotic voice as she repeatedly jabbed the call icon: "Phone. Three of four. Double tap to open. Phone. Phone. Phone. Three of four. Double tap to open."

She growled softly. "It's glitching."

He chuckled and held out a hand. "No, it's not. I turned on VoiceOver. It uses different gestures and takes some getting used to. Here." When she handed him the phone, he navigated to the right spot and felt her lean in to watch as he tapped out a phone number by heart.

"How can you understand what it's saying? It's so fast."

He lifted a shoulder. "Sounds normal to me." He tapped the call icon, then put it on speaker.

Lucy sucked in a sharp breath as it rang and grabbed his wrist. "Oh my God, it's working. Who are you calling?"

"Zak. I figure 911 is overwhelmed, and we'll have a better chance at reaching—"

"Hello?" Zak answered with an edge of suspicion in his voice.

"Zak—"

"Holy fucking hell!" Zak exclaimed, then shouted to someone off the line: "I got him! It's Sawyer!" Then he came back. "Where the fuck are you? Are you safe? Are Pierce and Raszta with—" There was a staticky moment and Zak's voice cut out.

He tightened his grip on the phone, willing the signal to hold out. "Come on. Come on."

"—injured?" Zak finished.

Sawyer lifted the phone toward his mouth and hoped the connection was strong enough that Zak could hear him through the static. "I'm on the mountain with Lucy Harper. Pierce isn't here. We're about..." He trailed off, unsure exactly where they were.

"Five miles east of Blue Mountain Fire Lookout," Lucy finished for him. "I had a tour group with me when the earthquake hit, and we've picked up a few others since. We have four adult males, one adult female, and one juvenile male with a broken leg. We left them all at the lookout to find help."

Static snapped and popped over the line. "Veronica and Conn—Blue—ower—was—"

Sawyer shook his head in frustration and raised the phone to his mouth again. "Bad copy. Say again, Zak."

"Veronica and Connelly just flew up to Blue Mountain," Zak repeated. "The tower was abandoned."

Lucy's grip on his arm loosened in shock. "Impossible," she whispered. "Joel can't walk. Where would they go?"

"We expected to find *you* there, Sawyer," Zak said, and even through the static, Sawyer heard the emotion choking his voice. "Ash said you radioed him from there, but all they found was a woman's body."

Sawyer swore. If they had stayed put, Lucy would be safe now. Or... maybe they would be dead like Maya, victims of the killer.

Where the hell was everyone?

Why would they risk leaving the tower?

"I wasn't sure Ash heard me," he said into the phone. "And then our radio died, so we hiked toward the nearest cell phone tower to try and get a signal."

Zak's sigh was explosive. "Okay. All right. I'm going to reroute Vee and Connelly to the cell tower. Do you have anything to signal them?"

"I have a flare," Lucy said. "Hopefully it still works after our swim in the river yesterday."

"Jesus," Zak muttered. "Okay, hunker down. No more dips in the river. We're coming for you. As soon as you hear the rotor—" Static cut him off and the line went dead.

"Fuck." Sawyer tried calling again, but the phone had stopped responding to his touch. "Is the screen black?"

"Yes," Lucy said with a heavy sigh. "The battery must have died. It didn't have much left when I looked at it yesterday. But at least we got through. They know where we are and they're on their way."

"One problem." He looked toward her voice and hated to extinguish the hope he heard there. "The moment we set off that flare—if it works—we pinpoint our location."

"Isn't that the point?"

"Yes, but more than Veronica and Connelly will be able to find us."

"Oh," she said softly, and he heard her drop onto a nearby boulder as the realization hit. "Oh, shit. The shooter."

chapter
twenty-three

LUCY STUDIED Sawyer from the corner of her eye as they waited. He seemed back to his old self, all chiseled determination and steady composure, but she kept picturing how he was last night, vulnerable and in pain.

She had been so scared. More scared than she'd ever been in her life, and she'd been kidnapped by a serial killer. But seeing him weak and hurting had triggered something in her, something deep and fierce and utterly terrifying.

Sawyer was one of the strongest people she knew. He was always steady and sure, always joking and laughing in the face of danger or hardship. She'd seen him do things that most people would find impossible. He was blind, but he never let his lack of sight hold him back. And he never complained.

But last night...

Despite his near superhuman ability to remain steady

in the face of danger, last night had reminded her he was just a man.

God, she had never felt so helpless.

He sat against a tree with Zelda faithfully at his side, his face raised toward the sun. He looked relaxed, like he was just enjoying a beautiful dawn on the mountain. But she knew better. He was simultaneously listening for the helicopter and focusing on any unusual sounds that might signal the shooter's approach. Every now and then, he would rub his swollen knee and wince.

Lucy shifted nervously, casting worried glances at the sky. Rescue was so close, yet felt a million miles away. She couldn't make herself believe this nightmare was finally over until she and Sawyer were safely inside the helicopter and headed home.

The silence was eerie, as if the forest itself was holding its breath in anticipation. Dew-drenched leaves glistened under the golden shafts of sunlight. Normally, it would be beautiful, but—and she never thought she'd think this —she'd had more than enough of nature for a while. She pulled her jacket tighter against herself, despite the chill of the fog not really being the reason for her shivers.

"A penny for your thoughts?" Sawyer broke the silence, looking in her direction but not directly at her.

Lucy snorted. "You can't afford my thoughts, Murphy," she said with a forced half-smile. His constant attempts at levity in stressful situations, though irritating, were comforting in a way.

His laughter echoed through the clearing, breaking

the heavy tension that had settled. The sound was warm and familiar.

"Fair enough," he conceded while his attention shifted back to the sky above them. "But mine are free, if you're curious."

She didn't want to be. She was already far too close to him. Any closer, and she'd completely lose her heart. She shifted toward him. "Okay. What are you thinking about?"

He grinned. "Getting you naked again."

She rolled her eyes. "Of course you are."

"When we get home, I plan to keep you in my bed for days. I want to take my time and explore every inch of you. I want to know what you taste like when you come. I want your smell all over my sheets, my skin." His grinned turned wicked. "Your breathing changed. Are you wet thinking about it?"

She was, and squeezed her thighs together. "No."

His head tilted as if he could hear the rush of her pulse. "Liar."

Damn him. The man had a way of sweeping away her defenses, making her forget for a moment the very real danger lurking in the wilderness around them.

Before she could respond—not that she had any idea what to say to that—the *whup-whup-whup* of an approaching helicopter snagged her attention. She popped to her feet and exhaled in a rush of giddy relief as the bird appeared over a ridge, its blades chopping through the morning fog. The sight of it, blocky and solidly real and safe, made something tight in her chest loosen.

"Send up the flare," Sawyer said, getting to his feet with a wince. "We're getting off this fucking mountain."

She nodded and reached for the flare gun. As she loaded it, her hands shook from a combination of nerves and relief.

It was over.

Finally.

She aimed the flare up towards the sky and pulled the trigger. The shot exploded into the air in a vibrant red streak, painting the dawn sky with its urgent message. She watched it arc high before starting to descend slowly, the trailing smoke weaving intricate patterns in the clear blue sky.

The helicopter tilted slightly to their direction.

They had been seen.

Sawyer turned towards her, his face lit by the flare's reddish glow. Up close, she could see the lines of fatigue etching themselves deeper into his rugged features, but his eyes held a spark of triumph.

"We made it," he said softly, reaching out toward her.

She laced her fingers through his. Tears welled up and spilled over, but these were tears of relief instead of fear.

They were going home.

Then, just as the helicopter lowered itself into the clearing, an ear-splitting crack echoed through the valley. The sound was so sudden, so violently loud, that both Lucy and Sawyer froze in place. Zelda growled low in her throat.

It took a second for Lucy to realize what had happened. "Gunshot!" she shouted over the thunderous whirring of the helicopter blades. She grabbed Sawyer's arm and yanked him down behind a large boulder.

"Sawyer?" a voice blared from the helicopter's loudspeaker and Lucy looked up, spotting a man clad in the red RWCR uniform leaning out of the chopper's open door. His face was obscured by the visor of his helmet, but she recognized his voice—Connelly Davis, former pararescue jumper, now a bestselling author and RWCR's part-time medic.

"Pull up!" she shouted, waving an arm at him without exposing her position behind the boulder. "Shooter!"

Just then a bullet pinged off the skid near Connelly's boot. He ducked back inside. She couldn't hear him, but she was sure he was swearing. The helicopter veered away, and her heart sank as she watched it go.

They were so close. But the shooter was still out there.

Sawyer's hand gripped hers tight as if to ground her. "Are you hurt?"

"No," she said, looking down at him. "Are you?"

He shook his head.

She let out a small sigh of relief. They were okay. For now.

"We can't sit here. We need to move." He struggled to his feet. His swollen knee trembled under the strain, but he ignored the pain and pushed himself upright. Zelda whined at his side, her tail tucked between her legs. She knew something was wrong and Lucy could see fear in her expressive hazel eyes.

"You're okay, girl," she whispered and gave the dog a kiss on her forehead. "We're okay." She looked up at Sawyer. "Where can we go?"

"Is there higher ground nearby?"

"Higher than here?"

"Anywhere we have a better chance of not getting shot."

She scanned their surroundings, her gaze landing on a cliff a good distance away. One side was vertical, but the other was a more manageable slope. It would still be a difficult climb, especially with Sawyer's injured knee, and they would be exposed on its rocky side until they reached the top. But once there, they would have the advantage of a view over their entire surroundings. The shooter wouldn't be able to sneak up on them.

"Yes," she said finally. "There's a ridge maybe half a mile to the north. It's a stretch, but it's our best shot."

His jaw clenched. "Any cover?"

"Some trees between here and there... but once we're on the rock, not much until we reach the top."

Another gunshot rang out then, closer this time, echoing sharply off the surrounding hills and making both of them flinch. Zelda whined again but stayed obediently at Sawyer's side.

"Fuck!" Sawyer cursed as the echo faded. "We don't have much choice, do we?"

Lucy glanced back at the ridge, her mind already calculating their route. "Just get to the trees first, then we'll worry about the climb. The shooter can't hit what they can't see."

"Then we go on my count," Sawyer said, the resignation in his voice punctuated by another gunshot, this one ricocheting off their boulder with a sharp ping.

Lucy nodded, tightening her grip on his hand. Her heart pounded in her chest, her breath coming short and quick with fear.

Sawyer leaned closer, pressing his forehead to hers. "Breathe, Lucy," he said, and she closed her eyes, focusing on the sound of his voice over the chaos around them. "We are going to make it. We have to."

She opened her eyes and met his distant gaze. Just once she wished she could look into his eyes and see him looking back. "Okay," she whispered.

He gave her hand a reassuring squeeze. "Three... two... go!"

Without another word, she took off, angling their path toward the cluster of trees dotting the terrain between them and the ridge. His grip was tight on her hand as they weaved through shrubs and rocky outcroppings, their boots thudding against the uneven forest floor. Branches cracked underfoot and leaves rustled in their wake, each noise a potential giveaway to their location.

They'd covered about half the distance to the trees when another gunshot shattered the tense quiet. The bullet kicked up dirt just a few yards away from where they were running. She let out a strangled gasp, but she didn't stop moving. If she let fear win, they were dead.

The shot had come from their left. The shooter was moving, trying to get into position to trap them against the ridge. Clever, calculating... and ruthless.

Just as they neared the treeline, another shot rang out. Lucy flinched as it whizzed past them, close enough to make her ears ring. It was followed by another crack, then another.

They stumbled into the cover of the trees just as the barrage ended in an eerie silence. Panting, she turned back to look at Sawyer.

He squatted

down next to Zelda, his hand resting on her head as he struggled to catch his breath. "That was too fucking close," he muttered, wiping sweat off his forehead with the back of his free hand.

Lucy nodded, pressing her back against a gnarled conifer and gulping in the sharp, pine-scented air. Her heart thrummed in her ears, and she could feel adrenaline coursing through her veins, leaving a tang of copper on her tongue.

"Are you okay?" Sawyer asked, reaching out toward her with a hand speckled with dirt.

"I'm okay." She was half-surprised to find that she was telling the truth. She was terrified, yes. Exhausted, absolutely. But not injured. "You?"

She'd noticed his limp had become more pronounced.

He shrugged and a wry smile twisted his lips. "Same as before. I'll live."

"Good, because I'm not carrying your sorry ass up that ridge."

His smile widened. "If I remember correctly, you liked my ass the other night. Nothing sorry about it."

She heard a noise in the woods and looked up, scanning the sparse grove of trees. She didn't see anything, but she didn't dare wait any longer. She grabbed his hand again. "Less flirting, more running."

"Roger that," Sawyer said, still grinning. The crazy man.

They didn't speak again as they darted across the open ground toward the base of the ridge. It loomed over them, an unforgiving slant of earth and stone under a slowly darkening sky. It was much steeper than it had looked from the distance; they would have to scramble up most of it on all fours.

Nothing like free soloing with a blind man, a dog, and a killer on their asses.

Okay, that was an exaggeration. But, still, it was going to be dangerous.

"We need to be fast and stay low," Lucy murmured as she calculated the best path up.

"Hey." He caught her hand and pulled her to him. Their mouths crashed together in a quick, hard kiss.

When he pulled back, his breath fanned across her lips. "If I don't make it—"

She cut him off. "You're going to make it."

"I love you, Lucy Harper," he murmured. "I am so crazy head-over-heels for you. You're all I can think about. Even now. I need you to know that before we go any further."

The words hit her like a bucket of cold water.

"Don't say that like a goodbye." She gripped his jacket, her fingers digging into the rough fabric. "We're not having this conversation, Sawyer. We are both getting off this goddamn mountain. Now, move."

He gave her that half smile again, the one that did funny things to her heart. "That's my girl. Lead the way."

They started the ascent. Zelda took the lead, her powerful body scrambling over rocks and loose soil with ease. Lucy followed behind, using the bark of a tree to hoist herself up a particularly steep section of the ridge. She glanced back at Sawyer. He was moving slowly, feeling his way, grim determination in every line of his dust-streaked face.

The whole world seemed to hold its breath as they climbed. The only sounds were the harsh raggedness of their breaths and the occasional dislodging of small stones under their boots. Her muscles burned, and her lungs screamed for air, but there was no time for rest. They were too exposed on the pale gray rock.

Gunfire ripped through the stillness, peppering the ledge right where she was about to place her hand. She jerked back as hot pain blasted through her thigh...

And lost her grip.

chapter
twenty-four

THE SHOOTER HAD FOUND THEM.

Sawyer ducked, pressing himself tight against the ground, the taste of chalky dirt coating his mouth.

The gunfire stopped.

Dirt and pebbles rained down around his shoulders, and then something slid by him, going fast.

"Lucy!" He reached out blindly where she had been just moments ago, fingers scrabbling against loose earth and sharp rocks. He found nothing but air.

Lucy must have fallen.

Jesus. She hadn't made a sound. Had she been shot?

Fear choked him, and he pushed himself backward, descending as quickly as he could until the slope started to level off. He straightened, and his injured knee screamed in protest with each jarring step he took. He could feel blood trickling down his shin, could smell the metallic scent of it. But none of that mattered. All that mattered was finding Lucy and making sure she was safe.

He squinted at his surroundings, willing something to move and orientate him, but it was all just static, vaguely tree-like shapes in weird colors that didn't make sense.

His fucking brain. Why wouldn't it work right, just this once?

Somewhere up the slope, Zelda whined.

"Stay there, girl," he called. Her training and instincts would be telling her to come back to him, to help him, but he didn't want her anywhere near the killer. "Stay."

He reached out, swiping his hand back and forth through the air. "Lucy?"

Something moved in his periphery. He spun toward it, but it had stopped moving again. His gut tightened with dread. The shooter, whoever they were, knew he could only see movement and was using it as camouflage.

"I know you're there."

The voice that answered him was chillingly familiar. "Course you do, Murphy. You've got a sixth sense for trouble."

Sawyer froze, blood in his veins boiling over with rage. "Grant."

There was a pause, then: "Not my real name."

"What have you done with Lucy?"

"She's here. Say hello to your boy toy, Luce."

There was short scuffle and for a moment, Lucy and Grant appeared. He had his arm locked around her neck and she was trying to fight him off. Blood covered her face. Then Grant hit her in the stomach, grabbed her around the throat, and they stopped moving, disappearing into the hazy stillness once again.

"Let her go, Grant," he said, his voice steady despite the maelstrom of terror and anger inside him. "Throw away your weapon and let her go."

"You're not really in a position to be making demands, Murphy."

Sawyer bared his teeth in a feral grin. "You'd be surprised what I'm capable of."

Grant scoffed. "What are *you* going to do to *me*?"

A flicker of movement caught his eye. Was that… fingers? Yes. Lucy was wiggling her fingers at her side.

"Who are you?" he asked to keep Grant distracted while he tried to interrupt her hand signals.

"My name doesn't matter. I'm just a hired gun."

"Then why haven't you killed us yet?" *C'mon, Luce,* he urged silently. *What are you trying to tell me?*

She bladed her hand, pointing like a flight attendant, then made her fingers into a gun before they faded from his sight again.

"I need to know what you know first," Grant said.

Sawyer slid a step in the direction she'd indicated, and his foot nudged something. Her backpack. "I know you're a fucking coward, hiding from a blind guy behind a woman."

Grant growled. "Where is Pierce St. James?"

Sawyer froze. "What the fuck does Pierce have to do with this?"

That question seemed to piss Grant off, because the next thing Sawyer knew, there was a gun pressing into his forehead. "Don't play games with me, Murphy. I know he's in Steam Valley. Word on the street is he's involved with your little dog show. Redwood Coast Rescue. Where is he?" Grant pressed the muzzle harder into his forehead. "What has he told you?"

Sawyer dropped to his knees. The impact jarred his already aching body, but it put him closer to Lucy's pack. His hand brushed something partially buried in the dirt and his heart pounded in his chest as he realized what it was—the gun he'd given Lucy. *That* was what she was trying to tell him.

"I told you before when you attacked me, I don't know where Pierce is." He figured the truth was his best option for distraction as his hand closed around the gun. "I came up here looking for him, too."

"You expect me to believe that?" Grant's voice was a low growl, the pressure on his forehead relenting a little.

"It's the truth." Sawyer gritted his teeth, ignoring the sharp pain radiating from his knee. The sleek metal of the gun nestled into his palm like an old friend, its weight comforting and familiar. He kept it hidden in the dirt as he considered his options.

He could shoot Grant, but he didn't know where Lucy was. Did he really want to run the risk of hitting her, too?

Suddenly Grant's foot crunched down on his hand, and he bit back a shout of pain. He wasn't going to give the bastard the satisfaction.

"You're not being as stealthy as you think you are." Grant yanked the gun from under his hand and then pressed more of his weight down on Sawyer's hand. "My employers *will* get what they're after, one way or another."

Sawyer gritted his teeth against the pain. "They won't get it from me."

"Then I have no use for you anymore." For a moment, Grant shifted his weight, easing the pressure on Sawyer's hand. It was a brief moment of relief that Sawyer would have savored if he wasn't suddenly aware of something else— Lucy's presence.

She was close.

"Sawyer, duck!"

His body moved on pure instinct, dropping flat to the ground as a gunshot exploded way too close to his head.

Jesus, if she hadn't told him to move...

Ears ringing, he rolled and grabbed a handful of pebbles and dirt, flinging them toward where he last saw Grant. There was a grunt of surprise, then another wild gunshot. Something heavy fell at his side. He felt around until his fingers touched cool metal—the gun Grant had taken from him.

He held it up. "Lucy!"

Lucy lunged for the gun in Sawyer's hand, getting to it milliseconds before Grant. He bared his teeth at her. His eyes were red and irritated from the dirt Sawyer had thrown at him. A small cut had opened up above his eyebrow and streamed blood down his face.

She didn't give him time to react—just shoved the gun at his chest and fired.

Nothing happened.

The gun was jammed.

Grant laughed, an ugly sound, and ripped it out of her hand, then backhanded her so hard she tumbled backwards. Her head hit the ground hard, stars exploding in her vision. Through the haze of pain and dizziness, she heard him say, "You really thought that would work?"

Something whistled through the air, followed by a sharp crack as it connected with Grant's skull. He stumbled back, releasing his grip on Lucy's ankle. Sawyer surged forward, swinging what looked like a fallen branch at Grant again. The makeshift weapon connected with force, sending Grant sprawling in the dirt.

But the bastard didn't stay down. He sprang back up, launching himself at Sawyer. They grappled for a moment before Grant landed a hard blow to Sawyer's stomach. Sawyer doubled over, dropping to one knee. Grant stood over him, swaying unsteady, the working gun back in his hand. He raised it to Sawyer's head.

No!

Pushing the nausea down, Lucy surged forward with a scream and slammed into him with all of her strength. They both tumbled to the ground, wrestling for control of the gun. It was a frantic struggle—dirt and blood mixing with sweat as they grappled.

Above them, Zelda's furious barking echoed through the valley.

And beyond that, distantly, another sound—the steady thrum of helicopter blades closing in.

Rescue was coming. They just had to hold on for a few more seconds.

With renewed strength, Lucy twisted beneath Grant, managing to get the upper hand for a split second. She slammed her hand into his face, feeling his nose crunch under the blow. He cursed, the gun slipping from his grasp and landing just out of reach.

Ignoring the blood streaming down her face from a fresh cut on her forehead, she turned and crawled towards it. Her hand closed around it just as Grant lunged for her again, catching her around her hips.

No. She was *not* going to be a victim again.

Every muscle screamed as she twisted and fired.

The recoil sent pain singing through her every nerve ending, but the satisfaction as Grant jerked back, clutching at his shoulder where the bullet hit him, made it worth it.

Staggering back, he fell to his knees, clutching his bleeding shoulder. "You bitch," he spat out.

Lucy took another shaky step back, clutching the gun in shaking hands. He looked up at her, the shadows deepening the lines on his face and making him look even more monstrous.

"Go ahead," he said hoarsely.

She swallowed hard, staring down at him with a mix

of fear and disgust. Then she tightened her grip on the gun and raised it.

Grant flinched, but the shot never came.

Instead, she stumbled back and dropped to her knees next to Sawyer. He was still on the ground where Grant had left him, dry heaving into the dirt, where it looked like he'd already emptied his stomach. His face was pale under a layer of sweat and grime.

Grant made a move as if to stand, but Lucy pointed the gun back at him without hesitation. "Stay down!"

The helicopter was getting louder now, the chopping blades echoing through the valley and drowning out everything else. Lucy squinted against the wind kicked up by the propellers as a rope dropped from the sky, quickly followed by several figures zipping down a line. As the first man hit the ground, he immediately reached behind him to unclip a mean-looking Shepard with yellow eyes from his harness. The dog bounded toward them, stopping short of Lucy and growling at Grant.

Relief swept through Lucy, followed by a profound wave of exhaustion. Her legs wobbled and gave out as the men and dogs of Redwood Coast Rescue surrounded and secured Grant. She crawled over to where Sawyer has collapsed and cupped her face in his hands.

His pale eyes fluttered open, but his gaze was more unfocused than usual. He was shocky, she realized. And maybe so was she.

"Sawyer," she said, her voice breaking with relief. "We made it."

He tried to smile through the pain, but the corners of

his mouth twitched with effort. "I'd...hoped to give you...a better second date."

Lucy let out a shaky laugh and leaned down to press her lips against his forehead. "This is definitely our third."

His hands covered hers. "The fourth will be better."

"Promises, promises."

"Jesus Christ, Sawyer," one of their rescuers said. He was a big, intimidating man covered in tattoos. Lucy knew his name, but it had escaped her at that moment. "Why didn't you invite us to the party sooner?"

Sawyer gave a weak chuckle. "You guys always have all the fun, Van. I thought it was my turn."

Zak Hendricks crouched down beside them. "You two all right?"

Lucy looked at him, her vision blurring slightly. "Define all right."

Zak's gaze was steady, assessing. "Still breathing?"

"Yes," she said, letting out a shaky laugh.

"Good. But I think we'll still get you checked out." He straightened and signaled Connelly over. "Sawyer's in pretty rough shape. Lucy's not much better."

Lucy felt Connelly's hands on her, checking for injuries. She mostly responded to his quiet questions and gentle prodding with nods and grunts.

Sawyer was lifted onto a stretcher, his face pinched with pain. As they carried him toward the helicopter, Lucy tried to stand up, but a wave of dizziness made her stumble.

"Easy there," Connelly said, steadying her with a firm

grip around her waist. "Let someone else be the hero now."

She gave him a shaky smile but didn't reply. Her focus was on Sawyer as he was loaded into the helicopter. "Will he be okay?"

"Oh, yeah. Some rest, some painkillers, and ice for that knee, and he'll be back to his usual charming self in no time," Connelly reassured her. His gaze landed on her leg and sharpened with concern. "Jesus. Were you shot?"

"Oh." She looked down at her thigh and poked a finger at the very obvious bullet hole in her pants. "I don't feel it."

Even as she said the words, her vision dimmed. The last thing she heard was Connelly's curse, and then the world spun out of her control. She was barely aware of the hard grip catching her as she collapsed.

DEJA VU.

Once again, Sawyer was sitting at Lucy's bedside. But this time, he had no intention of leaving her. Ever. He was with her when they rolled her into surgery, and he stayed in that sterile waiting room until the doctors emerged with news. The bullet had barely missed her femoral artery, a stroke of luck in an otherwise shitty situation, but she'd lost a lot of blood. Now, she was out of surgery, safe, but still unconscious.

Sawyer ran his hand through his disheveled hair and blew out a breath. Zelda sat by his feet, her head resting on his bandaged knee. She whimpered softly, and he reached down, stroking her head in reassurance even as frustration chewed at him. He wished he could've seen the danger. He should've seen that she was bleeding so heavily. He should've been protecting her, not the other way around.

"What are you doing in here?"

He frowned at Ash Rawlings' gruff voice. "Waiting for her to wake up."

"Weren't you discharged an hour ago?"

"Yeah, and what's your point?" Sawyer retorted.

"You need to go home and rest." There was a moment's pause, some shuffling of clothes like he was digging in a pocket, then he said, "Yeah, he's in her room."

"Calling in reinforcements?" Sawyer asked bitterly.

"Have a feeling I'll need them to cart your stubborn ass out of here."

"I'm not leaving." He reached out until he found Lucy's cold hand, then tucked it between both of his to warm it. "You didn't leave when Rose was in the hospital."

"The difference was I hadn't sustained your injuries hours beforehand."

"Doesn't matter. I'm fine."

Ash's exhale told him the man was striving for patience. "Look, I talked to her doctor. She's going to be okay. They got the bullet out, and it didn't cause as much damage as they feared, but she's on a heavy dose of pain meds and won't be waking up until morning."

He tightened his grip on Lucy's hand. "Then I'll be here when she does."

Before Ash could respond, the door opened again.

"What part of 'you need rest' do you not understand?" a female voice asked tersely.

Anna Hendricks.

Sawyer sighed. "Not you, too."

"Yes, me too," she retorted. "Someone has to keep you bullheaded alpha males in line. Sawyer, you're no good to anyone if you're flat on your back because you ignored doctor's orders."

He was quiet for a long moment, stroking Lucy's hand, a lump rising in his throat, choking him. "I can't leave her again, Anna."

"You're not," she replied, softer now. "You'll be back first thing in the morning. Ash will drive you. Right, Ash?"

Ash grunted something that might have been agreement. At least, Anna seemed to take it as such, and nobody knew the taciturn sheriff's grunts better than his twin sister.

She placed a gentle hand on Sawyer's shoulder. "You have to take care of yourself for Lucy. She'll need you when she wakes up, but not a version of you that's half-dead from exhaustion."

Part of him recognized the truth in her words— he wasn't in the best shape, and staying here wouldn't help Lucy if he ended up collapsing beside her.

But... he just couldn't bring himself to leave.

"I'll stay with her," Anna said. "I'll call if anything changes."

The offer eased some of the worry roiling inside him. Anna was strong, resourceful, and had a stubborn streak to rival his own. She wouldn't let anything happen to Lucy.

Sawyer took a deep breath, the tension in his body

deflating just a fraction. "Okay," he finally agreed. "But you call me the second she wakes up."

"Deal," Anna said, patting his shoulder reassuringly.

Ash shifted from where he'd been leaning against the wall and moved toward the door. "All right, Murphy. Let's get you out of here before you fall over."

It took all of Sawyer's willpower to relinquish Lucy's hand and push himself to stand. His knee protested, pain flaring hot and sharp, but he gritted his teeth and pushed through it. Zelda moved from her spot by his feet to guide him out of the room.

He'd be back in a few hours.

Anna was with her.

There was nothing to worry about.

So why couldn't he shake off the gnawing dread in his gut?

Something was off. Something he couldn't quite put his finger on. He paused in the doorway, taking one last look toward the bed. He knew she was there, but she was so still that without having his hand on her, he couldn't tell. All he could see was the steady spike of her heart rate moving across the screen behind her bed. He watched it for a long moment.

Anna waved a hand, drawing his attention. "Go. Shoo. I've got her."

"Come on," Ash said softly, nudging his shoulder.

He sucked in a steadying breath and stepped into the hallway.

"Left," Ash said.

He turned in the direction and stopped short when

he heard a familiar, grating voice that set his teeth on edge. "You found Chuck."

"And his son," Ash confirmed. "The boy's in a room down the hall recovering from surgery."

While he was relieved to hear that Joel was okay, he really didn't want to deal with Chuck right now. "Any chance we can avoid him?"

"Unfortunately, no. He's right by the elevators."

"Great," he muttered. "Why not add a cherry on top of this shit sundae?"

If he wasn't mistaken, the sound Ash made was a laugh. "He's too busy berating the staff to notice you."

As they moved forward, Chuck's voice boomed down the hallway. He was arguing with a nurse by the sound of it, his words loud and belligerent.

"Don't tell me what's best for my son!"

"Mr. Grassley, we need to—"

"I don't give two shits what you need! You better find a goddamn doctor who actually knows what they're doing."

It was tempting to keep his head down and ignore the man as they passed, but his pride won over. He wasn't a coward.

"Chuck," he called.

Chuck paused in his ranting. "Sawyer?" He felt the man's gaze slide over him. "You look like hell."

And you still look like a jackass.

Sawyer suppressed a smile at the thought. If he said that, no doubt Chuck would take another jab at his blindness, so instead, he asked, "How's Joel?"

The hostility drained out of Chuck's voice, replaced by something that might have been worry. "They keep saying he might lose his leg."

Sawyer swallowed a twinge of guilt. He knew what it felt like to get that kind of life-changing news and wished the kid didn't have to suffer through it. "I'm sorry to hear that."

"Yeah," Chuck muttered, the bravado he usually wore like a second skin now noticeably absent. "Me, too."

Sawyer figured the conversation was over and nudged Zelda forward, but Chuck called out, "Hey, Sawyer?"

He paused but didn't turn back. "Yeah?"

"What you did up there on the mountain, fixin' the radio, callin' for help..." He swallowed hard like the words were difficult to squeeze out. "It's the reason my boy still has a shot at keepin' the leg. Thank you."

Now, he did turn, his curiosity winning out over his distaste for the guy. "What happened after Lucy and I left?"

Chuck was silent for an uncomfortable moment. "Everyone else left, too. Grant followed you, then Ethan dug up Maya's body and took her Christ knows where. That twerp Theodore decided he didn't wanna sit around waitin', so he and Bea took off into the woods. Joel and I waited, and a few hours later, a rescue team reached us on foot. Said they overheard your radio call. So, yeah, thank you." Some of the bluster returned to his voice. "Now that's done, and I'm not gonna say it again. My boy and I are going home."

With that, Chuck turned and disappeared into his son's hospital room.

A weird feeling threaded its way through Sawyer—not quite satisfaction, but close. Chuck Grassley had just thanked him, and although he'd spat out the words as if they were poison, he was still going to count it as a win.

"All right, let's go," Ash said, nudging him forward. "You're swaying on your feet, and I'm not carrying you."

"Have you found any of the others?" he asked Ash as they caught the elevator. "Theodore? Bea? Ethan?"

"No," the sheriff said grimly. "Unfortunately, there are a lot of missing people right now and not enough people to look for them."

"What about Grant? Have you gotten anything out of him? Like why he's looking for Pierce?"

Ash said nothing until the elevator slowed and the doors started to slide open. Then he sighed like a man who was carrying the weight of the world on his shoulders. "Grant killed himself in custody."

The words dropped like a stone, hitting Sawyer hard. His head buzzed, and for a moment, the walls of the elevator seemed to close in on him. "What?"

"He had some kind of poison on him. We didn't find it, and he took it as soon as we put him in a cell. We tried to revive him, but there was nothing we could do." Ash's hand landed on his shoulder. "I'm sorry. I know you were hoping for answers. We all were."

Sawyer nodded, feeling a strange mix of emotions. Disbelief, anger, disappointment - all swirling around inside him like a rogue tornado. He'd been hoping Grant had answers. About Ethan and Maya. About Pierce. About why Grant had targeted him and Lucy...

And now, they would never know.

Back at home, Sawyer tried to sleep. He really did, but his brain wouldn't shut off.

Something about his conversation with Chuck kept replaying in his mind, a puzzle piece that didn't quite fit with the rest. After a restless hour, he sat up in bed and swung his legs over the edge. He held out a hand, and Zelda nuzzled his palm. "There's my girl. Let's take a walk over to the command center."

He felt around for her harness. When he held it up, she poked her nose through the neck loop, and he kissed her muzzle as he fastened it around her belly.

Zelda led him out of the apartment and across the grounds of Redwood Coast Rescue. He used to have an apartment in town, but since he couldn't drive and the small town didn't have a bus system, it became difficult to find rides to work. After a wildfire destroyed the original rescue two years ago, they'd had to rebuild from scratch, and Zak offered to build him an apart-ment on the grounds to make his commute easier. He was glad for it. After he was blinded, he'd wrapped himself in solitude like a shield, which hadn't been good for his mental health. Living here, he couldn't do that. He had his friends, the dogs, and Zak and Anna's adopted girls, Bella and Poppy, to keep him from wallowing.

The command center was his domain, where he ruled from his desk in front of a wall of computers, and it wasn't far from his apartment.

Thanks to his years of working for the rescue, Sawyer knew the layout by heart—the radio equipment near the front, the lockers along one wall, the large table strewn with maps and search plans...

He made his way toward what he knew was a corkboard full of photos and notes. He didn't need to see it, but he reached out anyway, fingertips brushing over pins and paper edges. His mind formed an image of the board based on memory— dozens of Polaroids, some old, some new; countless scraps of paper with hastily scribbled notes; and at its center, a printout with "Redwood Coast Rescue" boldly typed across it.

The chatter of radio communications filled the room during the day, but now it was silent.

"Sawyer?" Zak's voice broke the silence.

Sawyer startled. "Zak? What are you doing here?"

"Couldn't sleep," Zak replied gruffly. "You?"

"The same." Zak's prosthetic leg hit the floor with a heavy thud. As usual, he'd been lounging at his desk with his feet up. "I don't like it when Anna's not home."

Sawyer winced. "It wasn't my idea to have her stay with Lucy. If I had it my way, I'd still be there."

Zak chuckled. "Of course not. It was all Anna's. She was afraid you were gonna keel over or something. Which—" He paused, and Sawyer felt his considering gaze. "You look like you might." A chair scraped over the floor. "Sit down."

Sawyer felt his way to the seat and sank into it. He'd be lying if he said he wasn't grateful to be off his feet. He let himself enjoy it for a moment, then sat forward. "Is my backpack here, or did it get left on the mountain?"

"No, it's here."

"Lucy's?"

"Yeah, hers too. Why?"

Sawyer shook his head. He couldn't explain it. "Just an itch I need to scratch before I can rest. Can I see them?"

"Sure," Zak said with a shrug in his voice. He walked across the room, and there was some shuffling. Then, he came back and put both bags on the table in front of Sawyer. "Looking for anything in particular?"

"A phone."

Zak grunted and rummaged through the bags. "Your phone is here."

"Not looking for mine."

"Lucy's, too."

"Not hers, either." He stood, grabbed the first bag his hand hit, and upended it. He heard the other phones clatter out onto the table.

"Jesus. How many phones are you hoarding in there?" Zak asked.

"Help me find charging cords for all of these."

"The hell for?" Zak grumbled. Despite his sleep-deprived irritation, there was a layer of concern lacing his tone that only Sawyer could pick out.

"A hunch?"

"You don't sound too sure about that," Zak said but moved away to find cords.

"Because I don't know what's bugging me about this whole thing." Slowly, he felt over each phone, mentally categorizing them by size and brand, hoping to place Bea's distinctive case. When he finally found it—smaller than Lucy's, slightly chipped on one corner—relief washed over him. "We need to charge this one first."

It took a few minutes after they plugged it in, but the screen finally flickered to life with a robotic voice intoning, "VoiceOver on. iPhone. 10:05 PM. Notification from Messages: New message from Vince Walker. Notification from Mail: New email from Halston." It continued listing off more notifications from both Walker and Halston.

"Vince Walker," Zak muttered, and the chair behind his desk squeaked as he settled back into it. He tapped on his keyboard, the clicks of the keys loud in the silent room. "Why is that name ringing a bell?"

"I don't know," Sawyer said. "But Halston is a military contractor. Before I was injured, they were trying to wine and dine me into joining them when my enlistment was up. I told them to shove it. I hadn't heard good things about them. Then I was shot, and they lost all interest." He tapped into the messages on the iPhone.

"Messages," the phone said. "Vince Walker. Message, 'You don't need to come. I have it handled.' Received Friday at 3:45 PM."

"That was right before the earthquake," Zak said. "Is there a reply?"

"No. Bea never received any of these." He navigated to the email and opened it.

"Mail," the phone said. "Halston. Subject: Mission Update. 'What the fuck is going on? Walker says you're there. Why the fuck did you take the client there? Theodore Carter is valuable. If anything happens to him, the blowback won't just be on you. Get him off the mountain and report back immediately. Do not fuck this up.' Received Saturday at 2:30 AM."

"Wait," Zak said suddenly and snapped his figures. "Vince Walker. He was black ops. He left the military before I did and hung out his shingle as a hitman."

And the pieces clicked into place in Sawyer's head. He sat back. "Grant told me he was using an alias. I bet Vince Walker was his real name... and he knew Bea and Theodore. They were all fucking lying."

The phone chimed. "Video Message. Unknown Sender. 'You want to see your women again? Bring us Pierce St. James. Further instruction to come.' Received just now."

Zak shoved out of his chair so hard it clattered on the floor, startling Zelda. "Jesus. Anna!" He snatched the phone from Sawyer's hand.

"Playing video message from unknown sender," the phone said.

Sawyer strained his ears, but the video had no sound.

"They have her." Zak's voice was a raw wound, his pain palpable. "Fuck. Sawyer, they have them both."

chapter
twenty-six

LUCY CAME AWAKE SLOWLY, and pain swamped her. God. Where was she? Where was Sawyer? She strained to think, but the last thing she remembered was watching Sawyer get loaded onto a helicopter. And then...

Nothing.

Just a black hole.

She struggled to sit up.

And that's when she felt the cuffs on her wrists, cool metal biting into her skin. She was bound to something hard and unyielding. She tugged and pulled, but the cuffs held firm.

She listened for anything that might give her an idea of where she was. All she could hear was a soft humming noise, like an air conditioning unit, and the distant murmur of voices. She had no idea if they were friend or foe.

Panic ripped through her. She yanked on the cuffs,

making them clatter against whatever she was bound to. A pipe of some kind.

"Lucy," a soft voice said. A woman, and she was close. She sounded familiar, but Lucy couldn't place her. "It's okay."

It was definitely not okay. She was cuffed to a fucking pipe! "Where's Sawyer?"

"He's safe."

"What happened?"

"You were in the hospital. I told Sawyer I'd stay with you so he could get some sleep. He didn't want to leave you, but I convinced him. When he left... God." Her voice broke. "A nurse came in. I didn't suspect a thing. She injected me with something, and I woke up here. I'm so sorry."

Some of the panicked disorientation faded as she focused on the other woman's voice. "Who are you?"

"Anna."

Zak Hendricks' wife. She'd never met Anna before, but she knew of her. "You offered to sit with me when we've never met?"

"Yeah, of course," Anna said. "Sawyer loves you. That makes you family."

Sawyer loves you.

Her heart flipped. The statement, so matter-of-fact and sincere, was both terrifying and comforting. She remembered he'd told her he loved her on the mountain, but it had been in the middle of a life-or-death situation. She'd convinced herself it was just the adrenaline talking and he'd come to his senses.

But, instead, he'd told other people.

Like Anna, a stranger to her.

She didn't know what to do with that information, so she tucked it away for later consideration. "Why are we here?" she asked, fear gripping her throat so tight it made it hard to breathe.

"I'm not sure," Anna said, her voice shaking slightly. "But they want Pierce."

"God. Not this again. We don't know where he is!"

"None of us do." She sounded sad. "Wherever he is, I hope he's okay."

A door opened, spilling a square of light into their darkened cell, momentarily blinding Lucy. She blinked as two figures stepped into the room. One was a small man, the other a big woman with a military bearing.

Theodore and Bea.

"I'm sorry for all of this, ladies," Theodore said, taking off his glasses to clean the lens. "But it should all be over soon. Your men won't keep protecting Pierce now that we have you. We're making an exchange in a few hours, so just sit tight. You'll be home by dawn."

Lucy stared at him in disbelief, then her gaze shifted to Bea. She had thought the woman was kind and warm, if a little rough around the edges, but she saw none of that on Bea's hard face now. Those were the eyes of a stone-cold killer.

She shifted her attention back to Theodore. "What's so important about Pierce?"

"He has information I need." His gaze flicked over to Bea in disgust. "I originally hired help to track him down, but they proved unreliable. And then the earthquake threw a wrench in the works. Hence, the... change in tactics. I needed to speed this whole affair up."

"What happens to us once you have him?" Anna asked.

Theodore smiled, but it didn't reach his eyes. "I told you already. You'll be free to go," he said, his voice smooth as oil.

He was lying.

A glance over at Anna showed Lucy that she knew it, too. Theodore had no intention of letting anyone walk away from this alive.

Theodore's gaze turned cold as he took in their disbelieving expressions. His smile tightened, an almost cruel bent to his lips. "You don't look convinced," he said, a faux innocence lacing his words. "You really needn't worry, ladies."

Bea stood there silent, arms folded across her chest, her facial expression almost bored. But Lucy could see the tension in her stance, the way her gaze followed Theodore's every move.

"Bea and I are not monsters," Theodore continued, setting his clean glasses back on his face. "We simply require something that your friends are being unreasonably stubborn about surrendering."

"Pierce is a human being, not a thing to be tossed around for your convenience," Anna said icily.

Abruptly, Theodore turned away and Bea followed, the door closing behind them with finality. The space fell into an oppressive silence again—the humming of the air conditioning unit even more deafening now.

Lucy pulled her chains again. It was more for the sake of doing something than anything else.

Anna groaned softly. "Zak's gotta be losing his mind. We can't wait around for them to come back. We need a plan."

"This is stupid and dangerous," Ash said darkly.

"Have you ever known me to be smart and careful?" Zak said, voice tight as he and Sawyer pulled on bulletproof vests and slid into lightweight jackets.

"We know where they are," Ash reasoned. "My deputies can surround them and—"

"Your deputies that were supposed to be watching the hospital?" Zak snapped. "The deputies that these fuckers kidnapped two women out from under?"

"Come on, Zak. I know my deputies haven't had the best track record, but these were some of the good ones."

"How did it happen?" Sawyer asked.

Ash growled softly. "It was a woman dressed in scrubs with a nurse's ID. She walked by with Lucy on a stretcher, saying the doctor wanted another X-ray, and they didn't have any reason to be suspicious until they realized Anna had disappeared, too. They think she was subdued first and taken out through a stairwell. We did what we could to secure the place, but it's chaos there right now. Half the hospital is in ruins—" He broke off, sounding tortured. "But you're right. I should've done more."

"Godammit," Zak muttered, then added more softly, "It's not your fault. It's these fuckers' fault, and we're going to make them pay."

"But if they see any cops, they'll kill the girls," Sawyer said. "Then themselves, just like Grant or Walker or whatever his name was. Whatever Pierce is twisted up in, it's big enough that people are not only willing to kill for it but die for it. We don't have a choice, Ash."

Ash growled. "Then use Donovan as the decoy. At least he can see!"

Sawyer chose to ignore that last bit and pulled on the hood Zak handed him. His vision dimmed from a splash of indistinct colors to darkness. "We have to assume they know what Pierce looks like. Donovan's too big to pass as him. We're the same height and roughly the same weight. They won't know I'm not him until it's too late."

"Ash," Zak said, and there was a rare note of seriousness in his tone. "When I married Anna, I promised you I'd always protect her, and I don't plan on breaking that promise. I'll bring your sister home."

Ash groaned softly. Then, "Fuck it." Something clattered to the floor. Through the gap at the bottom of his hood, Sawyer saw Ash's badge spin across the floor, coming to rest by his boot. "I'm coming, too. Give me a gun that's not police issue."

Zak chuckled, but there was no humor in it. "Careful, Ash. Your inner bad boy is peeking out."

"Fuck off, Zak. Let's move."

chapter
twenty-seven

SAWYER SAT in the cramped backseat of Zak's truck, jammed between Donovan and Connelly, his hands loosely bound in front of him with a zip tie. When the time came, he'd be able to break free.

"Remember to put on a show," Donovan murmured. "If we were really betraying Pierce, he wouldn't go easily."

"I know it." His throat tightened.

Pierce had been missing for nearly a week now and nobody knew why, or where he'd gone, but Sawyer wanted to assume his friend had a good reason for disappearing. Pierce was... complicated, and often made decisions that were hard for others to understand.

But now those decisions had put them all in danger. Had put Lucy in danger, and Sawyer didn't know if he'd ever be able to forgive Pierce for it.

If Pierce was even still alive.

"This is all so fucked up," Connelly said.

"That coming from the horror writer," Donovan said, a grim laugh rumbling in his throat. "You couldn't make this shit up."

"Wouldn't want to," Conn muttered. "I'm seriously considering a career change. Maybe children's books."

"Yeah, well, let's just hope the ending is happier than some of your plots," Zak said from the driver's seat.

There was a shared silence, then a collective inhale as the truck pulled off the highway onto a rutted, dirt road. Coordinates had arrived in another message, and they pointed to an abandoned mill deep in the heart of the redwood forest. The place had a history of fires and accidents, which had eventually led to its closure—just the sort of eerie backdrop that fell neatly into Sawyer's nightmares. A perfect setting for a horror story, not a rescue mission.

"Game faces on," Zak said.

Sawyer nodded, his heart pounding hard in his chest. His palms were sweaty against the zip tie, and he told himself it was the cheap material, not fear. He was going into the lion's den blind, and God knew if he'd come out of it alive.

But it didn't matter, as long as Lucy and Anna survived.

The truck pulled to a stop outside the mill, and Sawyer was immediately shoved out of the vehicle without preamble or warning. Donovan's big hand was rough on his arm, and he fought against it, making it look good.

A punch to his gut had him doubling over, breathless. The sharp pain was real, and it took a moment for him to recover.

"Easy," he hissed.

"Gotta make it look good," Zak said through his teeth.

Yeah, that was more than for show. Zak was pissed he'd dragged Anna into this. Rightly so, but... Jesus. His body was still one giant bruise, his knee singing with every step.

Someone shoved him and he stumbled forward, landing hard on his knees in the dirt. He felt the barrel of a gun press against his temple and although he'd been expecting it, fear still coursed through him, sharp and cold. He closed his eyes, drew in a slow breath, trying to keep his calm.

"Bring the women out," Zak called, his voice hard as steel. "Or we kill him."

A moment of tense silence followed his words, stretching until it seemed almost unbearable. Then, the heavy sound of a door being thrown open echoed through the night and Sawyer heard the soft rustle of movement. His heart hammered in his chest as he counted the beats of silence—one, two, three...

Footsteps approached, crunching against gravel and straw. He heard Lucy's sharp intake of breath, followed by a soft sob, and something in him went cold and heavy.

They were hurting her.

He curled his hand around the knife hidden at his waistband and waited.

"We can be civil about this," Theodore said even as Bea shoved Lucy and Anna to their knees in front of the men of Redwood Coast Rescue. "It doesn't have to end badly."

Lucy stared at the men. Donovan, Connelly, and the sheriff flanked Zak, who was holding a gun to—

Her breath caught in her throat.

God. That was Sawyer. She knew it even with the hood over his head. She'd recognize him anywhere, any time. She'd know him from the way he held himself, the set of his shoulders, the faint scar on his left hand visible even in the dim light of dawn.

She blinked back tears, lips pressed into a thin line to stop herself from crying out.

He was here.

She didn't know whether to be relieved or horrified.

Once again, he was throwing himself into harm's way.

"Now, don't do anything rash, and we can all walk away from this." Theodore adjusted his glasses nervously, his eyes darting to Bea, who stood tall and menacing by his side, a gun in each hand, pointed to the backs of Lucy's and Anna's heads. "All we want is Pierce."

"Yeah," Zak called out, his voice echoing around the hollowed-out mill. "We're all real civil here, Theodore. Now, let's get those girls walking, and you can have him."

Lucy's eyes flicked to Sawyer. Was that the plan? To swap Sawyer for her and Anna, in hopes the captors wouldn't realize they'd been duped until it was too late? If so, it was a plan she found horrifyingly terrifying and incredibly brave.

Theodore shook his head. "Once we have Pierce, we'll let your women go."

"No," Zak growled. "They walk first."

A tense silence fell over the group. Lucy glanced at Anna, who was looking straight ahead, a determined set to her mouth. Her hands were shaking slightly but her eyes were steady and hard. She was just as tough as her husband, but it was a quiet kind of strength.

Lucy's gaze went back to Sawyer. His head was bowed beneath the hood, but she knew he was aware of everything, every move, every whisper. His body was taut as a bowstring, and she could almost feel the tension radiating off him.

Suddenly, the butt of Bea's gun hit Lucy sharply in the back of her shoulder, and she let out a gasp of surprise and pain. "Unless you want me to put a bullet in their pretty little heads, I suggest you hand him over."

Lucy's hands curled into fits at her sides as fury blasted through her, burning away the fear and pain.

She. Was. Not. A. Victim.

"I liked you, Bea," she said, keeping her voice soft and scared. "I liked both of you."

"That was your mistake," Bea said.

"Why are you doing this to us?"

"Shut up." Bea raised the gun as if to hit her again.

She didn't give the woman the chance. She reared back, knocking the top of her head into Bea's face.

It hurt.

God, it hurt, and she immediately bent forward, dry-heaving from the pain of it.

Chaos erupted.

Bea stumbled backwards from the blow, and at the same time, Anna shoved Theodore toward the men. Sawyer broke free of the zip ties around his wrists and slammed into Theodore, a knife flashing in the pale dawn light an instant before it plunged unerringly into Theodore's throat.

Theodore fell to the ground with a gurgle, his hands clutching at his neck as blood bubbled up around the blade.

"Your mistake," Sawyer said, his voice quiet, deadly, "was thinking we'd ever betray our friend." Then he pulled the knife free, and Theodore spluttered, blood spraying from his mouth with each struggling breath.

"Anna!" Zak's shout was raw, full of fear.

Anna scrambled to her feet and launched herself into his arms. He gave her one hard kiss, then pushed her toward Ash, who whisked her over to their waiting car as the men converged on Bea, weapons raised.

"It's over," Donovan said.

"No, it's not." She smiled, blood leaking down her face from her broken nose. "More will come." Then she raised her gun to her chin and pulled the trigger.

Lucy flinched at the gunshot and averted her gaze as the men all swore. She didn't want to see it. She crawled over to where Sawyer still knelt next to Theodore's body.

"Sawyer—" A sob choked off her words.

He reached out, hands swiping through the air until he found her. He yanked her into his arms with blood-stained hands and held her tight. "Shh, I got you."

Lucy gripped him back, her fingers digging into his jacket as she fought to control the nauseating swirl of fear and relief that threatened to devour her. Her face pressed against his chest, desperate to block out the horrific memory of Theodore's death and Bea's suicide.

The men moved in the flurry of activity around them. Ash had his phone out, barking orders into it, while Connelly was trying to save Bea for some unknown reason. As far as Lucy was concerned, the woman could rot in hell.

Zak strode over to the truck and pulled his wife out of the seat into his arms. He held her tight, kissing her repeatedly while she tried to assure him she was okay.

That was love.

There was so much love between Zak and Anna, it almost hurt to look at.

Did Sawyer love her like that?

Was she ready for a love like that?

Lucy drew back and realized Sawyer still wore the hood over his head. She carefully pulled it off and found his pale eyes streaming tears.

"Oh God, Luce," he whispered hoarsely, his fingers moving to cradle her face. "I thought I'd lost you."

"You..." Her voice came out raw, and she swallowed

hard. "Why do you keep throwing yourself into danger for me?"

His hands stilled on her cheeks. "Because I love you," he murmured, almost as if the words were torn from him by force. "And there's no danger in the world that could keep me away from you."

Tears welled up in her eyes, flowing over and making tracks in the dirt on her cheeks. She grasped his wrist, lowering his hand from her face as she stepped back. He tried to follow, but she held him back with a firm hand on his chest.

"Sawyer," she said, her voice shaky. "You... you can't."

"Can't what?" he whispered. "I can't love you? Too late for that."

"No," she said, shaking her head. "You can't keep risking your life for me. I don't want you to."

"Luce—" He reached for her, but she backed away, leaving his hand to meet only air.

His pale eyes clouded with confusion and hurt. Then the confusion gave way to understanding and his eyes widened in disbelief before they hardened into something akin to resignation. He opened his mouth to speak, but no words came out. A haunted look crossed his features and she hated that she'd put that look on his face.

She turned around, walking briskly toward Ash. She didn't look back. She didn't want to see him standing there, all alone. She didn't want to see the pain in his eyes or the way his shoulders slumped in defeat.

Ash looked up from his phone call and frowned. "What's wrong?" Then his gaze went to Sawyer and his frown softened into understanding, but he didn't comment.

She blinked back the sudden flood of tears. "Can I go home?"

"No," he said and waved to one of his deputies, who had just pulled up. "But Delgado will take you back to the hospital and guard you."

"Hi, I'm Izzy," the woman deputy said and gently wrapped an arm around her. "How about we get you out of here?"

As Izzy bundled her into the front seat of the patrol car, she couldn't help but spare a glance at Sawyer.

He looked like his entire world had just crashed down around him. But this was for the best, she told herself. He would keep throwing himself between her and the world and it would eventually get him killed.

And she'd rather live in a world without Sawyer's love than a world without Sawyer in it at all.

"Ready?" Izzy asked, sliding in behind the wheel.

Lucy tore her gaze away from him and leaned back in the seat, closing her eyes. "Yes. Let's go."

chapter
twenty-eight

WEDNESDAYS WERE FOR GROUP THERAPY
—THE day of the week that the Redwood Coast Rescue
team crowded into the community center and unloaded
their trauma. Sawyer used to look forward to the meet-
ings. He used to enjoy the camaraderie, the shared stories,
the sense of collective healing.

But now?

It had been three days since the standoff at the mill.
Three days since he'd last heard her voice or held her in
his arms. Three fucking miserable days, and he didn't
want to talk about it. He wanted to wallow.

He still couldn't believe Lucy had retreated from him
after everything they'd been through. When he tried to
talk to her about it later at the hospital, all she would say
was that she needed time, but there had been a finality in
her voice that sucker-punched him right in the gut. She
didn't want time. She wanted to run. She wanted to lock

herself in behind those protective walls of hers and never come out.

And why wouldn't she? Sawyer thought bitterly. He'd failed her, hadn't he? He couldn't keep her safe. He was useless. Broken. He tried to keep those thoughts at bay, but they gnawed at him like Zelda gnawed on a particularly juicy bone.

He stood behind his usual chair, fingers tapping rhythmically on the metal back. Zelda was antsy, too. She sat at his side like she was trained to, but she was panting anxiously.

If he sat down, he was committing himself to talking...

The room seemed too tight, the air too heavy.

No.

He couldn't be here.

He had to—

"Sawyer, you look like shit." Zak's hand clapped down on his shoulder in what was supposed to be a comforting gesture, but it only sparked off his temper like a match dropped in a can of gasoline.

He snarled and shook off the hand. "I just survived an earthquake, a landslide, jumping into whitewater, and hiking all over a mountain with not one, but three people trying to kill me." And having his heart ripped out and stomped on by the only woman he wanted. "I think I deserve to look a little rough."

Donovan whistled softly. "Woman trouble," he said without a shred of doubt.

"Definitely woman trouble," Zak agreed. "All that other shit? That's just a walk in the park for us. It's not why you're moping like someone just took away your favorite toy. It's Lucy that has you all tied up in knots."

Fuck. Why did they have to be so goddamn observant? "I don't want to talk about it."

"Oh, you're going to," Zak said with an edge of glee in his voice.

"That's why we're here," Donovan said. "It'll be nice to talk about something other than Uno's fucked up head for once."

"Or your impending midlife crisis," Zak shot back. "How's that bald spot coming?"

Donovan growled.

"Keep poking the bear, Zak," Veronica said as she breezed into the room on a soft cloud of vanilla. "I can't wait until he finally snaps and rearranges your pretty face."

Zak was unrepentant. "Aw, hear that? She thinks my face is pretty."

"For a Neanderthal."

Sawyer opened his mouth to tell them all to fuck off, but the door slammed open again and Shane Trevisano stalked in.

He was the newest member of their group, and still carried that flinty edge of a man not comfortable with attending therapy. "Let's get this over with. We all got work to do."

"Ry's not here yet," Zak pointed out.

"Rylan isn't coming," Shane said, and a chair scraped

across the floor as he pulled it into the circle. "He's out looking for his sister. We should all be out there helping, not in here talking about our fucking feelings."

"Ry would be the first to disagree with you about that. And we have been searching for her," Zak said. The whole mood in the room darkened. "Every minute from dawn until dusk, but we have to take care of ourselves, too. There's no sense in us killing ourselves to find her when she's most likely no longer alive."

There was an *umph* of an elbow hitting soft flesh and Veronica said chidingly, "Zak."

"What? We all know it. If she was at Rylan's apartment when the quake hit, she's been buried in rubble for a week. Better we face it now than be blindsided with it later. For once, Ry's going to need *us* to be *his* support."

"We could really use Pierce and Razzy right about now," Donovan muttered. "They'd find her."

A silence fell over the group.

Nobody wanted to say what they were all thinking: If Pierce was also buried somewhere, he wasn't ever coming back.

The air in the room became so heavy it was tangible, pressing on them from all sides. Sawyer rubbed his temples, the headache that had been simmering beneath the surface now blaring loud and persistent.

"Okay, let's... let's focus," Veronica said, her voice wavering just slightly as she took control. "Rylan would want us to have the meeting. Sawyer, do you want to talk about your recent breakup?"

Sawyer scowled, crossing his arms over his chest. "What's there to talk about? It's over."

"But do you want it to be?" Veronica pressed.

He opened his mouth to reply, but found no words came out. His chest tightened, and he had to force himself to swallow. "No," he admitted finally. "I don't. I'm all in, but every time I think she's right there with me, she pulls back. What if—" He stopped, the words catching in his throat.

"What if... what?" Donovan asked.

"What if it's because I'm blind?"

Zak scoffed. "Come on." But then after a heavy moment of silence, he asked incredulously, "Wait, you're serious?"

"Of course he's serious," Veronica said with a *duh* in her tone. "God. Are you sure you idiots aren't the blind ones? Sawyer's always been sensitive about it."

"He has?" Donovan said, nothing but confusion in his voice.

"But he's so... capable," Zak said.

He hated when people talked about him like he wasn't there, like his disability somehow made him invisible or unable to speak for himself. "I am still in the room, guys. Talk to me, not about me."

"Sorry," Zak and Donovan said at the same time.

"Why would you think your blindness has anything to do with it?" Zak asked.

Shame washed through him. "Because... I couldn't protect her."

"For real, dude?" Donovan said. "From what we saw,

you put up one hell of a fight. I know sighted people that can't do even half of what you did up there. Or, hell, on a daily basis. Ask me, you're a goddamn superhero, and if Lucy doesn't know that, she's not worth it."

"But she *is* worth it." The protest was instant.

"Why?" Zak asked.

"Why?" he echoed incredulously. "Because she's smart and tough and sweet and a little bit geeky and... everything I've ever wanted."

"A lot of women are all of those things," Donovan said. "What makes her so special?"

"It's...I can't explain it," Sawyer muttered, shifting uncomfortably on his feet. Zelda whined softly at his side, bumping his hand with her snout. He soothed his palm over her head. "It's just...her. It's always been her from the moment I met her."

Donovan grunted. "Still not good enough. If you love her, you know the real why."

Sawyer didn't have to think about it. He didn't have to search his heart or his mind for the answer. It was simple. It was pure. "Because she makes me feel alive."

He'd gone into the cave planning to save her. But, instead, she had saved him. He hadn't even realized how lonely he'd been until she came into his life, and the prospect of losing her now was unbearable.

Zak gave a low chuckle.

"What's so funny?" Sawyer demanded, not seeing the humor in the situation at all.

"Nothing," Zak said, obviously trying to smother his laughter. "It's just... Man, you're screwed."

Sawyer groaned and dropped his head into his hands, but he couldn't really argue. He was screwed. His heart was tied to a woman who seemed to be slipping further and further away from him every day.

"So what do I do?" he asked helplessly.

"Fight for her," Shane said from across the circle, his statement simple yet full of undeniable conviction.

"How? How do I make her see that I'm more than just... this?" He gestured loosely around his face.

"Well, for one, stop talking about yourself like you're broken."

"But I am."

Donovan grunted. "What you need is some confidence, my man."

Zak hummed in agreement. "You once told me we're all broken people carrying our busted pieces as best we can, and some days are harder than others. But every day, you have a choice to either let that break define you or use it as fuel to become something greater than the sum of your shattered parts. You forget that?"

Sawyer felt a small, unexpected smile tug at his mouth. As much as they sometimes annoyed him, he really did love these guys like family. "I didn't say that. I told you therapy works because we're all here to help you glue the pieces back together when you crack."

"Okay, so I paraphrased." Zak's chair creaked as he leaned forward in it. Sawyer saw him reach out a hand. "We're here with the glue. Let us help you put yourself back together into something even a stubborn woman like Lucy Harper can't resist."

Slowly, Sawyer reached out and grasped the proffered hand, surprised at the sudden surge of emotion that swept through him.

And for the first time since Lucy had walked away, Sawyer felt a glimmer of hope. The guys might be right. It wasn't going to be easy; hell, it could very well end up being the hardest thing he'd ever done. But Sawyer had never been one to back down from a challenge.

"I'm going to get her back."

Zak released his hand and settled back in his chair with a satisfied chuckle. "Good. So what's the plan, and how can we help?"

Sawyer scanned the room. He could pick out the shapes of his friends around the circle—Donovan's big, muscled frame, Zak's leaner one sprawled carelessly in his chair, Shane's military rigid posture, Veronica's curvaceous silhouette—and felt a surge of gratitude. "Okay, here's what we're going to do..."

The group leaned in as he laid out his plan.

Veronica broke into an abrupt laugh and shook her head. "This is either the cutest or stupidest thing I've ever heard."

He looked in her direction. "But will it work?"

Veronica said nothing for a moment. "If Lucy ran because she's afraid of what she feels for you..." She sighed. "Well, I know what that fear is like. I did the same thing with Connelly for years. I found reasons to be angry with him and push him away, but he wouldn't let me. He reminded me of how much he meant to me. He reminded me of how good we were together. That's what you need to do. Remind her that you're the guy who held her in your arms and kept her alive in that cave, the one who sat by her hospital bed, the one she clung to up there on the mountain when the world was going to hell around you. Make her remember that she already trusts you, Sawyer, and, yes, if she really loves you, it *will* work."

chapter
twenty-nine

THE ROAR of a motorcycle's engine drew Lucy to her front window. In the driveway sat a Harley. She vaguely recognized the tattooed man sitting astride it—one of the Redwood Coast Rescue guys—but she couldn't recall his name.

What was he doing here?

Oh, God. Was Sawyer okay?

She rushed to the door and yanked it open as the big man reached her porch. His leather boots thudded heavily on the wooden steps as he climbed them two at a time. He removed his helmet, revealing skull-trimmed hair and a series of wicked scars running across his head.

"Lucy?" His voice was a low rumble.

"What's going on?"

"Name's Donovan Scott."

Donovan. Right. He'd been there that night. The night she'd torn out her own heart to protect the man who meant more to her than anything. "What's wrong?"

"You need to come with me."

Her heart slammed against her ribs. He looked so serious, so grim. Oh God, something was wrong with Sawyer. She grabbed her coat, locked her door, and hurried after him. "Is Sawyer all right?"

He handed her a black helmet. "I've been instructed not to discuss it with you until we get there."

Lucy's stomach twisted into a knot as she buckled the helmet with shaking hands. He was told not discuss it? That could only mean bad news. Terrible news. She climbed onto the back of the motorcycle, the heat of the engine seeping through her jeans.

Donovan revved the throttle, and the bike lurched forward. Lucy grabbed his waist to keep from tumbling off the back. The wind whipped at her clothes as they sped through town, taking turns so sharply she thought they might tip right over.

Her mind raced as they wove through the quiet neighborhood streets and merged onto the highway heading north out of town.

What could have happened to Sawyer? Was he hurt? In trouble? A thousand terrible scenarios played out in her imagination.

Dying?

Already dead?

Oh, God. No.

They roared down the winding coastal road. Normally, she loved this stretch of highway with its breathtaking ocean views, and she was glad to see the earthquake hadn't caused much damage here, but she couldn't focus on the beauty of the ride. Her stomach churned with dread.

Why had she let her fears get the best of her?

Why had she pushed him away?

Had she lost him?

After what felt like an eternity, they pulled off the highway onto a barely there gravel road. Her hands fisted in Donovan's leather jacket. Where the hell was he taking her?

"Almost there," Donovan called over his shoulder.

Where was "there"? His cryptic words did nothing to halt the onslaught of fear that threatened to swallow her whole.

A few minutes later, Donovan abruptly slowed, pulled off the dirt road, and parked under a stand of towering redwoods. He killed the engine and swung his leg over the bike, gaze scanning their surroundings as if expecting an ambush.

He then turned to Lucy, his hardened features softening somewhat. "We can walk from here," he said, pulling off his helmet.

Lucy followed suit, her hands trembling as she unclipped her helmet.

The cool, salty ocean breeze was undercut with the earthy scent of the forest. She looked around the unfamiliar clearing. The only sounds were distant sea waves and the wind whispering through the towering trees. It felt... peaceful. But a sense of foreboding still lingered like an unwelcome shadow.

Donovan waited for her to dismount before beginning a silent trek deeper into the woods, his heavy boots crunching dried leaves and twigs underfoot. Lucy followed, a rush of adrenaline pumping through her veins with every beat of her racing heart.

Just when her anxiety was about to overtake her, Donovan stopped abruptly and stepped aside, holding out his arm. "We're here."

She walked past him and gasped. Below was a cove carved out of the cliffs, a private sanctuary with crashing waves, and a pristine beach. A small fire was burning, casting a warm orange glow against the coming twilight, and a familiar silhouette was seated next to it.

Sawyer.

The relief that flooded through her was so intense she nearly collapsed. Then she scowled at Donovan and gave his solid shoulder a hard shove. He didn't move. "You made me think he was hurt."

He grinned and held up his big hands. "All I did was take you on a nice motorcycle ride up the coast, as instructed."

She opened her mouth to retort, but the words caught in her throat as all the fear and worry of the last hour drained away, replaced by a rush of warmth and affection. "He... told you to take me on your motorcycle?"

"Bribed me," Donovan corrected, then grabbed her by the shoulders and turned her toward the path leading down to the beach.

Sawyer was seated on a picnic blanket near the shoreline. His head was tipped back, face directed towards the sky as though he were taking in the stars. Of course, she knew he couldn't see them—the fact never failed to make her heart ache.

Tears rushed into her eyes. She understood what was happening now. It was their date—the one Sawyer had promised her.

"Now go put that man out of his misery already," Donovan said, giving her a little push. "He's been moping for days."

Lucy swallowed hard, her throat tight with a mix of relief and anticipation. She glanced back at Donovan. "Bribe or not, thank you."

His grin softened, and she realized under his gruff exterior was a big romantic. "He's one of the best men I know and deserves some happiness."

Sawyer did deserve happiness. And, she realized, she would give anything to be the one who gave it to him.

"So do you, Lucy," Donovan added softly. "There are so many things to be afraid of in life, but love isn't one of them. Don't waste this opportunity."

With that, he turned away and strode back through the forest, leaving her alone on the cliff's edge overlooking the secluded cove. Taking a deep breath, she began her descent down the narrow, winding path toward the beach below, a flurry of emotions coursing through her. The relief of seeing Sawyer okay and the anger for the near heart attack she'd just suffered battled fiercely inside her chest. But underneath it all, there was a spark of joy. And an incredible surge of love.

As soon as her boots hit the sand, Sawyer seemed to

sense her presence. He turned toward the sound of her approach. "Lucy?"

"Sawyer," she breathed, bursting with feelings she couldn't contain any longer. She covered the distance between them in just a few strides.

He rose to meet her as she did him and opened his arms wide. She launched herself at him, wrapping her arms tightly around his neck, burying her face in his shoulder. He stumbled back a step, but caught his balance and held her close, his arms pressing her to him.

"Sawyer," she repeated his name like a prayer, the words slipping past choked sobs. "You... you jerk. You scared the hell out of me!" But there was no real heat in her voice.

Sawyer cupped the back of her head with one hand while his other slipped down to run the length of her spine in a soothing rhythm. "I'm sorry, Luce. I didn't mean to scare you. I just... needed you to come," he admitted in a low voice.

"You could have just asked me like a normal person."

Sawyer's face softened, a hint of a smile playing around his lips. "I thought Donovan would have made it clear that nothing was wrong."

Lucy rolled her eyes. "Donovan is about as clear as mud."

He winced. "Yeah, sorry. He can be..."

"Scary?"

He chuckled. "I was going to say gruff, but scary works, too. But at his heart, he's a good guy, and I needed him. I promised you a motorcycle ride and I obviously couldn't drive it myself."

Despite herself, she felt her lips twitch into a smile. "So... are you going to serenade me badly now with your non-existent guitar skills?"

He winced and released her long enough to pull her toward the picnic blanket. "I thought we'd skip that part, but we do have wine and cheese, as promised."

She stared at the spread. If her heart weren't already a puddle for him, it would've melted right then. "Sawyer?"

He half-turned, wine bottle in hand. "Yes?"

"I love you."

He fumbled the bottle. "Oh. Wow. Okay, I thought I was going to have to do a bit more work before I heard those words."

She stepped forward to take the bottle from him. "Well, I can make you work for it if you really want."

His pale blue eyes widened in surprise before crinkling at the corners as a grin spread across his face. "No, no," he said quickly, holding up his hands in surrender. "I'm absolutely fine with not having to work for it."

She laughed again and moved a little closer, her heart pounding wildly in her chest. The tension and fear from earlier had faded into something warm and sweet— a feeling she realized she wanted to hold onto forever.

Her voice was barely above a whisper when she asked, "Sawyer, do you still love me? I was such an ass. I shouldn't have pushed you away, but I was so scared."

He looked at her with such open affection in those unseeing eyes that it stole her breath away.

"Lucy Harper," he said softly, tracing his hands over her shoulders and up her neck to her face. He tucked a loose strand of hair behind her ear. "I've loved you since the moment I found you. It was dark, you were hurt, and you needed someone. And in that moment, I realized that I wanted to be that someone for you. Always." He leaned in closer, bringing their faces just inches apart. "And every day since then, I fell a little more in love with you. The way you laugh at my terrible jokes, how fiercely you fight for what you believe in, your stubbornness–God, Lucy, even your stubbornness... I love all of it." His voice fell to a whisper, his forehead resting gently against hers. "And I especially love how just when I think I've got you figured out, you surprise me all over again."

"Sawyer..." she began, her voice choked with emotion. But he placed a finger gently against her lips, silencing her.

"I'm not finished yet," he told her, his face serious. "You've made it clear that your past has made you wary of relationships. You've also made it clear that you're scared – scared of me leaving, scared of me getting hurt again." He took a deep breath before continuing. "I want you to know that I'm here for the long haul. I don't know what the future holds, but I know that whatever it is, I want to face it with you. And as for your past... we all have one. But it's just that—a past. It doesn't define us or dictate our future. I'm not your ex-husband, and I will spend every day for the rest of my life proving that to you."

The lump in her throat quadrupled in size, and she

felt tears well up in her eyes. "You don't need to. I already know it."

"Okay." His thumbs swept over her cheeks, catching her tears. "Good. But I still want to spend the rest of my life with you."

thirty

THERE ARE SO *many things to be afraid of in life, but love isn't one of them.*

Donovan was right. She'd spent so much of her life in fear, but she didn't want to be afraid anymore. Not of this. Not of Sawyer. Not of them together.

She pressed her lips to his. "Yes."

He started to return her kiss but then pulled his head back. "Wait, yes? As in, yes, you'll spend the rest of your life with me?"

She laughed, her heart light and full. "Yes, Sawyer. As in, I love you too, and I want to spend the rest of my life proving it to you just as much as you want to prove it to me."

Relief washed over his face. His grin was so bright it outshone the sun setting on the horizon as he leaned down and captured her lips with his.

She melted into him, and her hands curled in his

worn blue flannel shirt, tugging him toward the blanket behind them.

He chuckled against her lips. "I thought we'd at least eat first..."

"Hmm." She pushed him down to the blanket and straddled him. "Well, there is something I've been dying to taste."

His laughter came full and free, a sound that echoed through the secluded cove. His hands found their way to her waist, his thumb tracing the curve of her hip through the lightweight material of her jacket.

"And what might that be?"

She leaned down and dragged her open mouth down the muscle in his neck. "You."

His fingers dug into her hips, and he exhaled sharply as her teeth sank into the skin over his collarbone. "Far be it from me to deny you anything, love."

How could she have ever pushed this man away? How could she have let her fears, and her scars dictate her future when this is what it could be like?

She was struck by a sudden overwhelming need to make up for lost time.

She slid her hands under his shirt, tracing over the planes of his muscular chest as she pulled it off him. He was still bruised all over, the deep blues and purples fading to ugly greens and yellows—but he was still the most beautiful man she had ever seen. She kissed her way down his chest, stopping to tease his nipple with her tongue.

"I'm going to take you in my mouth and suck so

hard," she promised, blowing on his nipple and grinning when his back arched.

"Jesus, Luce." His voice was little more than a growl as his hand found her ponytail and gently tugged until her hair fell free. "I want to feel all this softness on my thighs while you suck me."

She silenced him with a searing kiss, her hand moving lower to grip him through his jeans. "Patience," she murmured, exhilarated by the ragged gasp Sawyer let out at her touch.

"Never had much use for it," he muttered and began to undo his belt. His voice was husky, gritty, filled with a raw desire that made her core clench with anticipation. He guided her head lower, his fingers tangling in her hair, his breath hitching as she traced a path of kisses down his abdomen. She took her time, savoring the taste of him, the twitch of his muscles under her palms, the way he squirmed.

She flicked open the button on his jeans and pulled down the zipper and found his cock hard and hot, straining the fabric of his boxers.

Slowly, she tugged the elastic waistband down, freeing him from his confinement. His cock sprang free, standing proudly against his lower stomach. She licked her lips at the sight of him, so hard and ready for her.

She chuckled softly, brushing her fingers over him. "Seems like somebody's eager."

He let out a shuddering breath, his grip tightening on her hair. "You have no idea."

He was large and thick, the head already glossy with

pre-come. She wrapped her fingers around him, her touch light and teasing. His hands tightened in her hair as she gave him a slow stroke that made him groan.

"Lucy," he groaned, his hips bucking into her hand. "You're killing me..."

Feeling incredibly powerful and more than a little bit wicked, she continued to stroke him slowly while lowering her mouth to his inner thigh and trailing kisses up towards his erection. She loved the way his stomach muscles clenched under her touch, the way he gasped and shivered as she came closer. When she finally swirled her tongue around the head of his cock before swallowing him whole, his strangled curse echoed through the quiet cove.

"Wait, wait." He tugged on her hair, forcing her to release him from her mouth with a wet pop. His chest heaved as he tried to steady his breathing. "This isn't fair."

She raised an eyebrow, tilting her head questioningly. "Oh? And why is that?"

Sawyer shifted beneath her, an impish grin tugging at the corners of his mouth. "Because I haven't gotten to taste you yet."

A shiver of anticipation ran down her spine as he flipped their positions, pinning her beneath him on the blanket. The warmth of his body seeped through her clothes, igniting a slow burn deep inside of her. Her heart pounded in anticipation, excitement coursing through her veins.

His hands roved across her body before coming to

rest on the zipper of her lightweight jacket. Slowly, almost teasingly, he eased it down to reveal the shirt she wore underneath. He bent down and pressed a long kiss to the exposed skin above the neckline of her shirt, the stubble on his chin scratching pleasingly against her. His hands slid under the hem, pulling the cotton fabric up and over her head in a single swift motion.

She bit her lip as his hands and lips roamed reverently over every inch of her exposed chest. He captured one of her breasts in his mouth through the lace of her bra and she arched into him, moaning as his teeth scraped over her nipple.

Her world narrowed down to the sensation of his mouth on her body, his hands moving over her skin. They seemed to be everywhere at once, and it was intoxicating, overwhelming in the most wonderful way possible.

"Sawyer," she gasped, tugging at the waistband of her jeans in a frenzied attempt to shed the last barrier between them. He obliged, sitting back on his heels to help her shimmy out of the tight denim, then he leaned down, pressing a trail of hot, open-mouthed kisses from her navel to the apex of her thighs. She writhed beneath him, panting and moaning as he spread her legs wider and settled between them. When his tongue finally stroked into her, she gasped, fingers digging into the blanket beneath them. He lapped at her with long, slow strokes, his hands clutching her hips to hold her still as she writhed and bucked.

"God, Sawyer…" The pleasure built like a tidal wave.

"I can't…" Her skin felt too tight, her senses too stretched. She was on the edge of something vast and terrifying and wonderful.

"You can." He swirled his tongue around her clit and then dipping it lower to plunge between her folds. Sudden tears sprang to her eyes as he hit a spot inside that made her tremble. For a second, she wondered if there was another earthquake.

"Sawyer," she pleaded, unable to say more than his name.

"Let go, Luce," he murmured against her skin, his fingers replacing his tongue and pushing deep inside to stroke that sweet spot again. His tongue flicked over her sensitive clit rapidly, spurring her closer and closer to the edge.

Everything inside her coiled tighter, her breath hitching as the pleasure swirled into a hot, dizzying storm. With one last sweep of his tongue and a deep thrust of his fingers, she shattered.

His low growl of satisfaction sent vibrations through her body that made her arch even harder against him, and he didn't stop until she was spent, his touches becoming gentler as she came down from her high. His fingers slowly withdrew from her, making her whimper at the loss. But then he was moving up her body, his hands and lips leaving a trail of heat against her skin. He kissed her deeply, his tongue stroking hers in a mimicry of what he had just done to her. She could taste herself on him, and it sent a jolt of desire curling in her belly.

"Now, it's fair," he murmured against her lips, his blue eyes twinkling with mischief.

She felt the broad head of his cock nudge at her entrance and opened her thighs wider hooking her ankles around his back. He sank in slowly, letting out a low, guttural groan that sent a fresh wave of heat coursing through her.

"God, Luce," he whispered in her ear, pressing his forehead to hers. "You're so tight, so wet…" He began to move then, pulling out nearly all the way before surging forward again in a slow, deliberate rhythm.

Each stroke rubbed against her still-sensitive nerves, drawing out tremors of pleasure that had her clenching her hands in his hair and wrapping her legs tighter around his waist. His thrusts grew faster and harder, the erotic slap of skin on skin echoing in the stillness around them.

Sawyer hooked an arm under her knee and changed the angle of his thrusts, hitting a spot inside her that had lights dancing behind her eyelids. She could feel the familiar coil of pleasure winding tighter in the pit of her stomach, ready to snap at any moment, but she didn't want it. Not yet.

She surged up, catching him off guard and knocking him back. She straddled him as he landed on the blanket with a surprised laugh. His eyes widened, and he let out a strangled groan as she sank down onto him. The new angle let her control the pace, and she set a rhythm that was tortuously slow, grinding down onto him each time she lowered herself. His hands clamped on her hips, his fingers digging into her skin

"God, look at you," he whispered. "You're so goddamn beautiful."

She looked down and met his gaze. For once, he wasn't looking past her, but those pale blue eyes were focused right on her with a mixture of awe and hot desire.

He could see her.

She froze in shock, and he let out a choked sound of disappointment.

"Don't stop moving. I want to see you when you come."

God. He could see her when she rode him. Heat flooded through her as she lifted herself and sank down on him again and watched his eyes follow her movements.

The sight of him sprawled beneath her, the moonlight catching on his body and highlighting the muscles in his abdomen and arms, galvanized her. A wicked smile curled the edges of her lips. She placed her hands flat against his chest, feeling his heart pound against her palm as she quickened the pace, pistoning up and down on his cock in a way that had him swearing and gripping the blanket underneath them. His hips were thrusting upwards to meet hers, each movement making his breath hitch and pleasure coil tighter in her gut.

"Sawyer," she gasped, leaning forward to brace herself on his shoulders.

She picked up the pace, grinding down onto him

faster and harder. His head tilted back, exposing the column of his throat as he groaned, but he kept his blue eyes on her. Watching her every move, greedily drinking in the sight of her as she took him.

"Keep moving," he urged hoarsely, his gaze locked on her swaying breasts. His calloused fingers brushed over her nipples, pinching and teasing. He sat up suddenly, wrapping one arm around her waist to draw her closer. His mouth latched onto a taut nipple, his teeth scraping lightly against the sensitive bud.

Lucy gasped, the sensation spiraling through her like a shockwave. Sparks danced in front of her eyes and as Sawyer continued to suckle and tease, his other hand slipped between their bodies to stroke her clit.

"Come on, Luce," he murmured against her nipple, then lay back again, keeping his hand between her legs, stroking where they were joined. "I'm close, but I want to watch you come first."

His words, raw and charged with desire, shattered her last bit of control. Her hips jerked and she cried out his name as a wave of pleasure swept through her, leaving her gasping and shuddering. Sawyer held her tight as she shook, his fingers still working between her legs to prolong the intensity of her climax.

As the waves receded, leaving her panting and spent, he rolled them over until she was beneath him again. His thrusts became more frantic as he chased his own release. He buried his face in the crook of her neck with a low growl that sent another wave of pleasure coursing through her.

And then he stilled, clutching her tightly as he came in a series of pulsing shudders, his body going rigid before finally collapsing onto hers.

For a long moment, they lay together in silence, their bodies tangled together as they tried to catch their breaths. Sawyer nuzzled the side of her neck lazily, his rough stubble scratching gently against her skin.

"God, Luce," he murmured sleepily into her ear, still struggling for breath. "I've never... That was..." He couldn't seem to find the words, but the awestruck look on his face as he pulled back said more than any words could. "I... I saw you. I saw you, Luce," he repeated, his voice choked and raw. "And you are more beautiful than I ever imagined. You're perfect." His thumb traced her jaw to the dimple in her chin, then caressed her lower lip.

She opened her mouth to capture it between her teeth, drawing a soft groan from him. "Who would've guessed sex is the cure for blindness?"

His laugh rumbled in his chest, the vibration seeping into her skin. "I'm still blind. But for those few minutes... it didn't feel like I was."

"Well, then, I guess I'll have to be on top more often."

"You can be on top whenever you want, Harper."

Despite his teasing, she heard the undercurrent of vulnerability in his voice. She hated that, deep down, under all of his charm and the confidence he showed the world, he still felt so insecure about his disability.

Tenderly, she cupped his face in her hands and looked into his unseeing blue eyes. "I heard a quote once that has always stuck with me, and I'm probably going to butcher it, but... love isn't about seeing the perfect person. It's about seeing an imperfect person perfectly." She kissed him, pouring all her love into the gentle brush of her lips against his. "I don't need your sight. I don't care if you can see me or not. I'm here, and I see you, Sawyer Murphy. Every scar, every flaw, every imperfection. And I love you because of all of them."

His face softened, the corners of his lips turning up in that smile of his that she loved so much. "And I love you, Lucy Harper," he said quietly, "with all my scars and imperfections."

chapter
thirty-one

LUCY LOVED HIM.

Sawyer woke the next morning on the beach with her curled up by his side, and he knew with absolute certainty that he wanted to wake up like this every morning for the rest of his life.

As the sun rose and warmed their bodies, he slipped his hand between her thighs and woke her up with a lazy morning orgasm that she eagerly reciprocated.

His phone alerted with a message from Zak, but he was moving inside his woman, breathing her in, listening to her cries as she came, and couldn't care less about the outside world. He buried his face in her neck, inhaling the scent of her skin mixed with the salty tang of the ocean air.

The phone rang.

"Ignore it," she panted, wrapping her legs around his waist to pull him deeper inside her. Her nails dug into his shoulder blades as she met him thrust for thrust, urging him on. "Don't stop."

He had no intention of stopping. Not when Lucy's heated walls were squeezing him so deliciously, and her fingers were touching where they were connected, furiously strumming herself to another climax.

She came hard, her body arching off the blanket, a choked cry leaving her lips. Her inner walls contracted around him, and with a few more frantic thrusts, he followed her over the edge, his body shuddering as he poured himself into her.

Sawyer slid out of her with a groan, collapsing onto the blanket next to her. Lucy curled into his side with a happy sigh and trailed a hand down his body, tracing the lines of his muscles with gentle fingers.

"God," she whispered. "You're still one big bruise."

He held her tighter. "Don't get scared and run off again. I'm fine."

"I know."

"And even if I wasn't, you agreed to marry me."

"Oh, did I?"

"Yeah, somewhere between orgasms three and four. So you're stuck with me now, Future Mrs. Murphy."

She sank her teeth lightly into his shoulder. "Who says I'm going to take your name?"

He opened his mouth to respond, but his phone alerted again.

"Incoming call," the phone said. "Zak Hendricks."

"Fucking Zak," he muttered.

Lucy laughed and sat up. "You should answer it."

He groped around until he found the vibrating phone in his discarded jeans pocket. "What?"

"Good morning to you too, lover boy," Zak said. "I figured you'd be in a better mood this morning. Donovan said when he left last night, things were looking up for you and Lucy."

"I *am* in a good mood."

"Yeah? Doesn't sound it."

"Because your timing sucks."

"Ah." Zak laughed. "Well, sorry, but you'll have to put the lovefest on hold for a bit. Team meeting, half hour. Donovan's already on his way to pick you guys up."

The command center was buzzing with anxious energy when Sawyer and Lucy entered with Donovan twenty minutes later. Men, women, dogs. It was chaos.

"Hey!" When Anna spotted them, she launched herself into Lucy's arms. "How are you?"

"I'm good," Lucy said, awkwardly patting her back.

"Better than good." Sawyer's arm snaked around her and pulled her possessively into his side. He raised his voice. "We're getting married."

A stunned silence hung for a moment before the room erupted in cheers and happy barks.

Anna squealed with delight, her eyes shining as she hugged Lucy again. "Oh my God! Congratulations! Welcome to the family!"

Family.

Lucy had never really had one of those, but as she looked around the crowded room filled with beaming faces, raucous laughter, and the soft, occasional whine of excited dogs, she felt warm. Safe. The kind of feeling she imagined people often associated with family.

She looked at Sawyer, and her heart felt too big for her chest. Sensing her gaze, his hand came up, searching for her cheek. She caught it, pressed it to her lips instead, and stared into those pale blue eyes.

"I love you," he whispered for her ears alone.

She rose up on her toes and kissed him, causing more cheers and some catcalls.

"All right, all right," Zak finally shouted over the noise. "We're all happy for them, and we'll definitely celebrate later. But right now, we need to settle down and focus. We have a lead on Pierce."

Everyone found their seats, and the mood shifted.

Sawyer didn't release his grip on her, but she could tell Zak had his full attention now. She turned in his arms and saw a still from a security video pop up on the main screen at the front of the room. It showed a man with a baseball cap pulled low over his eyes, keeping his face turned away from the camera as he filled up his gas tank. In the corner of the image, one furry paw hung out the Ford Bronco's side window.

"Pierce and Raszta were spotted at a gas station outside Eureka the day of the quake." Zak paused and met each gaze for a moment before continuing. "So let's go find our boys and bring them home."

epilogue

one week earlier: the day of the earthquake

PIERCE'S PAST had finally caught up to him.

He'd known it was chasing him, nipping right at his heels. He'd known it was only a matter of time before it lunged, tearing open old wounds and secrets he'd tried to bury. But he hadn't expected it to hit him like a freight train, throwing him into a situation far removed from the solitary life he'd carved for himself in Steam Valley.

He couldn't stay.

He'd put all of his friends—his only family—in danger.

His original plan had been to hike up the mountain and disappear into the wilderness, but halfway up the trail, he'd spotted a familiar face and realized it wasn't an option.

They knew he was here.

He had to leave Steam Valley altogether.

Probably California.

Hell, maybe the States.

If he got far enough away, maybe the past would finally stop biting.

Yeah, right, he thought.

They'd never stop looking for him. They'd never let him be. They were like hounds, relentless and unforgiving. If they smelled blood, they'd hunt him to the ends of the earth.

So Pierce returned to his comfortable apartment above a sweet old lady's garage and packed his bag—bare minimum, essentials only. He tossed a few protein bars into the mix and filled his flask with water from the kitchen tap. He yanked his duffel bag over his shoulder, the worn leather straps fitting comfortably.

Jesus. For a few years there, he'd thought he was finally done running, finally done living out of a bag. His heart clenched at the thought. He'd found a home in Steam Valley, something he hadn't even known he was missing till he'd stumbled into it. He almost laughed at his own naivety. Who was he kidding? A man like him could never escape his sins. The sins that had marked him, scarred him, taken away his voice and his ability to indulge in pretty fantasies, things like a home.

Raszta sat at his feet, panting anxiously. Smart dog knew something was up.

Picking up his keys, he headed out the door. He gave Razzy the hand signal to stay even though it broke his

ized. The air no longer felt like sandpaper against his throat. Why was that when moments ago he thought he might pass out from lack of oxygen?

Bewildered, he ran his hand over his short hair. Rhiannon had the same air of calm as her brother—the same soothing and steady presence that encouraged you to drop your walls, to unwind, to trust. It was a trait that had annoyed Pierce when he first met Rylan, but with Rhiannon, it seemed different, somehow. More appealing. With her, it felt like a soothing balm to wounds he didn't even know were still open. This woman, this stranger who was not a stranger, made him want to trust her, and that went against everything that had kept him alive for the past few years.

He couldn't let down his guard. He had been blindsided before by people who seemed harmless.

He lifted his hands to tell her he needed to go, but the ground beneath him lurched violently, throwing him off balance. The air filled with a cacophony of car alarms and panicked shouts as the world shifted and buckled. A nearby telephone pole snapped like a toothpick, slamming into a parked car with a sickening crunch.

Rhiannon staggered, arms flailing for balance. She barely managed to keep her feet under her as Raszta yelped. Pierce reached out and grabbed hold of her arm, pulling her toward him just as the ground gave another ferocious lurch that sent them both sprawling. He curled around her, cushioning her fall, and his head hit the asphalt hard. Stars danced in his vision. Raszta huddled against them, shaking with each tremor.

Then, just as suddenly as it began, the earthquake stopped.

For a moment, there was just silence– an eerie calm following the earth's violent tantrum. Pierce's ears rang, his heart thundering as he lay on the asphalt with Rhiannon sprawled on top of him. Her body was warm against his, her quick, shallow breaths matching his own. His senses were hyper-aware; the smell of hot asphalt and disturbed earth filled his nostrils, and he could taste dust and blood on his tongue from where he'd bitten down during the quake.

"Are you okay?" he signed to Rhiannon when he saw that her eyes were open, and she was staring down at him with wide-eyed shock. She blinked at him, dazed and silent, before finally nodding and pushing off him.

Pierce expelled a shaky breath of relief. Having her so close had been...disconcerting. It rattled him more than the quake.

He sat up, swaying slightly as a wave of dizziness washed over him.

Fuck.

He massaged his aching head before finally looking around at the damage. The nearby telephone pole was now a splintered remnant, live wires sparking dangerously on the ground. Cars were askew, tossed like a child's discarded toys. Cracks spiderwebbed through the asphalt beneath them.

He hadn't realized when he pulled in, but this rest stop was more like a roadside attraction, with a chintzy gift shop built into the side of a cliff. The shop was intact except for a few shattered windows and people slowly emerged looking dazed and terrified, faces pale under a layer of dust and debris.

Raszta was shaking, his tail tucked between his legs. Pierce reached out to calm the dog, scratching behind his ears in an attempt to reassure him.

"Pierce," Rhiannon's hoarse voice cut through the strange stillness. "Look at the hill."

Pierce followed her gaze to the hill overlooking the rest stop. The whole side of it was moving, shifting like a monstrous wave.

Landslide.

He grabbed her hand, picked up his dog, and ran for the shelter of the gift shop as a cascade of rocks and dirt rolled toward them with an ominous, deafening roar.

The Redwood Coast Rescue adventure continues with Pierce's book, Searching for Secrets.

Make sure you never miss a new release!
Sign up for Tonya's newsletter at tonyaburrows.com/ newsletter.